By Danielle Steel

PALAZZO • THE WEDDING PLANNER • WORTHY OPPONENTS
WITHOUT A TRACE • THE WHITTIERS • THE HIGH NOTES
THE CHALLENGE • SUSPECTS • BEAUTIFUL • HIGH STAKES
INVISIBLE • FLYING ANGELS • THE BUTLER • COMPLICATIONS
NINE LIVES • FINDING ASHLEY • THE AFFAIR • NEIGHBORS
ALL THAT GLITTERS • ROYAL • DADDY'S GIRLS
THE WEDDING DRESS • THE NUMBERS GAME • MORAL COMPASS
SPY • CHILD'S PLAY • THE DARK SIDE • LOST AND FOUND
BLESSING IN DISGUISE • SILENT NIGHT • TURNING POINT
BEAUCHAMP HALL • IN HIS FATHER'S FOOTSTEPS • THE GOOD FIGHT
THE CAST • ACCIDENTAL HEROES • FALL FROM GRACE
PAST PERFECT • FAIRYTALE • THE RIGHT TIME • THE DUCHESS
AGAINST ALL ODDS • DANGEROUS GAMES • THE MISTRESS
THE AWARD • RUSHING WATERS • MAGIC • THE APARTMENT
PROPERTY OF A NOBLEWOMAN • BLUE • PRECIOUS GIFTS
UNDERCOVER • COUNTRY • PRODIGAL SON • PEGASUS
A PERFECT LIFE • POWER PLAY • WINNERS • FIRST SIGHT
UNTIL THE END OF TIME • THE SINS OF THE MOTHER
FRIENDS FOREVER • BETRAYAL • HOTEL VENDÔME
HAPPY BIRTHDAY • 44 CHARLES STREET • LEGACY • FAMILY TIES
BIG GIRL • SOUTHERN LIGHTS • MATTERS OF THE HEART
ONE DAY AT A TIME • A GOOD WOMAN • ROGUE • HONOR THYSELF
AMAZING GRACE • BUNGALOW 2 • SISTERS • H.R.H. • COMING OUT
THE HOUSE • TOXIC BACHELORS • MIRACLE • IMPOSSIBLE
ECHOES • SECOND CHANCE • RANSOM • SAFE HARBOUR
JOHNNY ANGEL • DATING GAME • ANSWERED PRAYERS
SUNSET IN ST. TROPEZ • THE COTTAGE • THE KISS • LEAP OF FAITH
LONE EAGLE • JOURNEY • THE HOUSE ON HOPE STREET
THE WEDDING • IRRESISTIBLE FORCES • GRANNY DAN
BITTERSWEET • MIRROR IMAGE • THE KLONE AND I
THE LONG ROAD HOME • THE GHOST • SPECIAL DELIVERY
THE RANCH • SILENT HONOR • MALICE • FIVE DAYS IN PARIS
LIGHTNING • WINGS • THE GIFT • ACCIDENT • VANISHED
MIXED BLESSINGS • JEWELS • NO GREATER LOVE • HEARTBEAT
MESSAGE FROM NAM • DADDY STAR • ZOYA • KALEIDOSCOPE
FINE THINGS • WANDERLUST • SECRETS • FAMILY ALBUM
FULL CIRCLE • CHANGES • THURSTON HOUSE • CROSSINGS
ONCE IN A LIFETIME • A PERFECT STRANGER • REMEMBRANCE
PALOMINO • LOVE: *POEMS* • THE RING • LOVING • TO LOVE AGAIN
SUMMER'S END • SEASON OF PASSION • THE PROMISE
NOW AND FOREVER • PASSION'S PROMISE • GOING HOME

Nonfiction
PURE JOY: *The Dogs We Love*
A GIFT OF HOPE: *Helping the Homeless*
HIS BRIGHT LIGHT: *The Story of Nick Traina*

For Children
PRETTY MINNIE IN PARIS
PRETTY MINNIE IN HOLLYWOOD

THE HIGH NOTES

5a

DANIELLE STEEL

THE HIGH NOTES

A Novel

Dell
New York

2023 Dell Mass Market Edition

Copyright © 2022 by Danielle Steel
Excerpt from *Happiness* by Danielle Steel
copyright © 2023 by Danielle Steel

Published in the United States by Dell,
an imprint of Random House, a division of
Penguin Random House LLC, New York.

DELL is a registered trademark and the D colophon is
a trademark of Penguin Random House LLC.

Originally published in hardcover in the United States
by Delacorte Press, an imprint of Random House,
a division of Penguin Random House LLC, in 2022.

This book contains an excerpt from the forthcoming
book *Happiness* by Danielle Steel. This excerpt has
been set for this edition only and may not reflect the
final content of the forthcoming edition.

ISBN 978-1-9848-2176-8
Ebook ISBN 978-1-9848-2175-1

Cover design: Eileen Carey
Cover images: © Shelly Perry/Stocksy (woman),
© Pixel Stories/Stocksy (lighting),
© Boris Jovanovic/Stocksy (microphone)

Printed in the United States of America

randomhousebooks.com

2 4 6 8 9 7 5 3 1

Dell mass market edition: July 2023

To Beatie, Trevor, Todd, Nick,
Samantha, Victoria, Vanessa,
Maxx, and Zara,

To my darling children,

May you be blessed and lucky and happy,
and may you find the right person to love you
    with all their heart,
and may you love them, with all yours.

With all my love,
Mom / d.s.

"The only lie I ever told you is that I liked you when I already knew I loved you."

—The Los Angeles–based street artist known as Wrdsmth

THE HIGH NOTES

Chapter 1

Iris Cooper was small for her age. She looked more like ten than twelve, in her cut-off jeans with ragged edges, a pink T-shirt, and scuffed pink cowboy boots her father, Chip, had bought at a yard sale.

She stood watching the horses tethered under a tree on a blazing hot day in Lake City, Texas, kicking pebbles with the toe of her cowboy boot.

She was humming to herself, as she always did. She could hear music in her head. She composed songs on her father's guitar, and they sounded pretty good. She'd gone to school in Lake City for four months. She'd been to three schools so far that year. Her father liked to move around a lot, looking for opportunities to make some money. He got tired of the towns they went to pretty fast. He rented a room for each of them in someone's house, stayed for a few months, and then they moved on. Iris liked it when they stayed in a town with a church. She could sing with the choir, and they were always happy to have her. She could hit the high notes better than anyone else. Once they heard her sing, they let her stay. She could go to the church socials and eat pot roast and fried chicken, potato salad or mashed potatoes. The rest of the time, they lived on fast food, and whatever her father could afford that day, sometimes just a can of beans or some chili.

Her name had been prophetic. She had deep blue eyes, the color of an iris, and a mass of soft blond hair that framed her face. She wore it in a braid that she could do herself.

Her mother, Violet, had left her and her father when she was two. He never told her, but she'd once heard him say that Violet was killed during a bar fight in East Texas after she left. She and her boyfriend had been at the bar when someone pulled out a gun, shot into the crowd during the fight, and killed them both. She and Chip had a rocky marriage. And when she left Chip, it was easier to leave Iris with him. Iris didn't remember her, so she didn't miss her. You couldn't miss someone you'd never known. But she missed having a mother, like other kids. Chip had grown up as an orphan, living with two unmarried uncles who

paid as little attention to him as possible, and
made him sleep outside when they brought women
home. Chip had left them at sixteen, and never
saw them again. He got work wherever he could
find it doing odd jobs, and used to ride the bulls
and broncos in the rodeo, until he got trampled by
a bull and hurt his leg. He walked with a limp now,
and his rodeo days were over. Iris liked going to
rodeos with him. Sometimes he saw old friends.
They lived now from the work he picked up wherever he found it, tending bar, doing carpentry,
working on a ranch when they needed extra help.
He always found something, and when there were
no jobs, they moved on to another town, and
started all over again. Iris's dream was to stay in
one town for a long time, like other people, and go
to the same school for years at a time. Her father
said they'd settle down one day, but they hadn't
yet. They'd been roaming around the small towns
in Texas for the last ten years. She wrote a song
about it that she played on his guitar.

She was still watching the horses when Chip
came out of the house where they were staying,
and told her to get in his truck. They were going
for a ride. It was an old green truck he'd had for as
long as she could remember. It got them from one
town to the next, with everything they owned in
boxes tied up in the back, a plastic sheet over
them, secured with ropes.

She hopped onto the passenger seat, and he

got in and started the engine. They drove off a minute later, down a back road in the direction of the town. She never asked where they were going. It didn't really matter. She watched the cattle and the horses as they drove past them. They stopped at a bar just outside of town. A red neon sign read "Harry's Bar." Chip parked and turned off the engine, and looked at her.

"Stay here. I'll come and get you," he said, and she nodded, and turned the radio on after he left. He had parked under a tree and the air was still and hot. There was no air-conditioning in the truck, and Iris watched as he limped into the bar. She wondered if he had gone in to have a beer, or if he was looking for work. They'd been eating canned beans again, so she knew he was short of money. If he didn't find work soon, they'd be moving on again. She hoped they wouldn't have to. She liked it here. The woman they rented rooms from was nice to her. She had a granddaughter the same age who was bigger than Iris, and she gave Iris her old clothes sometimes when her granddaughter outgrew them. Iris had never had anything new to wear. They got all her clothes at yard sales, secondhand shops, and church bazaars.

Chip Cooper limped up to the bar and glanced at the heavyset blond waitress. Her hair had black roots, but she had a friendly smile.

"Is Harry here?" he asked her, and she cocked her head toward the kitchen.

"He's fixing something. He'll be back in a minute. The dishwasher's broken. Coffee?" They served lunch and dinner. It was early to start drinking, although some did. Chip wanted a beer, but settled for a cup of coffee while he waited, and drank it standing at the bar. There was a small stage set up at the back of the room, and once in a while they had a live band. The ranch hands liked it, and when they had live music it drew a fair crowd.

Harry came back to the bar ten minutes later, wiping his hands on a rag, and told the waitress he'd fixed the dishwasher. He glanced at Chip. He'd seen him there before.

"Hey, how're you doing?" Chip asked him. They had an ancient air conditioner, which kept the place only slightly cooler than the temperature outside. "You've got a treat in store," Chip told him. Harry was short and stocky, bald, and somewhere in his fifties. His bar did well. They got a good crowd on the weekends. Chip had noticed that himself, which was why he was here.

"Yeah, how do you figure that?" Harry asked him with a suspicious glance.

"I've got a kid whose voice your customers will never forget. She can sing anything they want to hear. She's just a girl, but she sings better than any woman on the radio. She'll be a big star one day." Harry didn't look enthused at the prospect.

"How old is she?" Harry asked him, and Chip hesitated.

"She's twelve, but you forget it when you hear her. She can hit the high notes like nobody else."

"I can't have a twelve-year-old singing in a bar," Harry said, visibly annoyed at the suggestion. Pearl, the waitress, grinned and disappeared into the kitchen to load the dishwasher Harry had just repaired. They needed a new one, but he was keeping the old one alive. Harry liked making money, he just didn't like spending it. Pearl was still smiling at the idea of a twelve-year-old singing at his bar. That was never going to happen. Chip had the wrong guy for that.

"I've got her with me, if you want to have a listen," Chip persisted. "She doesn't need to hang around. I can bring her in right before she starts, and get her out as soon as she's finished." Harry could just imagine some tricked-out kid, wearing an inch of makeup, and dressed like a chorus girl from Vegas, none of which appealed to him at all. He didn't want every pedophile in Texas hanging out at his bar. He was a decent guy, and ran a respectable establishment. Families came for Sunday dinner, not just ranch hands wanting to get drunk. "Just let her sing you one song, you'll see what I mean."

"I can't hire a kid that age to sing here. It's not right," Harry said stubbornly, but Chip looked like he wouldn't leave until Harry finally heard her.

There were no customers at that hour, and just to get rid of Chip, Harry finally agreed to hear her. "Okay. Where is she?"

"Outside, in my truck."

"In this heat? Are you crazy? You got air-conditioning in your truck?" Chip shook his head, and was already halfway to the door. He was at the truck in a few long uneven strides, with his limp. Iris was sitting cross-legged on the seat, red-faced from the heat and singing along with the music on the radio.

"C'mon," he said when he opened the door. "I got you an audition."

"For what?" She looked surprised. She'd sung in churches and at church socials, but never at a bar.

"They have a setup for live music in the back." He took a boom box from the floor behind his seat, and Iris hopped out, and followed him back into the bar. She was flushed from the heat. Pearl poured her a Coke and handed it to her as soon as she saw her, while Harry stared at her.

"She's twelve?" he asked. She looked more like nine or ten, and she wasn't decked out in makeup and sexy clothes as he had feared. She looked like a normal, ordinary kid. "What's your name?" he asked her in a kind voice.

"Iris." She smiled at him and took a long sip of the ice-cold Coke, and thanked Pearl for it.

"Your dad says you have a knockout voice." She looked suddenly shy.

"I like to sing."

Chip set the boom box down on the bar. "I've got the instrumentals she sings to on here. She can sing anything you want. Ballads, country, western. She can sing requests. She knows everything on the radio." He signaled to Iris to back away a little, which she did. She set the glass down on a table, and Chip turned the machine on. Just before he did, he reminded her to hit the high notes, and she nodded. She got right into the first song without hesitating, an old cowboy song the ranch hands always loved, followed by "Somewhere Over the Rainbow," which gave Harry a sense of the range of her voice. The next one was a gospel song, and she did as her father had told her. She hit the high notes and held them. Harry and Pearl stared at her. Chip turned the machine off after the third song, and Harry looked at him skeptically. He had guessed what the trick was. She was lip-synching. No child could sing like that and few women were able to. The ones who could were famous.

"Okay," he said cynically. "Great performance. Now let's see what she can do without the music on." He was sure that they would beat a quick retreat after that, and Chip didn't look happy. She sounded better with the music, but he gave Iris the nod and she sang three more songs a cappella. Her voice was even stronger without the music. She had a voice that filled the entire room, and she hit high notes like he'd never heard before. Chip was right. Iris sang like a grown woman, but she was this slip of a girl, who didn't even look her age, and had a voice that ripped your heart out. Harry and Pearl stood mesmerized. Iris clearly wasn't lip-synching. Chip was right. She could sing anything, and hit the high notes like no one else.

"Your customers are going to go crazy when they hear that," Chip said, and Harry looked at her intently. He liked how clean and normal she looked. No makeup, no artifice, there was no suggestion of sex about her, and she still had the body of a child. Little girls dressed up like women and trying to be sexy made Harry uncomfortable, and he didn't want any part of that. There was nothing suggestive about her. She looked like an ordinary little girl.

"Have you had singing lessons?" Harry asked her, still amazed by what he'd heard, and Pearl handed her another Coke.

"No, I've just been singing all my life. I sing in church choirs sometimes, when we stay somewhere long enough," Iris told him. There was no way her father could have paid for singing lessons, but she didn't say that because it would embarrass him. "I listen to the radio a lot."

"She knows all the hit songs," Chip intervened again. "So what do you think?" he asked Harry.

"I think you have a prodigy on your hands." The contrast between the way she looked and the way she sang was utterly incongruous, and he didn't know how people would react, particularly since she was so small and looked so young.

"Why don't you try her for a couple of nights? I guarantee your customers will be begging you to get her back." It was entirely possible after what he had just heard. Live entertainment was hard to come by. They had to rely on the occasional cowboy band, or a group passing through on their way to somewhere else.

Harry turned to Chip and asked him, "What did you have in mind?" At night there were two waitresses, Pearl and Sally, and Harry tended bar. It was a small operation, but a profitable one. The ranch hands left pretty good tips when they drank. The food was decent and he had a loyal clientele. The cook came in at night. Harry made lunch himself.

"Six nights a week, twenty-five a night."

"Weeknights are slow. Maybe Thursday through Sunday," Harry countered.

"Five nights at thirty bucks a night," Chip said, "and she gets to keep her tips. You won't be sorry. And weeknights won't be slow if she's singing."

Harry wondered if Chip might be right, and he felt sorry for Iris, with her father dragging her around bars to have her sing, at her age.

"You'll keep an eye on her so no one hassles her?" He looked at Chip sternly, and he nodded. "We'll try it for a week and see how it goes. If people love it, she can have the job, five nights at twenty-five a night." That would give them five hundred dollars a month, which would make a big difference for them. It was easy money, and Harry could afford it.

"And I'll get her in and out. She can wait for me in the truck." It sounded like a miserable life for a kid her age, but she didn't look unhappy. While the men were talking, Pearl offered her a piece of peach pie with vanilla ice cream on top, and Iris stared at it hungrily. She sat down and gobbled it up immediately, and took the plate out to the kitchen. The equipment was old, but the place was clean.

Chip had a beer before they left, and told Iris to wait for him in the truck. She left quietly after thanking Harry and Pearl. After Chip left, Harry turned to Pearl and shook his head.

"That poor kid. He'd have her singing in a coal mine if it made him a buck. But her voice is a gift from God."

They'd agreed that she would go on at nine o'clock and do a full set. She would be starting in two days, on Wednesday.

"What if they don't like what I sing?" She looked at her father nervously as they pulled up at the house where they were living for now.

"They're going to love you. And you're going to be a big star one day. Don't forget that. What are you going to wear?"

"My blue dress." It was the only nice dress she had, and she rarely got a chance to wear it. She had a pair of sandals to go with it. She wore that when she sang in church.

"You'll make some money on tips too." Chip was smiling, pleased with himself. They needed the money, and this could be the start of her singing career. The possibilities were endless. He'd been waiting for this moment for years. She had found her voice at six.

"They're nice," Iris said, thinking of Harry and Pearl, and the peach pie and Cokes.

"So is the money." Chip grinned broadly, as they got out of the truck, and Iris went to check that her blue dress looked all right. She was nervous about singing at the bar, but she liked the idea too. As long as she got to sing, everything would be okay. Singing always fixed everything and made her happy.

On Wednesday night, Chip drove Iris to Harry's at eight-thirty. They got there in ten minutes, and he told Iris to wait in the truck, just as he had told Harry he would. Once inside, he sidled up to the bar, and had a beer with a whiskey chaser. By the time he finished, it was time for her to go on.

Harry told him to bring Iris in through the kitchen. The stage was set up for her with a microphone, and Chip plugged in the boom box for the instrumentals.

When Harry saw her walk in, in her little blue

dress the color of her eyes, he wondered what he was doing and if he was crazy. No one saw her arrive. He dimmed the lights, and got up on the stage himself and said that he had a surprise for his customers. They had a special guest with them that night, Iris Cooper.

She hopped onto the stage when Harry stepped down and smiled at the people finishing dinner and standing at the bar. Her father turned on her music. No one knew what to expect, and then she started to sing. She sang a few country songs made famous by well-known singers, moved into ballads, and some show tunes, sang a couple of current hits, and closed with a gospel song that had everyone applauding as soon as she finished. People were stunned by what they'd heard. She bowed and thanked them, and suddenly looked like a girl again. It was as though she morphed into an adult when she sang, and then turned back into a child again when it was over. She grinned from the stage, and said, "See ya'll soon!" then hopped down and disappeared into the kitchen, where Pearl handed her a plate of meatloaf and mashed potatoes to take back to the truck with her.

"You were fantastic!" Pearl whispered to her. "They loved you!"

"It was fun, and thank you for dinner," she said, before scampering back to the truck with the plate. Harry had left a bowl on the stage for people who wanted to leave a tip for her. Several people got up and dropped a dollar bill or two in the bowl. People talked about her for the rest of the night, and Harry grinned at Chip when the performance was over.

"She's a winner," he said to Chip.

"What did I tell you?" Chip said smugly. "She's going to be big one day." It seemed like a distinct possibility after listening to her for a whole set. "She can play requests on my guitar if you want her to."

"They loved it." Harry was beaming, still surprised.

Chip hung around the bar for an hour, and then went out to the truck where Iris was listening to the radio. She had finished the dinner Pearl had given her and taken the plate back into the kitchen. She'd had fun singing for their customers.

"How was it?" she asked her father when he drove her home.

"Pretty good," he said. "Don't forget to hit the high notes. They always love that."

"I did."

"You can go higher," he reminded her, and she grinned.

"I'll do it tomorrow," she promised.

"You should bring the guitar too, in case they want you to play requests." She nodded. This was going to be fun. It already was.

By the end of the week, everyone was talking about the amazing kid singing at Harry's, and people were coming just to see her. All the tables were filled on Saturday, after her Friday night performance. She had made five dollars in tips the first night, eight on Thursday, ten on Friday, and sixteen on Saturday. Her father said he would keep the money safe for her, so she gave it to him.

On Sunday night, still feeling a little crazy for having a twelve-year-old singer at the bar and restaurant, Harry hired her for five nights a week, at the twenty-five dollars a night they'd agreed on. His customers loved the performance and people were asking him about Iris. He said she was just a very talented kid. They agreed with him.

Iris raked in the money for the rest of the summer. It slowed down a little in the fall, when people stayed home more and the weather cooled, but she still filled the house every weekend, and had increased business on weeknights. Harry asked Chip if it would be a problem on school nights, and he responded that Iris did her homework before she came to work, and could sleep in the truck after she performed.

Pearl had made Iris a new dress by then. It was a plain navy blue dress. Her father had let her use some of her tip money to buy a pair of plain black leather flat shoes. Nothing sexy or too grown up. She looked beautiful in her new dress when she sang with her long blond hair down. She was a pretty little girl and Pearl said she would grow up to be a beauty. Chip had been a handsome man before he'd started looking so dissipated from too much hard living. And she'd seen in an old photograph of her mother that she was beautiful. Chip had thrown the photograph away. Iris had none of her mother.

They stayed in Lake City until Christmas, when Chip decided it was time to move on. He wanted to try their luck in a bigger town, where he thought there would be more opportunities.

Iris was sad to leave. She loved singing at Harry's, and Pearl and Sally, the other waitress, were so good to her. Harry was nice too. She'd have to go to a new school again when they moved to a new town. But Chip promised her he knew what he was doing. They'd make more money somewhere else.

Pearl made her a black velvet dress before they left. It had a white satin collar, and Sally gave her a headband to go with it, with little pearls she had sewn on it herself. Iris looked like Alice in Wonderland when she was onstage, and she sang like Barbra Streisand, or any of the big stars in Hollywood.

Pearl, Sally, and Harry had tears in their eyes on her last night, and Pearl hugged her tight. Iris had tears running down her cheeks when she left. She knew she'd never forget them.

"You need a bigger audience. More tips," Chip said, as he drove out of town. "We're heading for

Houston. This was only the beginning. You're going to be a big star one day . . . just keep hitting those high notes."

She nodded, but couldn't speak. She was too sad about leaving. Harry, Pearl, and Sally were the only family she had ever known. But her father had bigger dreams. He had a gold mine in his hands and he knew it. Harry worried about what would happen to her now, with a man like Chip as a father, who wanted only to exploit her. If she were to become a star one day, she had a long, hard road ahead.

Chapter 2

They hung around the Houston area for a few years, far enough outside the city that Chip could always find a bar where they'd let Iris perform. She was an oddity for the bars they found, a curiosity, but once they heard her sing, they would hire her. They'd stay for a few months, and then Chip would get the itch to move on. Iris went to a new school every time they got to a new town. She made a few friends, but not many. She knew they'd be leaving again soon, whenever her father got bored or heard about what he thought would be a better town with a better place for her to perform. He wasn't particular about where he let her sing, and once they heard her, the bar owners' objections melted like ice cream in the Texas sun. She was too good to pass up and their customers loved her. She still missed Harry, Sally, and Pearl, and dropped them a postcard from time to time. It reassured them. Harry would look at the cards she sent and shake his head.

"They moved again. That guy can't stay in one place for six months."

When she was sixteen, they went to Austin, which Iris loved. Chip didn't. It was too polished for him, with a university, and too sophisticated. He liked the dusty cowboy towns, which were more familiar. But the money was good in Austin, and Iris was finally looking more grown up, so seeing her perform in a bar wasn't as shocking. They figured she was a college student. She was still small, but she was starting to look more mature.

Her act stayed as clean as it had been when she was twelve. It was all about her voice, and the songs, and more and more she performed the ones she'd written. She wrote the lyrics and the music, and the messages were strong. She could nail a ballad like no one else, sing some old Elvis songs, newer hits, and country when the audiences requested it. Fame hadn't found her yet, but her talent dazzled everyone who heard her, and her father exploited her liberally.

Chip gave her pocket money, kept the rest and drank most of it. Sometimes she helped herself to some of the tips before he got his hands on them, but she never gave him a hard time. He was capable of some serious nastiness if he'd been drinking, and threatened to kick her ass. She grew up believing it was how most men behaved, with a few exceptions. She had no pie-in-the-sky dreams about wanting to buy expensive things. She would have just liked to stay in one place for a while. She had gone to eleven schools to get through high school. They stayed in Austin for nine months, the longest they'd been in any town. They spent a few months in Arizona, and then moved to Nevada for her senior year of high school. She got her high school diploma in a town fifty miles outside Las Vegas, after living in four towns before that.

There was a method to Chip's madness. By Iris's eighteenth birthday, he wanted to start booking her into nightclubs in Las Vegas and aim for the big time. Her beauty had reached full bloom by then. Her father had to keep a close eye that none of the men in the audience hassled her when she finished the set and left the stage. She wore simple clothes when she sang, usually black jeans and a black sweater, or a plain black dress, and she looked like an angel with her long blond hair, exquisite face, and big blue eyes. As always, she wanted to highlight the music and not herself. Chip was convinced that a good promoter would know what to do with the raw material and turn her into a star. She'd been singing in bars and roadside restaurants for six years by then.

Chip got his wish when two months after her eighteenth birthday, he booked her into a bar on a back street of Las Vegas, and a manager's scout happened to hear her one night and gave Chip his card. The bar owner had pointed him toward Chip when the scout asked to speak to Iris after her performance. "Her father handles everything."

The scout told Chip he worked for Billy Weston. Chip had never heard of Weston, and the scout told him his boss was always on the lookout for young talent. He recorded Iris with his cellphone that night, just to give Billy an idea of what he'd heard. Despite the poor quality of the recording, her voice soared, as it always did, straight up to the high notes. She'd taken some singing classes while she was in high school, and her delivery was more professional. Her voice had only gotten stronger as she matured. The high notes were easier for her than ever, and the songs she wrote were powerfully moving, with more sophisticated arrangements, all of which she did herself.

Chip called Billy Weston the next day, and he was waiting for his call. He promised to come and hear Iris himself. He came the next night and went crazy when he heard her, only spoke to Iris briefly, asked her a few questions about the material she sang, and made the deal with her father. Chip was only too happy to make the deal with Weston. As her self-appointed agent and manager, Chip co-signed a contract with Weston for five years for a touring deal on the road. Weston said he had groups touring all over the country. Chip didn't bother to check him out. The money looked good to him. He told Iris about it when he got to the house where they'd rented rooms. He had co-signed for her as an opening act on national tours, with the possibility of being the main feature for the last two years, if Weston felt the audience's receptivity and her performances warranted it. He made no solid promise to feature her, only to use her as an opener onstage before bigger bands. She was the teaser before the main event came on. He handled mid-range performers, and arranged tours to smaller cities around the country. He assured Chip verbally that her accommodations would be comfortable and she'd be treated well. He said the artists he represented were like his children and Iris would be one of them. Many of them were discovered on the road and went on to stardom from there. He didn't mention any names, but his promises were good enough for Chip.

Chip all but forced her to sign the contract, since she was eighteen and had to sign too. It sounded like a hard life to her. And five years of touring sounded like a lifetime. It was the life she had been living for years, with even shorter stays. She wanted to stay in one place for a while, and was hoping to audition for some of the big casinos, but she needed an agent for that. Her father had no connections to get her in. Chip said this was the next big step to stardom.

She signed the contract with Billy Weston with some misgivings, but her father convinced her that this was a phase she'd have to go through, as an opening act. He said that everyone did it, and there was a one-sided escape clause, which would allow Weston to fire her if he chose to, but she couldn't quit. She signed it, and left on her first tour a week later, in the Deep South. Weston hadn't told them that they would travel from city to city in a beaten-up van with another unknown act, that she would have to go on whether sick or not, that they would drive for fifteen- and twenty-hour stretches between towns, crammed into the ancient van, with the stench of sweat and un-washed bodies, and often drunk and drugged-out musicians recovering from the night before. When they spent the night, they were booked into the cheapest motel in each town, or had to get in the van as soon as the equipment was loaded right after a performance, and drive straight through the night and the next day to reach the next spot an hour or two before they went on, with no time to rehearse. It was a grueling, brutal life, and they played in filthy third-rate venues. She worked for a relatively low salary, with an insignificant raise at the beginning of each year. She got a small portion of each check to spend, the rest was sent to her father, as Chip had arranged, so he could save it for her.

Most of the time, there was an atmosphere of camaraderie among them, in their misery, but occasionally tempers ran short and the men got into fights. Injuries were of no consequence, and they had to go on anyway, or not get paid, or were even penalized for it if they couldn't perform. Tours were twelve weeks long, with two weeks at home in between, if they even had one.

Her father floated around while she was on tour, and most of the time, she didn't even know where he was. He checked in from time to time, and she discovered later that he was spending her money, not saving it for her as he was supposed to. At the end of her five-year contract with Billy Weston, she didn't have a penny. She'd had a few brief romances of no consequence with members of other bands. She learned early on that the men in that world were unreliable and the romances brief and disappointing. The women stuck together and became adept at protecting one another from the drunks who hit on them after the shows.

She felt that she had wasted her time and her talent for five years. They kept her as an opening act for four of the five years, and finally put her on as a feature for the last year of the tour, in the frigid Northwest in the dead of winter. They were the worst five years of her life. She had no money to pay a lawyer to try and break the contract. Her father didn't care.

When the contract ended, she flew back to Las Vegas with a little money she'd saved on the road to pay for a room in Vegas until she found work. She was determined to audition at the casinos this time. She had some experience under her belt now, with five years of tours, and as she made the rounds, she heard from other talent that Billy Weston was well known for exploiting young performers, abusing them in the worst ways possible. He wasn't respected in Las Vegas. She needed an agent, but didn't know how to find one. Her father was a bad joke. Weston sent him her paychecks, and he'd cashed them all at bars where they knew him, and spent the money. She had nothing to show for five years on the road.

There were waiting lists of highly experienced singers and musicians for the casinos, and Iris put her name on the list. It took her three weeks to locate her father when she got back. He finally turned up, and got her a gig in a halfway-decent bar where he knew the owner and spent a lot of his time when he was in town. It was a stopgap measure until she got a better job, and she had some new songs she'd written that she wanted to try out.

The audiences loved her songs. Her material just kept getting better. The only time she was happy was when she was singing. When she sang, she didn't care where she was. She had learned to become oblivious to her surroundings. It was just her and the music, and her voice soaring high above the crowd.

The second night she presented her new material, a manager's scout came to see her backstage after the show. The owner of the bar had called him. She was twenty-three years old and had a small dressing room, even though she was a seasoned performer by then after five years on tour, one of them as a featured act. She wasn't interested in what he had to say, after years under contract to Billy Weston. He'd called her several times to get her to sign on again, and she didn't return his calls. She knew better now, and what a liar he was. Her father had sold her to Weston like a slave. She wasn't going to fall into the same trap again. She had learned a lot about the business, the hard way.

She had made a few friends, but Weston shuffled the groups around, matching up opening acts with featured performers, and they rarely went on tour with the same people. It was hard to stay in touch with anyone. They all moved around too much. She'd dated one singer and a few musicians, and eventually learned her lesson about that too. Most of them just wanted someone to sleep with during the tour. Many of them were into drugs, which she wasn't. In the end, she just stayed in her hotel room, which she shared with one or two other women, wrote songs in her spare time, and concentrated on her music. She'd never had a serious long-term boyfriend. Her brief relationships had gone nowhere except in and out of bed, with no promise or substance for a future. It was impossible to maintain a serious relationship the way they lived.

They were all drifters, and many of them were younger than she was. Billy Weston was a master at exploiting young people, some of whom had real talent. He treated them like so much cattle. Some of them just walked away from their contracts and disappeared, and went back to wherever they came from, and gave up music. Only the hardiest and most dedicated stuck with it. Iris refused to let him beat her down. There were road managers who went with them, who were usually sleazy guys trying to hit on the girls. She managed to stay away from them too. It was a seedy world, with some of the worst elements in it. She rose above it with her music. She had no friends, no money, and no idea where her father was when she first got back. After checking with Weston's office, Chip knew when she finished her contract, and he found her in Vegas and got her the job at the bar, where the scout heard her sing, and waited for her after her second set. She was twenty-three years old, and still looked like she was in her teens. She had a freshness and innocent look about her that didn't exist in the world she was in. But she was willing to endure anything to stick with her music.

The scout's name was Earl Drake. He said he worked for Glen Hendrix, which was a name she'd heard. He was supposedly a step up from Billy Weston. Drake said he managed talented artists for quality tours, and it was a short step to stardom and the big leagues in Vegas after that. Iris already knew how hard it was to get on the inside track in Vegas, unless one had a powerful agent. The bottom-feeders were plentiful and easy to find, and the reputable agents and managers impossible to get to, unless you had connections, which she didn't. She knew no one in the upper ranks of her business, and was at the mercy of everyone she worked for, with no one to protect her. Earl Drake reminded her that she needed another "layer of experience" before she could get to the top. Sometimes she thought about just giving up, and getting a normal job somewhere, like others she had known who'd done that to escape the tours, but she couldn't live without her music, and didn't want to give up. She'd spent eleven years singing in bars, and terrible places all over the country. She didn't want to waste that. She had been paying her dues for years, and still hoped that one day it would pay off. She knew she had the talent, what she needed now was luck. The scout left her with his card, and told her that if she wanted to be a big star one day, she should call them. Glen Hendrix could help her get there. She didn't trust them.

She had lunch with her father the next day. He was living with a woman he had recently met, who was a stripper in a second-rate bar off the Strip. She told him about meeting Earl Drake, she had no one else to talk to. She had long since lost faith in her father, and neither trusted nor respected him, but he was the only living relative she had, and he had an opinion about everything. Once in a great while he was right. He offered to make the deal for her, and she looked at him and almost laughed, except that it wasn't funny.

"Yeah, and take ten percent off the top for yourself and spend the rest you were supposed to save for me, like you did last time, Dad?" She'd been eighteen then. She was grown up now and knew better.

"I was acting as your agent," he said righteously. "That's what agents get. I could have taken twenty."

"You spent the rest," she reminded him. "All of it. You cashed the checks, you told me so yourself."

"I never lie to you. I had some heavy expenses. And work's not as easy to find as it used to be."

"Maybe if you didn't drink so much, you'd find work a little easier." He'd lost a number of jobs because of his drinking.

Chip encouraged her to sign on with Hendrix. She'd save some money, since he had blown all of hers, and he said he'd heard Hendrix was a class act. Iris doubted it. Her father wouldn't know a class act if he saw one. She thought of calling Earl Drake, but she didn't want to.

She asked some of the musicians she knew what they'd heard about Glen Hendrix, and some of them said he was okay. He organized domestic tours in the United States and some in Europe and Asia, and she might get opportunities that she wouldn't otherwise. After five years on the road to every miserable small town in America for Weston, she wasn't enthused. The contracts were long, and some performers didn't stick it out for all of it and just disappeared, but most were intimidated enough to stay until the end, which gave tour managers a flock of long-term slaves to exploit and keep their tours moving.

But the job at the bar ended, the good casinos had no openings, and she had no way in, and no money. After two months of waitressing and doing odd jobs, she called Earl Drake and signed with Glen Hendrix, for another five-year contract, at a better rate than she'd had from Weston. Hendrix only wanted her to be an opening act for six months, until she proved herself, and then she would be a featured act, with a backup band he'd provide for her. It sounded hopeful, and she told her father about it when he dropped by the restaurant where she was still working as a waitress until she left on tour. She sat down with him during a break for a cup of coffee, and he ordered a beer, as usual. He started drinking beer at breakfast, and added a whiskey chaser to it at night, as he always did.

He was stunned to hear that she had signed a contract without him, and even more so that she had her own bank account, which he had no access to.

"I'm still your agent," he reminded her.

"Not anymore, Dad. Those days are over. I can't afford to have you clean me out again, while I work my ass off on tour." Her face was still innocent, but her eyes were wise now. She'd learned a lot about life in five years on tour.

"I started you on your career," he said, instantly irate. "You'd be nothing without me. You owe me big-time for that. I've been your manager for eleven years, and now you're trying to screw me!"

"You've got it ass backwards, Dad," she said quietly, not wanting to make a scene at the restaurant. "You screwed me out of every paycheck for the last five years. You never even gave me my tip money when I worked at Harry's when I was twelve."

"We needed that so we could eat," he said, indignant.

"And so you could drink," she said under her breath, and he looked at her in a fury. He'd been counting on cashing in on her next job, and if she went on tour. He needed the money. He always did. He had sold his truck and was even driving the car of the stripper he was living with.

"Are you going to give me a percentage of what Hendrix is paying you?" He put it to her bluntly, and he forced her to be equally so.

"I can't, Dad. You're not my manager or my agent. You're just my father, and you've been cashing in on me since I was twelve. I'm twenty-three, and I don't have a penny to my name. I need to save something to live on when I finish touring for Hendrix. I can't come home to an empty bank account again."

"And how am I supposed to live?" he said, outraged.

"I don't know. You'll have to figure it out, and do what you always did, get a job here and there. He's not paying me that much, and I need it too." The concept that he should be taking care of her was totally foreign to him. He barely fed her when she was a kid, he never bought anything for her, except old clothes at a garage sale or Goodwill. Harry and Pearl and Sally had been better to her than her own father had ever been.

"So that's it? You're cutting me out? You set up your own bank account and you think you're hot shit?"

"I'm twenty-three, Dad. I'm an adult," she said. He left no doubt in her mind that his only interest in her was in exploiting her, as he had for half her life. He had made her sing for her supper, literally, nearly all her life, and he wanted it to continue forever, and thought she owed him that.

"You're a bitch, just like your mother," he said fiercely, as he set down his empty beer bottle with a bang on the table. "Watch out you don't end up like her, dead in a bar fight in some shit town somewhere." She could have said the same to him, but didn't.

Iris was a profoundly kind person, the lyrics of her songs reeked of it, she had turned out to be honest and moral, hardworking, and a good person, in spite of everything she'd seen with him, and all the slimy characters she'd met with him, and since. None of it had touched her. Her integrity had remained intact. He never had any. He was a user to the core. He saw her as an opportunity and someone he could take advantage of. He wanted her to become a star, so he could cash in on her big-time then. He stood up and looked down at her, sitting at the small restaurant table. "Don't come whining to me if you need something or get into trouble. You think you don't need a father, well I don't need a daughter who's ungrateful for everything I've done for her. You're on your own," he said, turned his back on her, and walked out of the restaurant without looking back. But she knew only too well that she had always been on her own with him. It was a terrible feeling having him walk out on her. She was still young and she did need a father, just not one like him. He was the one person who should have protected her, and instead he wanted to exploit her more than anyone else and already had.

She bussed her cup and saucer, threw away his empty beer bottle, wiped off the table with a damp rag, and went back to work. She wondered if she'd ever see him again. Maybe not, now that she wouldn't give him a free hand with the money she made. He was entirely capable of abandoning her completely if she served no purpose for him. She had to take care of herself. She always had. Nothing had really changed.

Chapter 3

Iris didn't hear from her father again before she left on tour. She thought of trying to call him, but decided not to. He could hold a grudge longer than anyone she knew, and she was sure he was still furious at her. She had no one to say goodbye to when she left Las Vegas. She gave up the small room she'd rented, put one suitcase and a couple of boxes in a storage unit, and left a box of fragile items and small, sentimental things with her land-lady. Las Vegas was the closest thing she had to home now. She hadn't been back to Texas in years, and had no one there.

You could still hear the remnants of her soft drawl. It wasn't strong, but it was there, except when she sang. She accentuated it on the country songs, but there was no Texas twang in the rest of what she sang. Her father's accent was still strong.

Several of Glen Hendrix's tours left on the same day. They met at a garage, and she jumped in a stretch van with a young woman with jet-black hair, and four men, and all their equipment. The others were a featured act, the woman was the singer, and the men her band. One of the men was going to drive. There were four other groups leaving the same day. The tours were better organized than Billy Weston's had been, and the performers were a little older and more experienced than the kids Billy Weston trapped into contracts. And the performers on Hendrix's tours were slightly better paid. And her father wouldn't be getting her checks now. She was hoping to save some money.

They were heading north that day. It was eight in the morning and they had an eleven-hundred-mile drive ahead of them, an estimated eighteen hours. The four men were going to take turns driving, and they expected to arrive in Seattle around two A.M. the following morning, check into the hotel, sleep for a few hours, and then go to the venue to set up and rehearse, and play a concert that night. In all, three bands would be playing, with Iris as the opening act. The woman with the black hair had brought bags of snacks with her for all of them, and they had a cooler full of sodas.

She smiled at the woman as they hopped into the van, and took the middle row of seats.

"Hi, I'm Pattie Dixon." She had long shining jet-black hair and was wearing heavy eye makeup, even at eight A.M., but she had a sweet face and a gorgeous smile. She had the faintest trace of a Southern accent and said she was from Mississippi. As they drove onto the freeway, she told Iris she had been touring for twelve years. All Iris could think of was that she hoped she wouldn't still be touring seven years from now, but she was in for the next five, like a prison sentence. Pattie said that she was thirty, she had a seven-year-old son living in Mississippi with her mother, who took care of him, and she supported them both. "It's either this or work at the convenience store where my mama lives. The only thing I know how to do is sing," she said with her dazzling smile, and Iris smiled.

"Yeah, me too. I've been singing in bars since I was twelve."

"I'm lucky my mama takes care of my boy. I'd be screwed otherwise, I don't have anyone else to leave him with. His dad took off before he was born. He was a drummer in a band I was touring with. We never got married. He's a big deal in Nashville now. He's never seen our kid. So here we are," she said, glancing at the scenery as they reached the open road. "Where do you live when you're not on tour?" she asked Iris, who paused, thinking about it.

"Nowhere, actually. My stuff's in a storage unit in Vegas and with my landlady. I've been floating all my life. I'm not sure where I'd live if I had the choice. We lived in Austin for almost nine months when I was a kid. I liked it, and California looks pretty good, but I've only been in and out on tour."

"Have you been to Seattle yet?" Pattie asked her, and Iris shook her head.

"We never toured there, I was with Billy Weston before."

"The child abuser," Pattie said with a grin. "I hear he hires teenagers, works them to the bone, and treats them like shit."

Iris laughed at the description. "That's about right. I was eighteen. Supposedly Hendrix does better quality tours," she said, and Pattie looked cynical.

"Don't count on it. They're not the worst in the business, but they're not great either. None of these guys treat their performers right. They milk us for everything they can get, and make a bunch of money off us, and pay as little as they can get away with, while they have us loaded into vans all year, driving all day and night."

"Yeah, I thought we were getting a night in the hotel before we go on tomorrow night."

"Not likely," Pattie said knowingly. "We'll get a few hours before we have to set up and rehearse."

She had brought a pillow and a blanket so she could sleep on the trip. "We do country, what do you do?" Pattie asked. The two women had formed a bond as soon as they started talking. Iris liked Pattie immediately. There was something vulnerable and sweet about her, despite the hard-looking makeup. Physically, she was the opposite of Iris. She was tall, with a sexy, sensual body, with her dyed black hair. She was very theatrical looking, but normal when you talked to her. She was knitting a sweater for her son while they drove. The two men in front were talking in low voices, and the two men in the backseat were sleeping. They were all about the same age, older than Iris. "So what do you sing?" Pattie asked her again.

"Just about anything. Usually, a lot of hits, some Elvis, some Dolly Parton, Carrie Underwood, Taylor Swift, old favorites, and a lot of material I write myself. Sometimes I do gospel if the mood is right. It depends on the place and the crowd and where we are. I try to tailor it to the audience."

"A couple of my guys are playing backup for you. They're good," Pattie assured her.

The drive was long and boring through Nevada, and they drove north toward Oregon. The trees were tall and thick by then, and the air cooler. It was a pretty drive, and tedious, as the boys took turns at the wheel. They stopped at a truck stop to buy sandwiches for lunch, and ate them as they drove, and stopped again at dinnertime, and had burgers, as Iris realized she had just signed on for five more years of fast food.

By the time they got to Seattle at two-thirty in the morning, it was raining, and they were all exhausted.

They checked in to the hotel they'd been assigned to, and slept two to a room. Pattie had slept on the way, but Iris hadn't. She was grateful to fall onto her bed, and was asleep before Pattie came out of the bathroom in her pajamas. Iris was dead to the world. They had left all their sound equipment in the van, and would unload it at the venue that afternoon. They had agreed to meet up again at noon.

When Iris woke up in the morning, Pattie was already dressed and had her makeup on, and had been to Starbucks. She handed Iris a cup of coffee, which she took gratefully and sipped it. It was still steaming hot. It was nice to wake up feeling like she had a friend. Pattie said she had gotten up at five to FaceTime with her son before he went to school in Biloxi.

"He sees more of me on FaceTime than he does in real life. I go home between tours, but it's so little time. I keep telling him I'll come home to stay one of these days, but I don't know if I ever will. I make more doing this than I would working at 7-Eleven, making Slurpees. You gotta do what you gotta do, especially when you have a kid. I used to think I'd be a big star one day, now I'd be glad with a job at a nightclub in Vegas, but you've got to know someone to get those jobs."

"I know, I've tried. They put you on a waiting list, and you never hear from them again. I think it would work better if you had an agent, but I don't," Iris said simply, drinking her coffee. "I don't want to tour forever," she admitted.

"Neither do I, but braces for my kid, piano lessons, doctors' bills for my mom, new brakes for her car . . . and I sign up for another round of tours. Real life is a bitch, but at least I have my son. I have no regrets about that, even if his dad was an asshole. My Jimmy is the sweetest kid." She had shown Iris pictures of him on her phone the day before, in the first hour they met. He was a beautiful little boy.

"I don't have that excuse for being here," Iris said, "but I couldn't get any other job singing and it's all I want to do. I'm not ready to give up."

"You're right. At your age, I didn't want to either. Now with a kid, I'm torn. Sometimes I think I should quit and go home. I've got another three years in my contract, we'll see where things are then. If I got a steady job in Vegas, I could bring Jimmy and my mom out to live there, but I haven't found a regular job in Vegas yet. I don't know if I ever will."

"What about Nashville?" Iris asked her.

"It's a thought. I don't know if I want to live that close to my ex."

They left for the concert venue to set up and rehearse at eleven-thirty, with their clothes for the performance, since they wouldn't have time to come back, and they'd been told they'd have a dressing room. The hotel had been clean and decent, with no frills, but the sheets were clean and there were no rats or cockroaches, which they had both experienced before on tour. When they got to the concert hall, while the boys unloaded the equipment from the van, Pattie and Iris went to check out the dressing rooms. They were tiny, but big enough to change in. Sometimes they weren't.

"It's a glamorous life, isn't it?" Pattie said, and they both laughed as they looked at what must have been equipment closets in another life and turned into dressing rooms. Each one was just big enough for a rolling rack for their clothes, and a dressing table with a mirror and a chair to put their stage makeup on. Iris wore very little, but Pattie went on in full war paint in a low-cut black leather halter and tight black leather pants, and looked incredibly sexy when she was onstage. Iris wore black jeans and a black sweater, her long blond hair brushed straight, in order to draw the least amount of attention to herself. She wanted the songs and the music to speak for themselves. Their theories and their styles were completely different, but they got along anyway, and were each grateful to have a friend.

After they set up, Tom, Ben, Willy, and Judd

from the band went out for something to eat, and brought food back for Pattie and Iris. They rehearsed at four, and were finished at six. The concert started at eight. The other bands had arrived before that, and rehearsed before Pattie and her group.

Iris was nervous before she went on. The stage was completely dark when she took her place on a tall stool, with the two musicians from Pattie's band in the darkness behind her. Iris wanted the music to hang in the air and envelop the crowd and pull them in.

The audience was excited and hadn't settled down yet when she came on. She had to work when she started, and by the end of the first song, she knew she had them in her grip. Pattie watched her from the wings and was fascinated. Iris held them totally captive with the sheer power of her voice. She was a tiny, little thing with an angel's face, and as soon as she started singing, the crowd didn't move until frantic applause at the end. She warmed them up beautifully for Pattie, who exploded onto the stage. She gave a wildly athletic performance, which Iris thought was good enough for any show in Vegas, but no one had discovered her yet.

They all worked hard, and so did the other bands that night, and the crowd went home satisfied. The reviews were good the next day. And Iris was happy. The crowd had felt just right to her, and they had connected immediately. They compared Pattie to Beyoncé, which was high praise. They were both pleased the next day.

They spent four days in Seattle, and after their last performance, they drove to Portland that night, where they spent three days, and from there to San Francisco, for another four days, two days at the Oakland Arena, with a much bigger band headlining, and then another two days in San Jose. They were going to make their way slowly down the state, and then go to Arizona and Texas, and then head for the Midwest. By the time they left San Francisco, for L.A. and San Diego, they had another ten weeks of the tour left, but it was going well.

In L.A., Iris met Glen Hendrix himself for the first time, and nothing had prepared her for the barrage of abuse he heaped on them. They had done really well, and gotten good reviews. He came backstage after their first performance in L.A., and told them how pathetic they were. He told them they looked cheap and second rate, and he should fire all of them. They were an embarrassment to him. Iris looked shocked and he told her that her material was terrible and she'd never be more than an opening act. She was crushed as she listened to him berate Pattie and the band, after he had viciously attacked her. She was almost in tears.

"Nobody warned you?" Pattie asked her, after

he left backstage. Iris shook her head, as two lone tears slid down her cheeks, and Pattie handed her a tissue.

"That's his thing. He wants to convince us we're no good, and no one else will ever hire us, so he can pay us as little as possible, and we think we're dependent on him. Only the worst slime in the human race are managers in this business, except for a couple of guys on top whom we'll never be able to get to anyway. They're too busy with the really big stars to give us the time of day, so we wind up with the Billy Westons and the Glen Hendrixes who kick us in the teeth in order to exploit us and treat us like shit for another day."

"I never saw Billy Weston the whole time I toured for him," Iris said, and blew her nose on the tissue Pattie had given her.

"Hendrix likes to show up and surprise us, particularly if we get good reviews somewhere. He wants to make sure he keeps our self-confidence at sub-zero level. Don't believe a word he says."

"He said I'm going to be an opening act forever, and my original material is garbage. Do you think that's true?" Iris looked devastated. "I've been playing in lousy venues for so long, maybe that's all I'm good enough to do."

"What does the audience tell you?" Pattie asked her. "Do they sound bored? Are they talking while you sing? Your songs make me cry, and when you sing gospel, I feel like I'm going straight to Heaven.

You even make the guys in the band cry, and they're tough critics. Don't let that jerk fool you. That's just what he wants, to beat you down and make you doubt yourself and believe you need him. You don't. He needs *you!*" Pattie gave her a hug, and Iris felt better. They went out for something to eat afterward with the band, and got back to their hotel late. They were staying at a fairly sleazy hotel off Sunset Strip, and they'd been to an all-night diner, and drowned their sorrows in French fries, chili, and ketchup. Some of the boys in the band told Iris the things Hendrix had said to them over the years that were even worse than what he'd told her. It was hard to imagine why anyone would do that, but Pattie's explanation made sense. It was disgusting of him, but apparently par for the course.

"Don't worry, he'll be back again. He shows up whenever he feels like it, just to beat us down, particularly if the press and the audience are loving us. I don't think there's a decent manager in this business."

Pattie was right with her prediction. He showed up again in Dallas and Atlanta, and was just as insulting. There was talk of a European tour by then, which all of them would have liked to do, but it was only a rumor for the moment. There was another rumor about an Asian tour, to Tokyo, Hong Kong, and Seoul. But Iris had no idea if she'd be asked to go on either of them, and neither did Pattie. But it was something to dream of.

The tour ended in Boston right before Christmas, and Pattie flew home to Biloxi to spend two weeks with her son. Not knowing where else to go, and not wanting to stay in Boston, knowing no one, Iris flew back to Las Vegas. She had no one to spend the holidays with, and hadn't heard from her father in three months, ever since she told him she didn't want to be his cash cow, and didn't want him as her agent.

She had sent him a couple of text messages, but he hadn't answered. When she stopped at his stripper girlfriend's house on the outskirts of town, she told Iris coldly that he didn't live there anymore, and she had no idea where he was. She added that he was a drunk and a deadbeat and Iris was better off without him. Iris couldn't disagree with her, but he was her father, whether he acted like one or not.

Pattie called her on Christmas to make sure she was okay. Iris went to a church she knew, and sang with the gospel choir that day, and got to sing "Silent Night" solo. It was the best moment of the holiday for her. The rest of the time, she didn't know what to do with herself, and wandered around the city and did some shopping. At least she had money in her bank account, since her father couldn't access it, not a lot, but enough to make her feel comfortable. It was the one advantage of signing a contract to tour. Her only friends were on the tour now, and she missed Pattie and the boys in her band. They had all exchanged small gifts before they left.

She spent the rest of the vacation working on new songs and lyrics, and had three ready to try by the time they left on tour again. She tried them out during a rehearsal with one of the band members accompanying her on piano, and she was pleased with how well they had turned out. She was going to sing two of them at their first performance. They were starting in Washington State this time, in the dead of winter, then on to the Dakotas, over to Michigan, eventually Chicago, and a number of smaller towns. The weather was going to be miserable, but the audiences would be grateful to see them. She and Pattie went shopping for warm down coats and boots before they took off. The drives would be even longer, and some of the roads dangerous. It seemed particularly cruel to book them into that part of the world at that time of year.

Iris hadn't heard from her father at all over the holidays, and she had no idea where he was, or even if he was alive. She doubted if anyone would call her if he died. It was a strange feeling not having any family at all now. She didn't know if she had a father or not.

"He'll probably turn up when you least want to see him," Pattie tried to comfort Iris when she mentioned it to her, "and he'll want money from you, from the sound of what you've said about him."

Iris smiled. "That sounds about right. What's upsetting is that he could be dead and I wouldn't even know it."

"How old is he?" Pattie asked her.

"Fifty-four, but he's led a hard life, and he drinks a lot."

"You've led a hard life too," Pattie reminded her, "thanks to him. He's probably fine, just pissed off somewhere that you won't let him rip you off anymore." Iris knew it was true. She also realized that she might never hear from him again.

By the second year of Iris's contract with Glen Hendrix, he promoted her to a featured act. It was a major step up, and she and Pattie celebrated that they were still on the same tour together. She got a raise to go with it. What Iris really wanted was an album. The scout who had found her for Glen Hendrix had hinted that that might be a possibility one day, but there was nothing about it in her contract. Her name was known in the smaller cities they went to, but an album would multiply ticket sales exponentially. And a hit album, or hit song, would catapult her to a whole other level, but there was no one to produce one for her.

Three years into her contract, Iris and Pattie

and several of the bands Hendrix had under contract were sent to tour England, Ireland, and Scot-
land for six weeks. They had a great time, but it
didn't change anything about how well she was
known. The fans loved Iris in England, but back in
the United States, having toured the U.K. didn't
change anything. None of it stopped Glen Hendrix
from showing up to insult them whenever he felt
like it. He rained insults down on them to the
point of abuse. Iris still wasn't used to it. Even
more shocking to her was the fact that she hadn't
heard from her father for three years. He had totally disappeared and she was beginning to be
convinced that he was dead. Surely he would have
surfaced by now if he weren't. She went to his favorite bars when she was in Las Vegas between
tours, and one bartender said he hadn't seen him
in about a year, the others said they hadn't seen
him in years.

"Maybe he went back to Texas," Pattie suggested. Iris wondered if that might be the case.

Iris was twenty-six years old by then, and had
had a near-serious romance with a guitarist in another band. They had met on tour, but he was
under contract to another manager and they saw
each other so seldom that it eventually fizzled out.

"You don't get to have much of a personal life
living like this," she commented. Pattie dated a guy
in Biloxi when she went home, but he saw other
women. She said he couldn't be faithful to a woman

who was only there a few weeks a year. "The only way you can have a relationship is if you sleep with one of the guys in your own band." They both laughed when she said it. There was great warmth and friendship with the four musicians they toured with, but one was married, another had two children with a woman he wasn't married to, one was gay, married to a male dancer in Las Vegas, and the fourth one was a sweet guy but nothing about him attracted either Iris or Pattie. It was easier just being friends with them, and not complicating things with romance. "Most of the women who tour the way we do either have one-night stands all over the country, or live like nuns." Iris didn't really care, as long as she had her music and could sing, and she still hadn't met anyone who had swept her off her feet anyway. Their life constantly on the road just wasn't conducive to it. It was a life of friendships and camaraderie, but not long-term relationships or romance. They each toured for a reason, usually financial, like Pattie, to support her mother and son. None of them enjoyed touring all the time, but they thought of it as temporary and a means to an end. Stardom shone like a bright star in the distance. It was hard to give up those dreams, so they all clung to them and kept going.

One of the things that irked Pattie was that Hendrix wouldn't pay for their stage costumes, whatever they wore to perform in. They had to pay for their own. It didn't present a problem for Iris, who always went onstage in the simplest dark clothes, black jeans and a blouse, or a plain black dress she had paid next to nothing for. She wanted her own looks to disappear so the music stood out. All one saw onstage was her face, and all one heard was her voice. The images she conjured up with the lyrics hung in space like dreams. She didn't need fancy clothes to do that, and didn't want them.

The costumes Pattie wore were more expensive, and distinctive, skintight leather pants, revealing tops that showed off her figure. Sequins, sparkles, see-through gauzy tops, and she had to be able to dance in them too. They weren't cheap, and she tried to get the touring company to pay for them every year, and the message came back that management had refused. It wasn't in her contract. And knowing Glen Hendrix and how tight he was, it never would be. The boys in the band wore T-shirts and jeans, mostly black like Iris. It was a look that worked well for her, and for them too.

They celebrated Iris's twenty-seventh birthday in Idaho, after performing at a small local theater. Glen stunned them by showing up, not to wish Iris a happy birthday, but simply because he had been staying with friends in Sun Valley, and it was a

relatively short drive to where they were performing. He thought he'd check up on them. His timing
was unfortunate. Pattie and her group, Iris, and
another band were looking forward to celebrating
Iris's birthday after the performance. They were in
a festive mood, and Iris was introducing three new
songs that night at a relatively small venue where
she could sense the reaction of the audience, and
share with them that the material was new, which
might make them feel special.

She had inspired Pattie to introduce a new song
and arrangement too. It was going to be an exciting performance. They didn't even know Glen was
there, until he walked backstage right after the
show, looking like a storm cloud. They were
shocked to see him. The audience's reception that
night had been warm and generous, and they gave
Iris a standing ovation after her three new songs.
She had really hit the high notes on the last one.
The audience had applauded frantically after she
did. Her voice had soared.

Pattie's new routine had been great. It had been
an exciting evening.

They all looked stunned when Glen strode onto
the stage after the performance like a dark angel
come to spread fear in their midst.

"What are you looking so happy about?" he
said, and they fell instantly silent. "That was one
of the worst performances I've ever seen. Good
thing you're in the middle of nowhere, in a bigger

venue, in a city, they'd run you out of town on a rail, and the reviews would kill you."

"The crowd loved it," Iris said bravely. Pattie had gone to her dressing room to get Iris's cake. One of the boys had picked it up in town.

"Where's Pattie?" he said, ignoring Iris's comment. He didn't know it was her birthday, or care. "Hiding in shame?" It was a nasty thing to say.

"It was one of our best performances," Iris persisted, unwilling to be put down by him again. She knew his game, and it was vicious. They worked hard for him, and he never had a kind word to say. All he did was demean them, in order to discourage them, keep them on a short leash, and make them believe that they had no other options than what he offered them, none of which was true. There were some very talented young people among his roster of performers, although he never admitted it to them.

"It was your best performance?" he said viciously to Iris. "You should head back to the cow town in Texas where you grew up. I'm sick of your maudlin songs. You get on the road and think you're independent, and can do whatever you want. You can't. You work for me. And you'd better not forget it or I will send you all back to the shit towns you came from. Try to get a job there. None of you will ever amount to a hill of shit, so you'd better watch your step or I'll cancel your contracts, all of you." And with that, he stormed over to where the dressing rooms were to berate Pattie. Iris was so incensed that she followed him, although the guys told her not to, and that Pattie was a big girl and could take care of herself. She was used to him, more so than Iris. They all knew why he berated them. It was all about abuse and control.

Iris walked into Pattie's dressing room seconds after Glen did, just in time to hear him unleash a torrent of abuse on Pattie for her performance that night. To Iris, he personified evil, and she leapt to her friend's defense.

"She was fabulous!" she said to him. "She was as good as any headliner in Vegas." Pattie looked touched, and startled by the surprise attack. Like the others, she hadn't expected him to show up there.

"Don't make me laugh," he said dismissively to Iris, and told Pattie that if she didn't watch out, he'd kick her off the tour.

"You can't do that," she said, hotly defending herself. "I tried out one new song. What's wrong with that?"

"You don't have the talent to create," he told her, his face inches from hers.

"What would you know?" she snapped back at him, and with an instant reaction, he hauled off and slapped her across the face. The mark of his hand was on her cheek, and she looked stunned, as Iris reached out to grab him if he tried it again.

He pushed her roughly away, as Pattie started to cry, and he stormed out of her dressing room, and left the building a few minutes later. He looked like a raging bull with wild eyes. Iris hugged Pattie. One of the boys commented that he must be back on coke again. It was an open secret that he had a cocaine habit.

"You should sue him!" Iris said, livid for her. He had no right to lay a hand on any of them, it was bad enough that he abused them verbally, and had them by the throats with their contracts.

"And then what?" Pattie said. "I'm out of a job, and no one will ever hire me again for suing him, and I can't pay my mom's rent, or buy shoes for my kid." The others came into the dressing room then, and commiserated with her, and they cut up Iris's cake after she blew out the candles, but the celebratory atmosphere was gone. Iris could still see the mark of Glen's hand on Pattie's face. It could have been her, or any of them. He treated them like dirt.

They went back to the hotel where they were staying, and the next morning, before they left to rehearse, an envelope arrived for Pattie. It had her name on it, and her hand shook when she opened it. She was sure she was being fired. Inside there was a thousand-dollar check with a Post-it on it, which said only "costume reimbursement," which Glen never paid. It was clearly to keep her from suing him for slapping her. She could have charged him with assault and battery and he knew it. She showed it to Iris, who wished Pattie could throw it in his face, but none of them could afford to. He had gotten away with it, and ran roughshod over her feelings in the process. There was no note of apology, just the check. Pattie folded it up and put it in her purse.

"I should let him slap me more often. I need the money. Jimmy's still wearing braces, and my mom needs new tires to drive him to school," she said with a sigh. But something about the whole incident made Iris feel sick. How much abuse were they supposed to take? How many years would it go on? Her father, Billy Weston, Glen Hendrix, all of them debasing the performers and their talent in order to control and exploit them. When did it end? How many times would they have to pay their dues just to be treated with respect, like human beings?

"I'm okay," Pattie told her, as they walked to the theater. But Iris wasn't. She had another year left in her contract. She had worked for Glen for four years, and the thought of another year working for him made her feel nauseous, and trapped. She hated what he had done to Pattie, what he did to all of them, what he had said about her new songs. What gave him the right to disrespect them all, and treat them like dirt under his feet? He was a disgusting human being, and abused them all just because he could.

Iris was quiet when they got to rehearsal, and spent the whole day thinking about what had happened the night before.

She slipped out and went to the drugstore that afternoon, and bought something she didn't even know if she'd use, but she didn't know if she could stand it one day longer. It was all too much. Her heart and soul were begging to be free. She couldn't hit the high notes for the likes of Glen Hendrix anymore.

Chapter 4

Iris's backup band could tell that her heart wasn't in it that night, in comparison to her brilliant performance the night before. She was disheartened by the way their manager had treated them, the vile things he had said, his lack of respect for their talent and how hard they worked, his abuse, and the slap across Pattie's face, which she had to tolerate because she needed the money she earned for her mother and son. They really were no better than slaves. It was a high price for Iris to pay just for the pleasure of singing her heart out, writing her own music, and hitting the high notes when she was onstage. She loved what she did, and the audiences who appreciated it, but the people she had worked for had held her in bondage, starting with her father, and had exploited her in every way.

She was getting ready to leave the theater with Pattie that night, when there was a knock on her dressing room door. It was Judd, her bass player, who played for Pattie too. They were leaving the next day, traveling to Wyoming, and into Nebraska, up into the Dakotas, and on to Minnesota, Wisconsin, Michigan, and Illinois. They had two months left in the tour, moving on every few days. And anytime he felt like it, Glen Hendrix could show up.

Judd looked awkward when she opened the door of her dressing room.

"What's up?" She smiled at him.

"I want to give you something," he said, with a piece of paper in his hands. He could see how fed up she was. And he had an odd feeling about it. She noticed that there was a name on the piece of paper and a phone number with an unfamiliar area code. The name on it was Clay Maddox. He was a god in the music world, one of the most important impresarios. He had discovered some of the biggest artists in the business.

"Go see him," Judd said in a whisper, and she looked sad.

"Are you crazy? He'd never see me. I don't even have a demo to give him." And Hendrix had never made the album he had promised. He had said it, but never put it in her contract.

"You've got reviews, great ones. You're one of the biggest talents I've ever worked with. Run like hell, Iris. Get out of here. You don't belong here, working for that asshole."

"If I walk out, he'll sue me," she said, thinking about what Pattie had said.

"So what? What's he going to get? Your guitar? Your running shoes? I've got a wife and kids, and I'm forty-two years old. Pattie has her boy and her mom. You're a baby. All you have is yourself. Go see him in New York." He pointed to the paper she was holding. "I want to say I knew you when." He smiled at her, and gave her a kiss on the cheek, and went back to the hole-in-the-wall dressing room he shared with the rest of the band. Iris closed the door behind him, and stood staring at the piece of paper. She knew Clay Maddox would never see her. She'd been singing for fifteen years by then, and what did she have to show for it? She was touring across the country, singing in small towns and beat-up auditoriums. At least Pattie had a home to go to between tours, and a child. She had nothing and no one. All she had was her voice. She had saved a little money this time, since her father couldn't get his hands on it. She shoved the paper Judd had given her into her purse, and she looked around the dressing room when she left, to make sure she hadn't forgotten anything since they weren't coming back.

She returned to the hotel with Pattie, who went to bed as soon as they got to their room. They were both tired after the upsetting visit from Glen the night before. It had stayed with them all day, and affected their performances that night. Pattie fell asleep as soon as she got into bed, and Iris quietly locked the bathroom door and got busy. They were both packed to leave the next day, so they'd have nothing to do in the morning except get into the van and drive farther into Wyoming. All they had to do was climb into their clothes, pick up their bags, and leave.

Iris took out the package she had bought at the drugstore that afternoon. She had made the decision, and there was no turning back now. She mixed the chemicals and shook the bottle. She winced as she did it. She spread the dye into her hair according to the directions, waited the appropriate amount of time, and then rinsed it off, and stood staring at herself in the mirror. She had selected a dark shade of brown. She had no idea where she would go, or what she would do, but if Glen Hendrix sent anyone to look for her, it would never occur to him to look for a woman with dark hair. With brown hair, she looked like an entirely different person. She shampooed it, and dried it with a towel, so she didn't wake Pattie with her hair dryer. She hardly recognized herself, but like this, if she took any jobs along the way, Glen's scouts wouldn't recognize her.

She dried her hair as best she could, and was just coming out of the bathroom when she walked straight into Pattie, who had woken up to go to the bathroom and screamed when she saw Iris. At first she thought it was a stranger in the room.

"Oh my God, what did you do?" Iris grinned sheepishly. Pattie would have seen the mess of stained towels in the morning anyway, and guessed. "What are you doing?" And then looking at her, she knew. Tears filled her eyes and she pulled Iris into her arms and hugged her. "Iris, don't . . . you can't leave."

"I have to. I can't do it anymore. I don't care if he sues me. We can't let ourselves be abused like this, and get taken advantage of by every manager we work for. It's not right." And Judd was right when he said what would Glen get from her anyway. She had nothing for him to take. Her father had taken five years of her earnings when she'd worked for Billy Weston. Someone was always trying to rip her off, exploit her, or abuse her. She felt squeezed to death, like a lemon. All she wanted to do was sing, and all they wanted to do was use her, find a way to make money from her God-given gift, and turn her into a money machine. She'd been putting up with it for fifteen years, since she was just a kid. And she couldn't let it go on forever.

It would kill her and destroy her soul and her music.

"Where will you go?" Pattie asked her and they sat down on her bed. It was two o'clock in the morning, and they were both wide-awake.

"I don't know. I'm going to buy a car, some old piece of junk, in Ketchum, and see where it takes me. New York maybe. I can get work there. I can wait on tables if I have to. I can't go to L.A., it's too close to Vegas, and he'll find me. I don't know how hard he'll look. I only have a year left in my contract."

They sat and talked for a while, and then Pattie went to sleep, and Iris lay on her bed, thinking of where she would go and what she would do. She was scared, but not as scared as she was of staying and what that would do to her. She wanted to leave before the others woke up. She left the room at six. She smiled at Pattie, sleeping soundly. She had promised to write to her when she settled somewhere, or send her a text to say she was okay. She walked to the bus station, and sat on a bench waiting for the first bus out of town. She boarded it at seven, and she climbed in with her one suitcase and her guitar.

She stayed on the bus for two hours, got off and took a cab to the nearest used car dealership, and bought an old Ford for seven hundred dollars. It had a hundred thousand miles on it, and the paint was chipping, but she hoped it would get her across the country without giving her any trouble. She had enough savings to cover it, and still be okay until she found a job somewhere. She knew she could make it all the way to New York and be there for a while without working. It was now or never. She was glad she'd done it. Another year of Glen's insults and abuse would have been too much. She admired Pattie for having the guts to stay, but she had no other choice with her mother and Jimmy to think of.

Pattie and the boys in the band were awake by then. The guys had gone out to breakfast, and Pattie looked at the mess of dye-stained towels in the bathroom and wondered where Iris was now. She met them at the van after they ate, and they looked at her expectantly.

"Where's Iris?"

"I don't know," Pattie said in a subdued voice, and they could tell that something had happened. "She was gone when I got up." She had to tell them.

"What do you mean gone?" their drummer, Willy Kieffer, asked her. "Did she leave a note?" She shook her head, and Judd looked at Pattie and nodded almost imperceptibly. Iris had done it. It was like knowing that one of their fellow prisoners had tunneled out and escaped, and he was glad for her. She had the least to lose by fleeing, no kids to support, no ex-wives, no sick parents, no one depending on her, not even a boyfriend. She was free. She had nothing to tie her down and no one to answer to.

"Who's going to tell Hendrix?" Judd asked them after they took off, with the GPS in the van set for Wheatland, Wyoming. It was going to be another long drive, and they were performing the next day.

"I will," Ben volunteered. He'd never liked him. "It will be a pleasure."

"He's going to have a fit," Willy warned him.

"Let him. I'll send him a text. We can do it tonight from Wheatland. I'll tell him I didn't have cell service till we got there. We can give her a head start before he puts out an alert for her with his scouts."

"I hope he doesn't find her," Pattie said softly, thinking of Iris's newly dark hair the night before. It was a good disguise, but nothing could hide that voice if she took a job singing somewhere. If she did, someone would hear her and tell him. She'd been touring long enough in the small towns that there were plenty of people who remembered her name. Pattie hoped she'd head for a big city where she could get lost and he wouldn't find her.

They rode in silence for a long time, each of them thinking about her. They were going to miss her.

"She'll be a big star one day," Judd said from

the backseat. He hoped she would call Clay Maddox. That was where she belonged, not touring for Glen Hendrix for too little money and too much abuse. It made him feel good just knowing she was free.

The car took off from the used car lot without a problem. Iris had put her suitcase and her guitar in the trunk, and stopped to buy a cup of coffee on the way out of town. The car didn't have a GPS, but she used the one on her phone. She drove due east, heading across the state toward Nebraska. She had a long trip ahead of her if New York was her final destination. She hadn't decided yet and she was in no hurry. She was free now. She didn't have to be anywhere, and the longer she stayed on the road, traveling, the less likely Glen was to find her, if he even cared. Maybe he wouldn't try. She was just another body, another voice. He had enough performers on the road to draw from to fill in the gap she left. She had almost convinced herself it wouldn't matter to him, when she checked in to a motel just off the highway.

She had bought a salad at a truck stop, set it down, and lay down on the bed, tired from the long day of driving, when her phone started ringing. Glen had just gotten Ben's text. He spoke to all of them, who claimed they had no idea where she went, which was true. And then he called Iris.

She saw his name come up on her iPhone and she didn't answer. He called her eight times that night. She finally put it on mute, so she didn't hear the calls when they came in. He sent her several texts too. "Where the hell are you?" "Get your ass back on tour before I fire you." "I'm going to dock your pay for not working tonight." "What kind of game are you playing?" There wasn't a single nice message in the bunch, but she didn't expect one from him. He sounded frantic and angry. She got a text from Pattie too, asking if she was okay. She texted her back and told her she was fine. Pattie didn't ask her where she was, and didn't mention Glen. She missed her but she wanted Iris to make a clean getaway if that was what she wanted. She deserved it. She'd been working like a dog for fifteen years, for people who didn't appreciate her, and her incredible talent. They just used her.

Iris slept like a baby that night, at a seedy motel. She had the bare necessities and nothing more, but it was cheap, and she wanted to be careful. She didn't know how long she'd be out of work. Maybe a long time. She started driving the next morning before the sun came up. When it did, it filled the sky with orange and pink and purple. She took it as a sign that she had done the right thing. Even the sky was celebrating her. She got to the Jackson Hole valley that night, and saw the Grand Teton Mountains looming above her. Jackson was a friendly picturesque little tourist town for skiers in the winter and hikers in the summer, and people who rode horses all year long. Some people had fancy homes there and flew in on private planes to get away to natural surroundings. She did none of those things, like riding or skiing. She'd never had an opportunity or the money to develop those skills, or do sports when she was a kid. Skiing and riding horses were for rich people, and she had been dirt poor. Her father couldn't have paid for horseback riding lessons, or tennis, or skiing. They barely had enough to eat. She remembered those days so clearly, waiting to see if she'd get more than a can of beans for dinner. Some days were better than others, and once she worked at Harry's, the waitresses had fed her well, and the meals were delicious.

They weren't delicious now that she was on the road, but she was sure they'd be better now. They had to serve hearty meals for the cowboys and ranch hands.

It felt weird to not be performing, to not be rushing into a town to start setting up, or going to dinner at a diner with Pattie and the boys in the band. You could tell that they were from a city. They looked it, and Iris was afraid that she did too, and someone would spot her here as an outsider. It was harder to just blend into the scenery. And she looked weird to herself with dark hair. It seemed like her most dominant feature, because it was striking and so new. It felt strange to see herself. It wasn't as dark as Pattie's, but it was a rich brown, and she looked radically different.

She turned on the TV as she lay in bed, as Glen continued to blow up her cellphone. She didn't bother to read his texts. She knew he'd be threatening and insulting and telling her to get her ass back to work. She was never going back to him for the rest of her life, even if she had to keep driving forever.

She was going to explore the town the next day, and she could hardly wait. She felt like a bird in the sky, spreading her wings. She missed singing that night, but she hoped she'd be singing again one day. And best of all, she was free now, for the first time in her life, with no one threatening her or trying to use her.

Chapter 5

Iris spent the day exploring Jackson Hole. It was a funny little tourist town, an odd mix of cowboys, ranch hands, skiers, nature lovers in hiking gear, and a few fancy locals with houses there, in fur parkas with good haircuts, who had come to lead their version of "the simple life" in their luxurious homes just outside of town. There was a general store that looked as though it had been there forever, some simple shops and other fancier ones with jewelry, or high-end, brand-name clothes. It seemed to be a melting pot of people and social levels, in the shadow of the gorgeous mountains that hovered over them. Iris felt totally at ease strolling around town, and no one seemed to notice her. She wasn't well-known or a big-name star, and there were a number of famous actors and actresses, Hollywood people, who lived there. There were many restaurants, again at all levels, and she stopped at a deli for a cup of soup and a sandwich at lunchtime. There was a fishing shop where you could rent equipment, and a stable where you could rent horses to ride on the trails. It was a perfect vacation spot, a place where you could hide away from the world.

A couple of ranch hands talked to her when she checked out the general store. She knew the look and the style of men like them. They reminded her of her father. They asked her if she was passing through and she said she was. They chatted for a few minutes, and one of them told her she should check out the Elk, on the way to a town called Moose just outside Jackson Hole. He said they had good live entertainment. They left and she checked out the souvenir shops for the tourists, with Native American dolls, bead necklaces, chaps and cowboy hats for kids, Ken dolls dressed as cowboys, and Barbies in full rodeo gear. It made her think of the rodeos she'd been to as a child with her father, and she wondered where he was now. The rodeos he'd taken her to, to look up his old friends, were among her happiest childhood memories, maybe the only ones. She hadn't seen him in four years, since she'd signed with Glen Hendrix. She wondered if he was alive somewhere, unless he'd had an accident, or had drunk himself to death. It was odd not knowing if she still had a father or not, but she'd gotten used to no longer having him in her life. She wondered if she'd run into him here, but it wasn't his kind of place. It was a little too upscale. One got the sense that there was a lot of money here, hiding discreetly. It wasn't sleazy enough for him. Las Vegas suited him better. And the women here were too wholesome and not his style. She had a gut feeling that he was either in Vegas or had gone back to Texas, if he was alive.

She had no desire to go back there, and no urge to revisit where she'd grown up, except maybe for Austin. In fact, she had no home, just a lot of places she had lived and gone to school, and no ties to any of them. Her father was the main link to her past. He'd always been a moving target, and now he was gone. She was like a ship without an anchor, particularly now, since she had cut the ropes that had moored her, and was drifting. She liked Jackson Hole, but it didn't feel like her destination. She was just passing through, as she had said to the ranch hands at the general store.

She bought another sandwich to take back to her hotel when it got dark, and she thought of the Elk on the way. She decided she might stop in later to check out the live entertainment the ranch hand had mentioned. It would be interesting to see what they played in local bars and how good the musicians were. They were probably locals.

She fell asleep for a while after she ate her sandwich in her room at the bed and breakfast where she was staying, woke up at ten o'clock, wide-awake and no longer tired, and decided to visit the Elk. She saw that she had four more texts from Glen, and erased them without reading them. She could guess what they said, and didn't need to have his threats spelled out to her. He ruled by fear and debasing the people who worked for him, some of them with real talent, although he tried to convince them otherwise, and often did. That way, they stayed in bondage to him, just as she had, and Pattie, and the others.

She drove the few miles to the Elk, and found that it was a large log cabin, with a neon sign. She stepped inside and the room was hot and cozy, filled to the rafters with locals, tourists, ranch people, a few of the fancier looking ones she'd seen in town. There was a long bar with people standing, mostly men, and crowded tables with people finishing dinner. The room smelled heavily of beer, and voices were raised in laughter and conversation. She stood to one side, and saw the stage set up at the back of the room. The place reminded her of a larger version of Harry's, where she sang when she was a kid, and she felt a sudden pang of missing Harry and Pearl, as she always did when she thought about them, even now, fifteen years after she'd last seen them. They were the closest thing she'd had to a family.

She ordered a glass of wine and sipped it as two men with long hair checked the sound equipment onstage and then disappeared again. Ten minutes later, three men came out, including the two who did the sound check, and a pretty girl in jeans and cowboy boots, a pink blouse and her hair in pigtails. She caught the men's attention immediately. One of the men was tall with a long blond ponytail. The girl introduced herself and the band. She said they were from Nashville and had come all the way to Jackson Hole to play for them. People lowered their voices as the music started, but they went on talking.

Iris listened raptly to what they played. The man with the ponytail sang some duets with the girl, named Annie. They were good, and people seemed to enjoy them. Eventually they paid closer attention, and stayed in their seats to listen. Annie sang a number of ballads. She had a sweet, true voice. The singer with the ponytail had a better voice, and then they moved into livelier country music again. They played a long set, and then got off the stage and said they'd be back in twenty minutes and disappeared. Iris had really enjoyed them. They weren't earth-shattering, but they were good. An opening act, but not strong enough to be a feature yet, she thought, analyzing their performance with a practiced ear. But they were young, and if they stayed together, they'd get there. She was curious about what they'd play for their second set, and decided to stay to hear them.

The restaurant and bar were even more crowded than when she had come in. People liked to congregate there late, and listen to the music. It was a warm, friendly place to hang out. A small table for one person freed up during their break. It was closer to the stage, and Iris took her glass of wine and sat down so she could see them better. There was a joyful abandon to the way they performed, their lack of polish was appealing. They were having fun together with the music. They hadn't been spoiled yet by grueling tours and concerts in bad places. Their love for the music was contagious, and they encouraged people to clap and stomp and sing along if they knew the songs, when they came back for their second set.

Having had enough to drink by then, people did as they were invited to, and at one point the whole room was singing, "We will. We will rock you!" an old Queen song. The room was vibrating with music and excitement, and Iris joined in and her voice soared above the others for a minute. She instantly caught herself and toned it down. The boy with the ponytail was staring at her with a questioning look. He had heard her, and on the next set, he beckoned her to come up, and she shook her head. He kept signaling her to join them and she knew the song they were playing, and had sung it hundreds of times herself. It was an old

Elvis song she'd sung since she was a kid. He finally stepped off the stage, came over, and held out a hand, and she took it and followed him back to the stage, and he pulled her up with a broad grin, and bent to the mike. "We have a talented audience here tonight. This young lady here is going to join us. What's your name, sweetheart?" he asked her, and she felt like it was her first time onstage, as she blushed and told him her first name. The audience was so close and personal, it really did feel like Harry's. She'd had more distance from her audiences for the past nine years, and more room to move around on the stage, and she had set the pace and tempo. Now they did. But they were easy to follow, and the girl in pigtails and the pink blouse, Annie, smiled broadly at her.

She slipped right into the song with them, careful not to unleash her voice to the fullest or she'd drown them out. There was an art to being a backup singer and singing with a group. She wasn't the lead singer here, or the star, and didn't want to be, but as they sailed into the end of the song, there was a place for the kind of singing she was best at, and Annie couldn't get there. Iris went straight up to the high notes she was known for, and everyone in the room was electrified and listened to her hold them and then float back to earth with ease as she joined the others for the finale. The singer with the ponytail stared at her when the song was over.

"Where'd you learn to sing like that, woman? You sounded like an angel fallen straight from Heaven. I'll bet you can kill a gospel song like nobody's business." She fumbled with her answers to him, thanked them, and was about to get off the stage, when Annie grabbed her hand and with big innocent blue eyes asked her to stay for the rest of the set. Iris hesitated, she didn't want to intrude on them, horn in, or steal their thunder, but all four of them asked her to finish the set with them, and she sang right along as backup, knew all their songs and only hit the high notes a few times. The applause was thunderous when they finished. Annie hugged Iris, and the ponytail guy was grinning.

"Man, you can sing, Iris. You need a job? We need you. Shit pay but free eats, they treat us pretty good here." He had a heavy Tennessee accent, and he had picked up on the remnants of Iris's Texas drawl, which came out more when she talked to other Southerners. He was the leader of the band, and the lead male singer, and played guitar. "My name is Boy, Boy Brady," he introduced himself, as they headed to an empty table near the kitchen for dinner. One of the waitresses brought it to them quickly, and bantered with them. The members of the band were friendly and likable, and they drew a big crowd for the owner, Moe, who looked a little like Harry, Iris thought when she met him.

"Boy's my real name, by the way, not a stage

name. My mama was fifteen when she had me and left me at the state adoption agency in Memphis. She never signed the relinquishment papers or named me, so I was state-raised in foster homes, but no one could ever adopt me. She showed up once in a while to check in. She moved away when I was fifteen, and I never saw her again. I got emancipated when I was sixteen, so I guess she figured I didn't need her anymore. But Boy is on my birth certificate, so I left it there. It's good enough for me." It sounded like he had had the same drifter's life that Iris had, except that she had one parent and he had none. But she might as well have been state-raised too. They had that in common. "Where'd you grow up? Is that Texas I hear?" He grinned at her as he dug into the meatloaf and mashed potatoes with gusto. Annie was holding hands with the drummer, and Iris could see they were a couple. Annie was twenty-one years old, and had a sweet, pure voice. Boy was the strongest singer in the group, and was twenty-nine.

"Yeah, it's Texas. You're from Memphis?" Iris asked him.

"I was fostered in Gatlinburg in the mountains, then sent to another family in Chattanooga, and made it to Nashville when I was sixteen. I've been singing ever since. You sound like a pro, Iris. Where've you been singing?"

"All over the country for the last nine years. I

want to settle down now, I haven't figured out where yet."

"Where are you headed?"

"New York, I think. I haven't decided. There's someone I want to see there."

"An old boyfriend?" he asked, and she laughed and shook her head.

"A rolling stone gathers no moss . . . and a singer on tour no boyfriends."

"You should come to Nashville and check it out. You'd like it. Lot of music there, lots of gigs, and you're good with country."

"I like it," she said. "I like doing other stuff now too. I write a lot of my own music and lyrics. That's the most fun for me." He looked at her carefully then. He had big green eyes, and was a handsome man. From what he said, she had guessed his age, two years older than she was.

"You really are a pro then. I just sing other people's songs. Writing is a real talent. I don't have that," he said modestly.

"A lot of singers don't. There's plenty of good material around. You don't need to write your own. I just enjoy it. I've been composing since I was a kid. My father would leave me in his truck for hours while he got drunk at a bar, or visited some woman, so I wrote songs to keep busy when I got tired of listening to the radio." She hadn't had an easy childhood either, and he understood it faster than most people would have, given his own history.

"Do you want to try a duet with me tomorrow? Annie doesn't like the song, and her voice is too low for it. We rehearse here mornings at ten-thirty, before the lunch crowd comes in." He told her what song it was, and she had always loved it.

"Sure."

"You can join us for the night if you want. We'd all love to have you. You can sing backup while Annie does her solos." He was fair to both of them, and Iris didn't mind singing backup. She was happy to be singing again. It was like an unexpected gift having met them.

They left the Elk together, and Iris promised to meet them at ten-thirty the next morning for rehearsal. Boy had said that they rehearsed every day, which was why Iris thought they were so good. Like all serious musicians, they were willing to work hard at it. They weren't just a casual bunch of friends who had gotten together to have some fun. The other two band members, Sean and Joe, were in their thirties, and had worked in Nashville for years. Annie was the youngest, and the least experienced, but she had good raw talent, which, with some practice and polish, she could turn into a music career if she stuck with it. She had dropped out of college to come to Wyoming with them, and was going to go back to Nashville with them. Boy teased her about being their groupie, since she was in love with Sean, their drummer, which was how they had met her. People who worked in music had a way of finding one another.

Iris was happy to have met them when she went back to her bed and breakfast. She kept thinking of songs she'd want to sing with them, that were adapted to their voices and the range they sang in. She wanted to try out one of her own songs with Boy. Maybe after they rehearsed the duet in the morning. Her head was filled with music again. It felt like destiny that she had met them. Maybe it was meant to be. She liked Boy and the others. He seemed like a straightforward person, and he was incredibly good-looking and talented too. She tried not to think about it. If they were going to work together, she didn't want to screw it up with complications. She wasn't a kid like Annie. She knew better. The work relationships that lasted weren't the romantic ones. And Boy hadn't come on to her. He just liked the way she sang, which was good enough for her.

She showed up five minutes early for rehearsal at the Elk the next day. She had the sheet music and arrangements for her own songs with her, with the lyrics, in case he wanted to try one or two, if they had time. She sat through their rehearsal, watching how they worked. Boy shone and stood out among them, with a powerful voice and beautiful delivery. Annie had a great voice but still had a lot to learn, which wasn't surprising at her age, and the two men in the band were good, solid musicians, with fine voices. They had Iris sing several songs with them as backup, and she knew where to tone it down, and when to let her voice soar, which she was so good at. After fifteen years, nine of them in concert, she was a pro, along with her own natural talent. Boy had her sing one solo and she shook the rafters, and had to pull her voice in at the end. It was too much for a small space like the Elk, but he was bowled over by her. Then they rehearsed the duet he wanted to do with her. It was a song she knew well, and their voices blended perfectly while their delivery of the lyrics ripped your heart out. He had her do another duet with him after that, with Annie standing offstage, which she didn't mind. She had no ego about it. She just enjoyed singing with them. When they were finished, Iris turned to Boy cautiously. They were all thrilled with the rehearsal so far. It was even better than they'd hoped.

"Do you want to try one of mine?" she asked him. "Do we have time?"

"Sure." They had sailed through the rehearsal in record time. "Do you have it with you?" he asked her, and she pulled the sheet music out of her bag for the band, and she handed him a sheet with the lyrics added. He read through it carefully. He had taught himself to read music as a kid, as she had. And she had honed her skills at the school she went to in Austin, when she took music classes for the only time in her life. Boy was impressed when he read the music, and nodded. The boys in the band played the chords and then started playing, and Boy sang it, reading the lyrics. Iris knew them by heart, and their delivery was flawless. He was grinning broadly when the song ended.

"Damn, you're good. I love it." It said everything he felt about loving a woman, and everything Iris thought love should be and had never experienced. "You got another one?" She nodded. She had brought two, just in case they had time, and the second one was even better, lighter in mood. He loved the melody, and she let her voice fly on that one, with gospel-quality high notes.

There was silence in the room when they finished, and then the waitresses who had come in and the bartender applauded.

"You guys are fantastic!" he shouted. They were thrilled with their rehearsal, and left the restaurant as the first lunch customers started to come in. Boy was on a high from singing with her, and how exhilarating it had been for both of them. What she wrote and composed was beautiful, and he was sure that if she ever got them on an album, they'd be a huge hit.

They were standing outside the Elk, when Annie looked at her as though trying to remember something. "I heard a girl in concert once, in Oklahoma, who had a voice like you. I never heard anyone else ever hit the high notes like that. I never forgot it. I always wanted to sing like that, but I can't get to those registers. My voice is too low," she said, still remembering. "Her name was Iris Cooper. She looked like an angel standing on-stage and had a voice like one. She had white blond hair, and those high notes," and as she said it she stared at Iris as though she'd seen a ghost. "Oh my God . . . Iris . . . that was you, wasn't it? Your hair is different . . . but that voice . . . Was that you?" Iris was about to deny it, and then decided not to. She liked them, and wanted to be honest with them. And they weren't going to tell anyone. They felt like friends now. Their music was their bond.

"It probably was. That's my name."

"And the voice," Annie said, in awe of her. "You're not really a blonde?"

"My hair's a little lighter than Boy's. It was almost white when I was a kid. I dyed it a few days ago, kind of an experiment."

"I think I liked it better blond," Annie said and Iris laughed.

"Yeah, me too." She didn't explain that she was

on the run from her manager and her contract, and didn't want any of his scouts spotting her if she did a gig like this one. Glen had scouts all over the country, in smaller towns than this, looking for new talent. "I'll let it grow back blond in a while," she said.

Annie and Sean went back to the house where they were staying then, and Joe went to buy groceries and get lunch.

"Want to go for a walk?" Boy asked Iris, and she nodded. He knew a pretty walking trail, and they set out together in silence at first. Then he looked down at her. "So what's the real story?" he asked her. "What are you running away from? A bad boyfriend? A husband?" He was curious about her, and she had an incredible voice. He loved singing with her, and couldn't wait to do the duets with her that night. They were going to do her two songs too, which Iris was excited about.

"Nothing that romantic," she said, as they sat down on a big rock for a few minutes. "I'm under contract to a rotten manager. I've been touring for four years and I have a year left in my contract. I couldn't take it anymore. He's an abusive son of a bitch, and he shows up during the tour to berate everyone, grind them down, humiliate them. He slapped one of the featured singers a few days ago. I figured I'd be next. He hates me. Hates us all. So I walked out, bought an old car, and hit the road. I have no idea where the hell I'm going. I've got the name of someone to see in New York, who probably won't even see me. I'm just floating for now. But I figure if he finds me, he'll force me to come back, or threaten me, or have someone beat me up. I think he's capable of it. So I'm hiding. He's been calling and texting, but I haven't answered."

Boy looked angry. "I won't let that happen," he said with a murderous look in his eyes. "No one's going to lay a hand on you if I'm around." He acted as though he'd known her forever and would protect her, and she got the feeling he might. He was that kind of guy. He didn't look as though he was afraid of anyone, and seemed like he could take care of himself. "You don't have to go back to him, Iris. What could he do to you now?"

"He always says he'll see to it that we'll never get another job if we leave, and he'll get us blackballed, or he'll sue us and garnishee our wages, till we earn out the contract. He's a bad guy. He probably would do all of those things. He's got scouts all over the country, which is why I dyed my hair."

"You can play with us if you want. I can pay you in cash," he said. "You can stay with us too. There's room in the little house we rented. I can sleep on the couch. We'll be here for a few more weeks. I'm not sure where we'll go from here. Eventually back to Nashville. You could get a really good job there. You do great with country."

"Glen would find me there for sure. I should probably lie low for a while, till he cools off, and I don't want to cause trouble for you," she said, smiling at him.

"You won't. I'll kick his ass if he or his scouts come near us, or you." She looked at him gratefully. She loved singing with him, and wouldn't mind hanging out with them for a while.

"Let's see how it goes. You may get tired of me."

He laughed. "Not likely. I've never had the chance to sing with anyone like you. You have an incredible voice, Iris, but you know that." It wasn't possible that she didn't. He couldn't imagine it.

"I don't know how I sing. I just sing what comes out," she said simply. "You have a pretty fantastic voice yourself," she said to him, and meant it. "I've never done duets onstage before. I was just an opening act for years, when I was under contract with Billy Weston. He treated us like dirt and slave labor too, but at least he wasn't abusive, like Hendrix. This guy is crazy, and rules by insults and terror." She was happy that she'd left, especially now that she was hanging out with Boy and his band, and she had a chance to sing with them. "How come the scouts have never picked you up, especially in Nashville?" she asked him.

"Not talented enough, I guess." He grinned at her. "Singers like me are a dime a dozen in Nashville. They're singing in every bar and on every street corner. I'm nothing special there," he said, and she shook her head.

"You're very special," she reassured him. "Your voice is pure gold. You just haven't run into the right one," nor had she, only scouts for sleazy managers, trying to trap young talent into signing bad contracts. She wondered if that would ever change. She still had Clay Maddox's number on the piece of paper in her purse that Judd Wallace had given her, but she didn't know if she'd ever use it. Maddox was too big and too important and she didn't feel ready for the big time in Hollywood or New York. Maybe Hendrix was right and she never would be. She was just a girl from Texas, good enough for a church choir and not much else. Her years of tours hadn't been confidence builders, but she was having a good time with Boy and his band. It was enough for now, and her first taste of freedom.

Boy dropped her off at her bed and breakfast, and she met up with them at the Elk later that night, before they went on. Annie looked pretty in a white lace blouse with her hair in pigtails again, and Boy's long blond hair hung straight down his back. It was almost as long as Iris's. It suited him. He had a lanky, sexy, cowboy look that went well with the songs he sang.

"Ready for our duets?" he asked her when she arrived. They were going to do two right after Annie's first song, and Iris's two songs with Boy, the ones she'd written, to close the show that night. She was nervous about it, and not sure how the audience would respond to them. She thought it would be hard to perform with people eating and talking, and not in a concert setup, but it was a good chance to try them out.

The audience loved their first two duets, and applauded enthusiastically after both songs, and they had settled down at the end of their meals by the time they sang Iris's songs. Watching them on-stage, it was easy to believe that they were deeply in love. There was a genuine, almost visible electricity between them, which brought the words and the music to life, and the audience was mesmerized when Iris hit the high notes and stunned them with her voice. There were tears in her eyes when they finished the last song. They carried with them all the heartache in Iris's life and the love she'd never had. Several people stood up to applaud them and Boy hugged her before they left the stage and whispered to her.

"You were incredible!"

"You too," she whispered back, and then they hopped off. Moe, the owner, came to tell them how great they were. His customers had loved her songs, and the whole performance that night. There was something special between the two of them, and one thing was sure, it was rare to see two talents like that together in a cowboy bar in Wyoming. Everyone in the restaurant that night agreed that they were two stars in the making and they were lucky to have been there. Boy was so happy he ate two helpings of meatloaf that night, and Iris was so excited that all she did was grin and never touched her dinner. Their performance had been perfect.

Chapter 6

Two weeks after Iris had left the tour with no explanation and no warning, she still hadn't answered Glen's calls or texts, and he was still livid. No one who worked for him had ever just disappeared like that, and he vowed that she wouldn't get away with it. Catching her, forcing her to come back, and punishing her became his obsession. He was in Vegas. He sent someone to her address, and the landlady said that Iris had called and asked her to keep the box she'd left there and she'd pick it up when she came through Vegas again, but she had no plans to return. She said that it was nothing of value or importance, just sentimental to her. The landlady said she had no idea where Iris was, she hadn't said when she'd called her.

The tour had made a last-minute stop that had been added, in Colorado, and Glen flew in to interrogate Pattie and her band to see if they knew where Iris was. No matter how much he berated and threatened them, they insisted they didn't. He flew back to Las Vegas and contacted a private detective he had used before when trying to track down people who owed him money. His name was Scott Campbell, he had a small business, but was dogged and had been successful finding the subjects every time. Glen brought half a dozen pictures of Iris with him to his meeting with Scott, and the private eye wondered why he wanted to find her. She was a beautiful girl and Glen said he wanted to find her dead or alive. He wondered if she was an ex-girlfriend who had stolen money from him.

"Have you called the police? Is she a missing person?" Scott looked intrigued and Hendrix shook his head.

"No. She's a little bitch and she broke her contract." His face was hard and angry.

"Did she steal money from you?" Hendrix shook his head and looked annoyed.

"Was there some kind of argument or fight with you or someone on the tour?" Scott asked, trying to figure out why Hendrix wanted her so badly. He was on a relentless manhunt for her, as though he wanted revenge for something.

"There was no fight. She's a troublemaker, and she can't get away with this. It sets a bad example to all the others. If they all get away with walking out like that, I'll have empty stages all over the country. She's toured for four years. She knows what's involved. And she worked for another tour manager for five years before I signed her."

"Maybe she was just tired of it. Did she have a boyfriend somewhere? Does anyone know?"

"I asked. They say she doesn't." It seemed like a wild goose chase to Scott, but he didn't want to say so. Glen Hendrix wasn't the sort of man you said no to. He expected to get what he wanted, and sounded like he expected Scott to deliver her head on a silver platter to make an example of her.

"Where is she from originally? Maybe she went home to her parents."

"She's from nowhere. Vegas between tours, Texas originally. No parents to speak of, she has a broken-down, ex-rodeo-rider father. They had some kind of falling out, and they don't speak." Her father had called Glen to complain about when she wouldn't give him access to her paychecks, and he tried to get Glen to give him access anyway, but he couldn't.

"Have you called the police to see if she was in an accident after she left the tour? She could have been killed or injured in a highway accident," Scott suggested, and Glen shook his head. He hadn't thought of that. "I'll check with the highway patrol in Wyoming, where she was when she left, and the surrounding states." Glen looked satisfied. "And what happens when you find her?" Scott asked, curious about Hendrix's determination and vindictiveness. He still thought she must have had some kind of romance with Hendrix and had rejected him. It made no sense to Scott that Glen was so hell-bent on finding her. She was just another singer.

"She comes back to work to finish out her contract or I sue her, and blackball her with every tour manager in Vegas," he said smugly.

"Is it worth the effort and the money?" Scott asked him and Glen nodded.

"I put out the word to the scouts I use all over the country. One of them will find her. She'll take a job in some dive somewhere, and they'll spot her. But maybe you'll find her first." Scott felt like a hit man or a bounty hunter as he listened to Glen. He thought Glen was over the top on this one, but a job was a job and business had been slow lately. He had trained with a detective agency in New York that did mostly corporate assignments, and had followed a woman to Las Vegas, in his own life, and stayed after they broke up. He was forty years old, and tired of dating showgirls.

There was something about Iris's photographs that captivated him. She had beautiful eyes, and there was something very sensitive, vulnerable, and touching about her. She looked like a nice person, a real one and not just a performer. He wondered why she had really walked away, leaving no trace behind her. She obviously didn't want anyone to find her, least of all Glen Hendrix, which Scott could understand. He wasn't a good guy, but he paid his bills on time. And Scott felt it wasn't up to him to decide if his assignments were worthy or not. Most of his searches were for people who had skipped town owing money, or guys who had dumped their wives and families to dodge child support, or had run off with their girlfriends. Iris's "crime" didn't seem heinous to him, and didn't seem worth pursuing, unless Glen was a rejected lover, but Scott couldn't imagine him in that role either. He looked like a man without a heart. And the beautiful blonde in the photographs on his desk looked like she was all heart.

Glen left his office a few minutes later, and Scott did what he said he would. He checked with the highway patrol in Idaho and Washington, Oregon, Nevada, Utah, Wyoming, and Montana. There were no accidents she'd been involved in, and they had no Jane Does who matched her description at the moment. He wondered if she was running away from another guy, and not Glen. But her friends had insisted she had no boyfriend, which seemed unusual to him too, for a girl who looked like Iris.

He pinned her photographs on a corkboard near his desk and glanced at her on and off all day.

She was beginning to haunt him. And given what he thought of Glen, he almost hoped he wouldn't find her, and wasn't sure what he'd do if he did.

In Jackson Hole, Iris was having fun singing with Boy's band. They tried out a few more of her songs.

By the third week, Boy and his band decided that maybe it was time to move on. They were packing the house at the Elk. Sean and Joe had a gig to go to in Nashville, and Annie wanted to take a few days to visit her parents. It felt like it was time to go. They didn't want to stay until people got bored with them. Boy was in no hurry to go back to Nashville, and he asked Iris what her plans were that night at dinner. There was a definite bond between them that had happened through their music, but Iris had stayed just out of reach, and thought it best for now. They were both going to go their separate ways and she didn't want to get her heart broken. They hadn't talked about it, but Boy understood and respected the boundaries between them. He liked her too much to hurt her or rush their fences or do something she wasn't ready for. She wasn't the kind of girl a good man would take lightly.

"I don't know," she answered him. "I've been having so much fun here, I kind of forgot about where I want to go next. The original plan was to head for New York. I haven't thought about it since

I got here, but if you guys are leaving, I guess I'll go too. Are you going back to Nashville with the others?" She assumed he was, and was sorry to see their time together come to an end. That's the way it was with performers on the road. She had lived that life for the past nine years, since she was eighteen, she knew it well.

"I don't have to," he said casually. "I'm not playing the same gig they are. I can take some time off. Do you want a passenger on the drive to New York? I can share the driving with you," he offered, and she thought about it. It sounded appealing. She liked being with him, and it was going to be a long drive across the country from Wyoming. She had planned to do it alone, but driving with Boy would be more fun, he was good company.

"You wouldn't mind?" she asked him.

"I'd love it. You're pretty nice to hang out with," he teased her, and she laughed. "Except when you hit those high notes. They hurt my ears."

"Bring earplugs. When do you want to leave?"

"In a few days. I think we've done it here. I'd like to leave them begging for more." It had been a good run and they'd all enjoyed it, especially after Iris joined them. She had added new dimension to their performance, and the audiences loved her. Moe said he was going to miss them when they left.

They played their hearts out for the next three days. Boy knew a dozen of Iris's songs now, and loved singing them with her, especially the duets. She let Annie try some of them, but she didn't have the range or power that Iris did, and the crowd loved it when Iris hit the high notes that soared up to the sky and back. She even sang a few gospel songs. Boy and the others were good backup for her. They had left Moe's customers with memories of evenings they would never forget, and Boy was sure they would remember her one day when they heard her name. From the moment Boy met her, he was sure she would be a star one day, which she didn't believe, but she thought the same thing about him.

Their last night at the Elk brought tears to Iris's eyes. Singing with Boy's group for the past few weeks had restored her self-confidence and made singing fun again. She no longer felt like a caged bird with clipped wings. She even looked better and happier, her hair was starting to grow out, and the brown was fading. She thought about dyeing it again, but she didn't have to worry about any of Glen's scouts seeing her once they were on the road. She and Boy weren't going to perform anywhere without Boy's band. They were taking all the sound equipment back to Nashville with them. Boy and Iris planned to be strictly civilians on the drive east, and would do all their singing in the car. Iris was looking forward to it, and so was Boy.

They thanked Moe on the last night, and gave

him a bottle of rare Scotch they'd bought at the general store. He said he'd drink it and think of them. He thanked them in return for the business they'd brought in. He'd made more money in three weeks than he had in the three months before.

On the morning they left Jackson Hole, Annie and Iris hugged, and then Iris hugged the boys. It was going to take them two full days of driving to get back to Nashville. They had sixteen hundred miles to cover. Boy and Iris had twenty-two hundred miles to travel to New York, but they were in no rush, and planned to take it slowly. They figured they'd do it in four or five days, and maybe stop along the way if they got to a place they liked. After all her years of touring, Iris was surprised how much she enjoyed just rolling along with Boy. They sang to the music on the radio, and then sang some of her songs. She was working on a new one now and turned off the radio while she wrote, and then pulled her guitar out of the backseat, and laid it on her lap, to try the melody with some chords. It sounded pretty good on the first try, and she sang the words to him.

"I like it." He glanced over at her and smiled, and then hummed along. She wrote the words down verse by verse, made a few corrections, and then played it again. It was a pretty song about flying along the road to freedom like a bird in the sky. You could almost feel the breeze and the sun on your face while she sang it, and he looked at her with admiration.

"Does that stuff just pour right out of your head like water?" She made it look so easy. She played some other songs then on her guitar, while he drove.

They stopped for lunch at a truck stop, and she drove after that, as he slept. They were comfortable with each other. He was easy to be with, and their love of music created a bond between them like no other.

As they drove along that night in Nebraska, he turned to her with a question. "What happens after New York? There's someone you want to see there, and then what?"

"I don't know," she said, looking pensive, "that's as far as the dream went. I never thought I'd get this far. It ended in New York."

"An old friend?" he asked her.

"No, someone I've never met. I don't even know if he'll see me. I got his name from a guy I sang with on tour who gave me his number. He probably won't even see me. I have his number in New York. If I can get up the guts, I'll call him anyway." She didn't want to say more. It seemed too crazy to her that she wanted to try and meet Clay Maddox just because she had his number. It was like reaching for the sky. She thought Boy would laugh at her or tell her she was nuts if she told him. But he wouldn't have. He thought all her dreams were justified, and she had a right to them. She deserved them. He was the exact opposite of all the men she'd ever known. She was tempted to give her heart to him, but she was afraid that their roads would split off in different directions and they'd get hurt. Their futures were too uncertain. For now anyway. If it was meant to be, it would happen in its own time. There was no rush. She was enjoying feeling comfortable with him and just being friends. It seemed the wisest course for now.

"You can come to Nashville with me, if things don't pan out in New York," he suggested gently.

"Thank you," she said. "I can come to visit if I stay in New York. I probably won't anyway." She was sure Clay Maddox would be out of reach.

Boy would have liked more than just a visit, but he didn't press her about it. She was on a path, which he respected, and he didn't want to spoil what they had. He had never met a woman like her. She was almost like a musical genius of some kind. She had a gift. And she thought he did too.

They found a motel to stay at that was clean and decent off the highway. They only had one room available, and Boy said he could sleep on the floor. He didn't mind, and had a sleeping bag in the car.

"Are you sure?" She felt bad about making him sleep on the floor. But she didn't trust either of them if they slept in the same bed, and neither did he. He could only restrain himself for so long.

They took the room, and he went to get his sleeping bag. They took turns taking showers, and sat on the bed, watching TV together like two kids. He bought a bag of popcorn in a vending machine, and she giggled when he brought it in.

"This is like a slumber party." She laughed, and he gave her a look.

"Don't push your luck, Cooper. I'm trying to be a gentleman. This is not like a slumber party. I'm trying to be a good guy."

"You're a great guy," she said, and kissed him on the cheek, and handed him a can of Coke while they watched a show on TV. He finally got off the bed when it was over, and climbed into his sleeping bag on the floor. She was already half asleep on the bed and he turned off the lights. They had both behaved admirably.

They woke up in the morning with the sun streaming into the room. They dressed quickly, had breakfast at a diner near the motel, and got back on the road. Iris was full of energy after a good night's sleep, and wrote another song, as Boy headed south into Missouri to avoid storm warnings in Iowa. They didn't drive as far that day, and stayed in another motel, in separate rooms that night, but they watched TV again in her room until they went to bed. The following day, they drove to St. Louis. She'd been there a few times on tour, and always loved it with the big paddleboats on the river. They took a ride on one. They spent the night there, and had a good dinner in a nice restaurant, and drove to Illinois the next day. They didn't drive as far north as Chicago, stayed at another motel and then drove to Indiana the next day and spent the night in Columbus, Ohio. They were taking their time. They went to Lancaster, Pennsylvania, the next day, to see the Amish Country and farms, which Iris had always wanted to see. They went to a farmer's market, and bought baskets of fruit they ate on the way. And from there they finally drove to New York. They both felt as though they'd gotten there too soon and wished they had stretched the trip longer. It had been a special time, suspended in their own world, singing, while Iris wrote songs. She had written four on the trip. He was stunned by how easily she did it, and by how the words and music flowed out of her and blended perfectly. It was what set her apart from the other singers he knew, who sang everyone else's songs and music, but not their own. They both knew that many of the famous singers had written their own songs.

He drove her to Times Square, which was the only area they both knew. It was nighttime and brightly lit, people were bustling along the sidewalks and they all seemed in a hurry to get somewhere.

They put their car in a garage, and found a

small hotel that looked clean on one of the side streets, and checked in to two rooms. And then went back out to the street to find a place to have dinner. They picked a Chinese restaurant a block away. There were dozens of choices, which all looked good.

"I ate at a cafeteria here when I was on tour. We didn't go to big cities much. I only came here once in four years," she said, and he nodded.

"I went to a Bruce Springsteen concert in Madison Square Garden with a bunch of guys from Nashville," he shared. "We got drunk and I don't remember where we had dinner, but we had a hell of a good time." He grinned and she laughed, as they dug into the food they had ordered. It was delicious and they were both starving after the last leg of their drive. "This looks like a fun city," he commented, "a little intimidating. I wouldn't want to live here."

"This part looks a little like Vegas, but it's all a lot bigger here, and I like the desert there better than the city. I lived in a bunch of places in Nevada with my dad. I went to a school in Tonopah, which I didn't like much."

"Sounds like my time in Tennessee before I went to Nashville. It's a pretty small city, and just about the right size for me. I'd get lost here," he said, and she nodded. She felt that way too.

"I have to do something with my hair," she commented to him as they left the restaurant. "I look like a tiger." It was streaked with the faded brown hair dye and her natural blond.

"I can't help you there. I don't do hair," he said, and she laughed. "Do you have to cut it to get rid of the brown part?"

"I don't know. I dyed it so none of Hendrix's scouts would recognize me. They won't look for me here, and they'd never find me if they did. It's a big place," she said, and was happy to get back to the hotel. She asked them at the desk and they told her about a hair salon a few blocks away. They told her she could just walk in.

She hung out in Boy's room for a while, and then she went to bed. It was comforting to have him there. She would have been lonely without him and was glad he had come. They always had something to talk about, and their silences were comfortable too.

Iris got up early the next morning, and went to the address they had given her for her hair. She walked in and they assigned her to a stylist who took one look at her hair and laughed.

"Oh, darling, welcome to the Big Apple, let's get rid of that alley cat look right away, shall we?"

"That's why I'm here. I wanted to see how I looked as a brunette, it wasn't so good."

"Most of the women I see are brunettes who want to be blondes. This is a whole new look. A lot of the brown looks like it's faded." It had been a good disguise while she needed it, but now she wanted to be herself. The stylist decided that the best solution was to bleach the whole thing back to her natural color, which was nearly platinum blond, and then she wouldn't have to cut the streaky dyed parts. And when it grew out, the dyed blond would blend with her natural color. It took three hours, but when he finished, it was a huge success. She was a blonde again, the exact color she'd been all her life.

"I had no idea it would be such a mess when I did it," she admitted to him. "I did it myself."

"I could tell," he said. She gave him a big tip, and felt like herself again as she walked back to the hotel, past street vendors selling hats, purses, jewelry, food. She walked into the hotel, took the elevator up, and knocked on Boy's room. He opened the door quickly and looked relieved when he saw her, and then his eyes widened when he saw her hair.

"Wow, you look gorgeous. Hello, Jean Harlow . . . or is it Marilyn? Is that your natural color?"

"All my life." She beamed at him. "He had to bleach it to get it back to my natural color, but this is it. I'm sorry it took so long."

"It was worth waiting for." He smiled at her. "Have you called the guy yet?" She shook her head. She was scared. She still hadn't told Boy who it was. He assumed it was some manager she'd heard about from a friend.

"I think I'll call him tomorrow. He's probably out to lunch now," she said, procrastinating.

"Chicken," he said with a grin. "Want to play tourist for a day?" She smiled broadly and nodded.

"I'd love it."

"Great, let's get lunch and go to the Statue of Liberty." They left the hotel, excited to have a day off to explore New York.

It had been a month since Iris had escaped the shackles of Glen Hendrix, and no trace of her had turned up. Glen had complained several times to Scott Campbell, who hadn't found out anything. There was no sign of her. Looking for Iris anywhere in the country was like trying to find the proverbial needle in a haystack. He had no idea where to look.

One of Glen's scouts finally called him the day Boy and Iris were discovering New York. The scout was in Denver, and was one of his best guys.

"I'm not sure it's her. I was in Jackson Hole last weekend. I went to a restaurant that's popular and they have a setup for live music they get from time to time. Everybody was talking about a band from Nashville that played here for a few weeks. Two women and three guys. Apparently, they were great, and one of the girls had a killer voice. People are still talking about them. They left about a week ago."

"Where did they go?" Glen sounded tense.

"Back to Nashville," the scout in Denver responded. "The girls in the band didn't match her description. The one with the voice was a brunette. The other girl was young, and kind of blond. Apparently the dark-haired one can hit notes no one had heard in these parts ever."

"That's her. I know it. Maybe she dyed her hair." It occurred to the scout that Glen sounded desperate to find her, as though she had committed a heinous crime and he wanted revenge. He couldn't figure out why Glen was so determined to find her.

"Well, if it's her, she's in Nashville by now. But the owner of the bar said they came from Nashville, so I'm not sure it's her."

"Maybe she hooked up with them once she was there. The bitch owes me another year, and I don't care if you have to drag her back in handcuffs, I want her back on tour." People had been asking for her by name, and several people had bought their tickets because of her, and wanted their money back when they discovered she was no longer on the tour. She had made a name for herself in the last nine years. Not a big name, but in the small towns across America, they knew who she was, and wanted to see her again. They all talked about her incredible voice. "I'll call my guys in Nashville," he said to the Denver scout and hung up without bothering to thank him for the information. He didn't waste time with the niceties with anyone, and never thanked anyone if he didn't have to. He figured they owed him. He had no fans, but he paid his scouts well for finding him new talent he could hire at bargain rates.

Glen called both his scouts in Nashville and told them to be on the lookout for her. Then he called Scott Campbell.

"I think she was in Jackson Hole until last week, playing at a restaurant there. She may be a brunette by now, but it sounds like her. No one has a voice like that. It's what people remember about her." He was sorry now that he hadn't made an album with her, while he'd had the chance. He didn't think he had to. And he didn't want to make her feel important. But there was no question in his mind now. She had been the draw on the tour she was on. He hadn't realized that before, and it made him even angrier that she left.

"What do you want me to do?" Scott asked him. "Do you want me to go to Nashville and look for her? Even if I find her, I can't drag her back with me. I'm not a cop, and as far as I know she didn't break any laws. She broke a contract, that's not a crime. And it doesn't sound like she'd be willing to come back, if she's being this careful not to be found, even dyeing her hair so she isn't recognized, if that's what she did."

Scott realized how badly Hendrix must have treated her to make her put so much effort into not being found. It sounded like a lost cause to him, and his heart wasn't in the project. If Iris Cooper wanted to escape him that badly, he hoped she would. She must have had a good reason to run away. Scott didn't like him.

"I don't want to spend the money to send you to Nashville yet," Glen said. "Let's see what my scouts turn up first." That sounded good to Scott, who didn't like the man who was paying him to find her, wherever she was hiding from him. He glanced at her photographs again on his pin board after he and Glen hung up.

"Keep hiding," he said to the photographs. "He'll get tired of looking for you sooner or later. Stay safe," he said to Iris's images. He had a bad feeling about it. Hendrix was too determined, and Scott was afraid he would try to harm her in some way, maybe beat her up, or drug her, or coerce her. Hendrix sounded a little nuts to him, which he never had before. But this time he sounded crazy. No one was going to walk out on him, and get away with it. He wanted to bring her back and make an example of her to the others and show them what happened when you broke one of his contracts and walked out on a tour. He was going to clean the floor with her and make her pay for what she'd done. That was exactly what Scott was afraid of, and why he didn't want to find her anymore. Run, Iris . . . run!

Chapter 7

Iris woke up early the next morning, and had to wait two hours for the office to open to make the call. She got the slip of paper with his number on it out of her purse and set it on the table next to the phone. She had touched it a hundred times since Judd had given her the number and told her to use it when she got to New York.

She was sure he wouldn't see her anyway. But she had to make the gesture. She had to try, just to prove to herself that she could. It was part of her fight for freedom. She had been put down and kept there by so many people, now she had to prove to herself that she could reach for the stars and had the guts to do it. It was more of a symbol to prove to herself that she was free, than an action she expected to get results. Whatever they told her when she called, even if they hung up on her, she had to do it.

She called at five minutes after nine, when she was sure he wouldn't be in the office anyway, so she would leave a message. He wouldn't call her back, and she would be done. And she could go to Nashville with Boy and see what kind of work she could get there, or maybe sing with his band if he wanted her. And then they'd see what would happen between them. Maybe nothing.

She called the number and was startled when a man answered. She was surprised he had a male assistant, and then she realized that she must have called a direct line, and Clay Maddox had picked it up himself.

"I . . . uh . . ." she stumbled for a minute, trying to regain her composure. "I was calling for Mr. Maddox," she said in a soft voice. "My name is Iris Cooper, he doesn't know me. A friend gave me his number, and I just want to leave him a message." The words came tumbling out and she felt breathless.

"You can talk to me," he said in a smooth, equally soft voice. "This is Clay." She nearly strangled when she heard him say it. "I know who you are, Iris. I've been following you for years. I've seen you perform twice. Once in Florida, about seven years ago. You were just a kid. And two years ago in Louisville, Kentucky. My scouts told me about your voice, you have incredible range, especially for the high notes. I inquired and was always told that you were under contract, so I never contacted you. Has that changed?"

"I . . . yes . . . well actually, no. I have another year in my contract to Glen Hendrix. I walked away from a tour a month ago. I just couldn't work for him anymore."

"How long was your contract?" he asked, and spoke to her as though he knew her. She was shocked that he knew her name and had seen her perform.

"Five years. I have eleven months left. I don't know if he'll sue me, but I can't go back."

"You lasted a lot longer than anyone should have to. I hear he treats his performers like dogs. We've gotten a few people out of his contracts. They're very badly written, and some clauses aren't even legal. I can have our lawyers take a look at yours if you like. What can I do for you?" He acted as though he'd been waiting to meet her. She was bowled over by what he'd said and that he'd seen her on tour.

"Could I meet you?" She managed to squeeze out the words, and didn't expect him to say yes.

"I always like meeting new talent," he said kindly, "especially someone with a voice like yours. I'm free at six o'clock today. Does that work for you?" She would have met him at midnight in a blizzard.

"Yes, of course. Thank you. I'm really grateful, thank you," and then she decided to go all the way. "I'm here with a friend. He sings too. Could I bring him? We sing duets of my original material," she added.

"You write your own songs?" Clay asked her.

"I do, when they let me. Glen didn't like me doing that. I write the lyrics and compose the music all the time. I have hundreds of songs I've written," she said in a burst of courage.

"Bring your friend, and anything you want me to hear." She didn't know it, but he never turned down an opportunity. It was how he had found some of his biggest stars and best artists. He already had an idea of how good she was since he'd seen her himself. He didn't think she was available. And if she had matured even more, all he had to do was free her from one of Hendrix's rotten contracts. He'd done it before, and Hendrix had folded like a letter in an envelope. He hadn't put up a fight for the others, but he might for her. She was very good, better than Hendrix deserved on his miserable tours. "See you at six," he said in a warm voice. "Do you know where to come?" He gave her the address. He had offices at Rockefeller Center, three floors of them, and a recording studio. Iris jotted it down with a shaking hand, thanked him again, and hung up.

She went straight to the next room and pounded on the door. Boy came to open it in boxers and a T-shirt, looking sleepy. She had seen him that way before on the trip.

"We have an appointment with Clay Maddox today at six!" she shouted at him, danced into the room and did a cartwheel, landed on the floor and looked up at him. He was bewildered and seemed confused.

"Who has an appointment with Clay Maddox? You do?" He broke into a smile then, happy for her.

"No, *we* do. I told him we do duets of my material. He wants to see you too."

"Oh my God, Iris. Are you crazy? I'm not in his league. He'll laugh me out of his studio, or his office, or wherever he's seeing you. You have to go alone. I'm not good enough for Clay Maddox. I'm just a run-of-the-mill singer from Nashville."

"You're coming with me, and shut up, by the way. I'm your agent now, and you have an interview with Clay Maddox."

"Holy shit, you're insane." But she also had a heart of gold, and he knew it. She was taking him with her, into her big break to meet Clay. "Did you tell him about your contract?" he asked her. They both sat down on the couch in his room. His legs were shaking, and so were hers. They were like two terrified, excited children who'd just been told they were going to the circus and could hardly wait.

"I did. He said he's broken Glen's contracts before, and they're terrible, and not always legal. I'm taking it with me, so his lawyers can look at it."

"How did you ever get to him?" Boy still couldn't believe it.

"One of the guys in my friend Pattie's band gave it to me. It turns out the number I have is his private line or something. He answered it himself. I didn't even know it was him at first. I thought it was an assistant."

"What do we wear?" Boy looked panicked. "All I have are T-shirts and jeans with me. Do I need to buy a suit?"

"No, silly. He represents people like us. He's used to the kind of stuff we wear." She had her clothes from the tour, and was going to wear black jeans and a black sweater the way she did onstage. She had already decided.

They were both in a panic all day. Iris thought to bring a folder with her contract, and some of her music in it. She brought half a dozen songs just in case. They decided to splurge on a cab so they didn't get lost on the way, and they arrived at Rockefeller Center five minutes early. Clay Maddox had told her what floor his office was on. Boy looked as nervous as she did, as they rode the elevator and got out on a reception floor that was teeming with activity and security. They walked up to the desk where two receptionists were directing people, and one of them took Boy's and Iris's photographs and fingerprints, and made badges for them to wear on a nylon rope around their necks, while one of the security men directed them to another elevator and they rode upstairs to the floor where Maddox's office was. Another receptionist at a desk there took their names and told them to take a seat. Boy looked so pale, Iris thought he was going to faint, which distracted her from her own nervousness.

"Breathe," she reminded him, and he nodded, and smiled wanly at her.

"Thank you for bringing me." She nodded. A pretty girl in jeans and a red sweater and high heels came to escort them to Clay Maddox's office. Boy stood up on shaking legs, and felt better as he walked down the hall behind Iris and the girl in the red sweater, and they were led into an enormous office, with a large seating area with comfortable chairs and couches. Clay came out from behind a large antique desk and walked toward them, smiling. The walls were covered with photographs of all the artists he represented, and they recognized all of them, going back more than twenty years. Some of them were no longer alive, but most of them were. Iris didn't know where to look. There was so much to see. He greeted them like old friends. She introduced Boy to him, and the three of them shook hands. Clay invited them to sit down, and his assistant took their drink orders. They both asked for water and nothing else.

"I can't believe you're sitting here in my office," he said, smiling first at Iris.

"Neither can I," she said, still stunned herself.

"Sooner or later, all the best talent winds up here," Clay said confidently, but it was true. He represented all the biggest stars in the music business, and had discovered many of them himself and started their careers.

"Did you bring the contract?" he asked her, and she took it out of the folder and handed it to him. He asked his assistant to make a copy of it when she brought their water, and then he chatted with both of them for half an hour as though he'd been waiting to meet them forever. He was just as welcoming to Boy as he was to her. "Would you like to play something, or sing one of your original pieces?" he asked Iris. She nodded, and he led them into a small sound studio adjacent to his office. There was a microphone set up, several tall stools, and an assortment of instruments, including a piano. Iris took one of her newest songs out of the folder, and Boy and Clay Maddox settled into chairs to listen to her. She played a guitar to accompany herself, and then she played a second song. Both were very moving. Clay closed his eyes for a minute as he listened, and spoke to her when she was finished.

"Your voice is so pure, Iris. It just flies straight up like it has wings. And I love your compositions."

"Would you like to hear a duet?" she asked him, wanting to give Boy a chance too, and Clay nodded.

"Sure." He was open to anything. This was how he found new talent. She handed Boy the guitar, and he felt better when he was holding it. She spoke softly to him before they started.

"Just like we did in the car, or at the Elk," she whispered to him, "play it for me," and he relaxed. Iris could see him connect with his inner voice, and he played the music for her, as she started singing, and in a few seconds he joined her and as soon as he did, they hit their stride together, as they had done before, and Clay listened closely. They were both in full form and control by the time they finished, and their nervousness vanished. Then Iris told Boy to play a song from his own repertoire so Clay could hear him on his own. He did, and sounded as good as he always did. Clay was impressed by both of them, although he focused more on Iris.

"I'd like to get a demo of both of you," he said when they stopped singing. "Do you have time to come in tomorrow?"

Iris looked at him, awestruck, and was honest

with him. "I came to New York to see you, Mr. Maddox. I can come anytime you want, and so can Boy." She spoke for both of them.

"Great, then we'll do a demo, and we'll hear something from the lawyers by then about your contract. How about eleven tomorrow?"

"We'll be here," she said, and Boy nodded, still dazed. Clay thanked them for coming and said he looked forward to seeing them tomorrow, and then it was over. They went back the way they came, and Boy let out a war whoop the minute they got to the street.

"Iris, you got me an audition with Clay Maddox! This is *insane*! I can't believe it!" He picked her up, twirled her around, and hugged her and wanted to kiss her full on the mouth, but he didn't. Even in his ecstasy he respected her boundaries.

They went to a Thai restaurant for dinner to celebrate, and the next day at eleven they were back at Rockefeller Center. They were taken to one of the recording studios to do their respective demos, and then they went back to Clay's office, after a short wait. They had each recorded the songs they were most comfortable with, and they thought the demos had been good.

Clay had already listened to them by the time they were back in his office. He said he was happy with both.

"Boy, if you're willing, I'd like you to record a single for us. I think that's going to be the best way to get you started. If we get you a couple of hit singles somewhere on the charts, I think an album would do really well then. You're not under contract to anyone, are you?"

"No, sir," Boy said politely, awestruck again.

"And, Iris, you're long overdue for an album. I'd like to work on that with you. We can start working on it as soon as you have time and you're ready. And after we do an album, then I'd like to plan a tour with you. Not like the ones you've been doing. I mean a major first-class tour. Maybe five or six important cities in optimum conditions. It will make sense after the album, and we'll do plenty of publicity for it. You'll be on tour a maximum of three weeks, maybe two. And we'll make it as easy as possible for you. Where are you both staying, by the way?"

"At a hotel off Times Square," she said simply.

"Let's get you somewhere more comfortable. Joanne, my assistant, will take care of it. We'll have contracts for you to look at in a few days. You can have a lawyer vet them for you. I want you to feel completely at ease with anything you sign. And, Iris, I've got good news for you on that front. Most of Glen Hendrix's contract isn't legal and is overreaching. I don't think we'll have any problem breaking it for you. Our lawyers can handle it if you'd like them to."

"I'd be really grateful if they would," she said politely. Everything was moving so quickly. Boy was going to do two singles, and she was going to do an album and after it a top-flight tour. She would have followed Clay Maddox to the end of the world, and done anything he told her. She trusted him completely and so did Boy. Being represented by him was every singer's dream. They had landed *in* the pot of gold. Clay said he'd be in touch about the recording. He wanted to round up the right musicians for her, and backup voices. He mentioned to Boy that when they got around to an album for him, he thought one duet on it with Iris would be a great idea. He left them a little while later. He had a lunch date. He gave Iris a hug and shook Boy's hand and they stared at each other as they walked out of his office.

"Did everything just happen the way I think it did? He's offering us both a contract, and I'm going to do two singles and eventually an album?" Boy stared at her in disbelief.

"And I'm doing an album and a tour." She grinned broadly at him.

"Holy shit, I don't believe it. We're going to work for Clay Maddox, thanks to you." Boy felt like he was dreaming. Joanne asked them if they would be able to change hotels that afternoon. She had a suite at the Plaza for each of them. She told them who to contact at the hotel. "The suites are yours until you finish recording, and after that, you'll probably want to go home." And the recordings would take time. Except that Iris had no home to go to, but she'd be there for quite a while to record the album. Boy had a studio apartment in Nashville, but he'd be in New York for some time too. And they were staying at the same hotel.

"I can't believe it," Iris said softly as they left. She owed the debt of a lifetime to Judd for giving her Clay's direct number. She was going to write to him and tell him what had happened. And Boy had never expected something like this to happen when he offered to drive to New York with her. In her inimitable way, Iris had swept him along with her own good fortune, and shared it with him. His life had changed in an instant, thanks to her.

They went back to the hotel and packed their things, drove to the Plaza in Iris's disreputable car, which they left with the doorman at the Plaza to have put in the garage. They looked like the Beverly Hillbillies moving into the hotel with their suitcases and guitars, and were escorted to their suites by an assistant manager. They were bowled over when they saw the suites Clay Maddox had treated them to. They were identical suites side by side, with a communicating door through their living rooms. They were very grand with a view of Central Park. They stood and looked at each other after the assistant manager left the room, and Boy started to laugh. He laughed so hard he couldn't stop for a minute.

"Am I in a movie or what? Iris Cooper, you are one amazing woman. You sure hit the high notes on this one, and I was right. You are going to be a star, a great big beautiful star."

"And so are you," she said softly, smiling at him. It was nearly impossible to believe all that had happened to them in the last twenty-four hours. After nine years of nightmare tours and being exploited by her managers, and her father all her life, her dreams were coming true. It had only taken fifteen years to get there, and no one had ever said truer words than Boy when he looked at her.

"Baby, you paid your dues." She wrote a song about it that night.

Chapter 8

Along with the luxuries Clay introduced Boy and Iris to, he expected them to work hard, which wasn't unfamiliar to either of them. They were exactly the kind of talent he looked for. Young people who loved their music, had a passion for it, and an unquenchable thirst to play better each time, and learn everything they could. They both spent countless hours at the studios they'd been assigned, perfecting their craft and improving the songs they were singing, recording over and over again to get it right. They'd been assigned studios on the same floor, and visited each other occasionally during a break. There were two floors of studios in constant use. Famous artists who came and went all day and night.

Clay stopped by for a few minutes sometimes too, but he didn't want them to feel that he was checking on them. He just enjoyed listening to them, and their progress on the recordings they were making. He had assigned separate producers to them, and they each had a backup band that Clay had chosen for them. The bands were what they needed to complement their voices. Clay had an unfailing ear for music, and an ability to spot raw talent, and turn singers who might have gone unnoticed into stars. It was like picking diamonds from the sand. He knew exactly what the audiences wanted and what they were waiting for.

He had dreamed of a career in music himself when he was young, growing up on a farm in Kentucky. He had gone to Nashville first, as a singer himself, and then New York, spent some time in L.A., and had discovered that he had a genius for finding talent in odd places. He had been doing it ever since.

He'd started by booking other singers he met into nightclubs, and he eventually gave up singing and became a booking agent. His first big win had been discovering Alice Blye, a huge star, until she died of an overdose, five years into her brilliant career. He'd found countless others who were legends now. That was his special gift, turning singers into stars, just as he was doing with Boy and Iris now. He always knew quality when he saw it, or heard it. He knew how to support young artists and help them grow. He watched over them like a loving father and protected them, shielded them, nurtured them. He was the exact opposite of Billy Weston and Glen Hendrix, who squeezed them like lemons, wore them down and brutalized them, and then threw them away, without getting out of them what he really should have, and helping them to polish their skills. Boy and Iris were thriving and blossoming under Clay's loving care. It was almost a sacred mission to Clay. He would help them become all they could, and discover more than they ever knew they had in them, and then present them to the world. What he did was a blessing for everyone, the artist, the audience, not just himself, and he fought like a lion to protect them, sometimes even from the risks they took and the damage they did to themselves. He valued young artists who worked as hard as Iris and Boy. He had seen Iris working in the studio until midnight sometimes. She never wanted to leave until she felt she'd gotten the song, the music, and the arrangement just right.

Clay was forty-eight years old, and was at the height of his own career as an impresario. He'd come a long way from the hills of Kentucky, and was polished and sophisticated, but had remained very modest, just like Iris herself. The temptations in his world were great. He'd been married twice, once to a singer he'd met on the road when he was singing in honky-tonk nightclubs in Nashville. They were both twenty-two years old, and she'd run off with a drummer who was dealing drugs and got her hooked. Clay had stayed away from that scene. He had no idea what became of her after they divorced, but he was sure it wasn't good. Three years later, when he was starting to book talent in L.A., he had married Frances, an actress. It had lasted for four years, and they had two daughters, Ellen and Margie, who were now twenty and twenty-two, and lived in L.A. with their mother. Her career as an actress had gone down the tubes by the time she was thirty. She was one of those eminently forgettable ingénues of which there were too many in L.A. She ran a cater-ing business now, and had been a decent mother to their girls, although she was sour about life, and eternally angry at Clay that he had become incred-ibly successful after their marriage and she hadn't. As she put it, she was just a fancy cook now, doing Hollywood events and weddings and bar mitz-vahs. She made a good living at it, and Clay was generous with her and his daughters.

They all lived in a beautiful home in Bel Air, which he had bought them. The girls had gone to the best private schools. His oldest daughter, Mar-gie, had graduated from USC and was working with her mother. Ellen, his youngest, was studying at UC Berkeley, and wanted to go to vet school at

UC Davis when she graduated. She was in her junior year at twenty. She picked up every stray she came across, and always had a flock of ragtag dogs around her, which drove her mother and sister crazy. She was more like her father than Margie was, who was more like her mother, always complaining about something, and jealous of others. Clay had a decent relationship with his daughters, although he felt he didn't see enough of them. He had strong paternal instincts, and used them to his young protégés' advantage, nurturing and helping them. He was almost like a father to them, and many of them had never had one, like Boy. He made the occasional subtle suggestion when he heard them perform, and they always found he was right.

Clay never took advantage of the young women he was shepherding and helping to launch their careers, which was unusual in their business. Most men his age, in his position, took full advantage of naïve young women who were only too willing to be used so they could get ahead. There were gorgeous women flocking to him everywhere he went, usually for the wrong reasons. He spotted it easily. There was no lack of users and opportunists in every facet of the business. One of the things he admired about Iris was that she had remained surprisingly pure and innocent despite the life she'd led and the bad people she had met and worked for. She was passionate about her music and nothing else. Her innocence and humility made her even more attractive to him, more even than her delicate beauty. He could tell that she led a clean life, didn't do drugs. He couldn't figure out what her relationship to Boy was, whether they were lovers or just friends, and he didn't want to ask. But either way, he never got romantically involved with his protégées. She was only five years older than his oldest daughter, who was twenty-two, but Iris seemed much younger with her simple, undemanding ways. His daughter Margie was decked out in Chanel from head to foot, even when working in her mother's catering kitchen. She drove a red Mercedes sports car he had paid for, and she wasn't shy about asking her father for whatever she wanted. Currently, she wanted him to buy her a house in Malibu. He wanted her to work for several years to earn it before he did, and she wasn't happy about it. He thought buying a twenty-two-year-old girl a ten-million-dollar house was ridiculous and inappropriate. He wanted his daughters to have real values, even though their mother, Frances, urged both girls to hit up their father for anything expensive they could think of. Frances told them he could afford it. He didn't think that was a good reason to go crazy.

Ellen never asked for the kinds of things her older sister did. She would ask him for donations to shelters for abused pets she was currently supporting, and was grateful for anything he gave her.

The two girls were very different. Their father had a real sense of values, and was generous when it was reasonable, which a ten-million-dollar house in Malibu for Margie wasn't. She was pissed at him for the moment and not speaking to him. She was pouting, as she always did when her father didn't give her what she wanted.

Her mother was even harsher when she didn't get her way, and Margie had learned it from her. Frances was livid that their marriage had fallen apart before he'd started to make really big money. She conveniently overlooked the fact that she was the one who left him. She thought he was wasting his time looking for young singers that he could develop in out-of-the-way places all over the country. He had turned his gift for spotting talent into a gold mine. He was now the hottest name in the music business, with the most famous stars on his client roster. Frances was furious that she hadn't gotten a piece of that when she walked out on him, looking for bigger fish, but she hadn't stayed long enough to cash in, lucky for him. He had never married again after Frances. They had divorced when he was twenty-nine years old, and just starting to become successful. He was somewhat suspicious now of most of the women who pursued him. They were transparent about what they wanted from him. At forty-eight, he had been single for nineteen years and liked it that way. He dated singers, models, and actresses. He enjoyed them, but no one had stolen his heart in twenty-three years. Frances had turned out to be a mistake. She was beautiful, but empty and greedy, but he was grateful for the two beautiful girls they had had during their brief time together. He tried hard to be a good father to them, and a responsible father figure to all the artists he represented.

He loved watching Iris work in the studio, singing her heart out for her album. She was a relentless taskmaster, always pushing herself harder and challenging herself to her limits and beyond. He was watching her one night, singing one of her own songs. She hit all the high notes, just like her father used to tell her to do when she sang the anthem at the rodeo, or performed at Harry's Bar when she was twelve, or hundreds of other places like it, over the years. Clay gave her the opportunity to work with the best sound equipment, the finest trained musicians and technicians, for an album that Clay knew would be an instant hit when they released it. And Boy was doing the same thing with his two singles that would come out on the radio, and hopefully would soar up the charts.

Clay watched Iris quietly. It was after midnight, and he could see that her musicians were getting tired, but Iris wasn't. She was tireless, driving herself, singing with her eyes closed and her headphones on. She was surprised to see Clay watching her when she opened her eyes when the song ended.

"I think your boys are going to fall asleep here if you don't let them go home," he said to her gently, and she glanced at the clock and turned to apologize to them. She could see that they looked tired, but she could have gone on all night. She let them go then, and told them to be back at nine the next morning. Clay waited for her to leave the studio a few minutes later and walked her out. "I think your backup boys may need a little more sleep than you do," he teased her and she looked sheepish.

"I want to get it right. I hate to leave before we do."

"There's always another day," he reminded her. He was wearing jeans and a black sweater, and she noticed that he looked handsome, and wondered if he had a girlfriend. He had dark brown hair with gray at his temples and green eyes. He seemed like a nice man, and she always saw him alone. But this was work, and she had no idea who he had at home, or even if he was married. She was wearing jeans and a blue T-shirt and tennis shoes, as she always did at rehearsals, with her long blond hair piled high on her head in a clip. She didn't care how she looked when she worked in the studio. She never wore makeup.

Iris looked about sixteen years old, not twenty-seven. She had a fresh, clean look to her, and was sexy because she didn't try to be, which made her even more appealing, to Clay at least. He loved her natural looks, but was careful not to show it to her. He didn't want to step over any lines or cross any boundaries, nor make a fool of himself if she was in love with Boy, which he didn't think he should ask her.

"There's no fool like an old fool," he reminded himself every time he saw her, and he didn't want to be one. He wasn't old, but he was twenty years older than she was, an entire lifetime. As young as she seemed, he couldn't imagine her being interested in him, even if she wasn't in love with Boy. He felt like an old letch, just thinking about it. He didn't want to abuse the fatherly role he had in her life. She needed him for that. He told her that they were meeting with the lawyers the next day about her contract, as he rode down the elevator with her. His car and driver were waiting outside, and he offered her a ride back to the hotel, which she accepted. He didn't want her taking a cab alone at that hour, although she worked late on most nights and often did.

The streets of New York were still busy, and it was a short drive back to the Plaza. Clay lived on Fifth Avenue in the Seventies, just north of the hotel.

"Will Boy still be up when you get home?" he asked her casually, and she shrugged as she looked out the window. She was more tired than she'd realized, and it was catching up to her. She had been standing at the mike for hours and singing hard.

"I don't know. I think he falls asleep watching TV. I don't see him when I work this late. He closes his door, and I don't see him till breakfast." Clay couldn't tell from what she said whether they were sleeping together or not, but he didn't want to make the wrong assumption.

"How long have you two been together?" He tried another tack. He just wanted to know if her heart was engaged, even if he never acted on it, and he was sure he wouldn't. He didn't want to make a fool of himself or take advantage of her.

"We're not 'together,' like that. We're just friends. I met him in Jackson Hole after I left the tour, so that's about two months now. Besides, I don't like mixing romance with work. It never works out, and it just messes things up. I guess we could have hooked up, but it would have been a mistake. It's much better like this," she said with her wide eyes and innocent face. She had given him hope with the first half of what she said, and dashed his hopes with the rest. She was right not to get involved with the people she worked with. He followed the same principle, but he was tempted to make an exception for her. She had brought him back to reality, like a bucket of ice over his head. He was too old for her anyway, he reminded himself. But it made him a little sad.

The one thing he couldn't buy was youth. He would have given anything to be her age again, or as old as Boy, and break down her resolve. Boy could have done it, but apparently had chosen not to. It wasn't the choice Clay would have made. He would have fought to win her if he'd had the chance, but he hadn't, so he reminded himself on the drive home that there was no point thinking about it. At least he knew her status now. She and Boy weren't in love. She was single and alone and married to her work. It was why she was so good at what she did. She had nothing to distract her from the main event. Clay's best artists were like that, although some of them had wild, turbulent personal lives. Iris would never be one of them. He could tell.

Joanne, Clay's senior assistant, came to get Iris in the studio where she was working the next day, and told her that Clay and the attorneys were waiting for her in the big conference room in Clay's office. She told her musicians they could take a break for lunch, and she followed Joanne to an enormous room, where Clay and two men were sitting at one end of a very long table, looking serious. They were there to talk about her contract with Glen Hendrix.

"Come on in, Iris." Clay smiled at her, waved her to a chair next to him, and introduced her to the two men. They were all wearing jeans and blazers, like a uniform, and open crisp white shirts. They looked businesslike and casual, and the lead lawyer, Paul Redmond, got right to the point.

"Some of it is standard boilerplate," he explained to her about the contract, "and a few clauses are within normal legal bounds, what you'd expect in any contract of this kind. But most of it violates your most basic rights. You have no right to any profits, and no information. You're expected to work well beyond the hours dictated by the labor laws, with no additional compensation. You're obliged to work if you're sick, or penalized financially if you don't. He has the right to dock your pay for any infraction he deems worthy of it with no explanation of what that infraction would be. You can't hold him responsible for any physical injury while you're on the tour, no matter what the cause is, faulty equipment, natural disasters, human error of some kind, and he can fire you at any time without notice, but you can't quit." The second lawyer, Andrew Stoddard, nodded as he listened. They had gone over the Hendrix contract carefully and were shocked. It was one of the worst contracts they'd ever seen, and gave one the measure of the man who had ordered it. Everything was in his favor and nothing in hers.

"Normally, some of these tour contracts can be hard to break, and take some negotiation to get out of, which we'd be prepared to do. We've done it before. But this Hendrix contract violates your basic human rights and all the labor laws which apply to this kind of activity so completely that there's no question in our minds that the contract isn't worth the paper it's written on." Her eyes lit up as she absorbed what he had said, and Clay looked pleased too.

"What do I have to do to get out of it?"

"Nothing," the lawyer reassured her. "He knows how bad his contract is. He couldn't defend it in court or in front of a labor board. We'll send him a letter declaring it void, and making it clear that we'll report him if he pursues you in any way. You're free to do as you want, as of now. You can sign a contract with Clay, if that's what you'd like to do, and you can have a lawyer of your own look at it before you sign. You should do that, to be sure you understand what you're agreeing to." Clay used a short form for young artists just starting out. Paul pushed it across the table to her. It was a two-page document, and unlike the Hendrix contract, the language was simple and clear. It stated that she wished Clay Maddox to represent her. Their agreement could be dissolved by either party with ninety days' notice in writing. Any salaries, profits, or royalties due her at that time would be paid in full. She was engaging to perform on a full-length album with the songs to be chosen by her and Clay in agreement on the material. A tour was to be negotiated at a later date, under conditions she agreed to with no obligation for her to tour if she didn't wish to. She was to receive an advance for the album that made her eyes pop as she read it and looked at Clay and he nodded.

"That's standard," he whispered to her.

She was to get a twenty-five percent royalty on the album, which was at the high end, with front- and back-end profits. She had an option for a second album, and all publicity and use of her image or name had to have her consent. It was all in black and white on the page, and she didn't need an attorney to tell her it was a great contract. Clay's contracts were always generous and fair. He wanted his artists to be happy and most of them were, except the greediest stars, to whom he made additional concessions when he thought they were worth it, and some were. Her contract also said that all costumes worn onstage or for publicity events were to be paid for by Clay. They had left nothing out. And Boy had been given a similar contract for his two singles, with an option for an album if the singles were a success.

"Where's a pen?" Iris asked, and the three men laughed.

"You really should have a lawyer look at it for you," Paul Redmond said gently.

"Why? I can read. Everything is right here. The only things I didn't get were a Rolls-Royce and a dog."

Clay slapped his head as she said it and looked

at his attorneys. "Damn! Did you forget those again?" He turned to Iris. "What kind of dog?"

"A white fluffy Chihuahua," she said, joking. She'd always wanted a dog as a kid, but there had been no way to have one with the life she led with her father. They had picked up a stray once, and he'd traveled in the truck with them for two weeks and then got hit by a car at a truck stop. Her father wasn't even responsible enough to take care of a dog, let alone a child.

Andy Stoddard handed her a pen as Clay nodded, and she signed her name on three copies, one for herself, one for Clay, and one for the office. Then she turned and kissed Clay on the cheek with a grateful look. "Thank you for being so good to me." He really was like a father to her, the kind one dreamed of and she'd never had. Then she turned to the two attorneys. "And thank you for getting rid of Glen Hendrix for me."

"Consider it done. We'll get the notice of termination letter out to him today. You'll never hear from him again. There's no way he can fight this. His contract is a disgrace." She nodded and believed them. He was a miserable human being.

She left Clay with the attorneys then, and ran into Boy in the hall, coming back from lunch.

"I just signed with Clay." She was grinning broadly. "And they're getting me out of my old contract."

"So did I." Boy looked jubilant too. "I got a fifty-thousand-dollar signing bonus," he said with awe. She had gotten a hundred-thousand-dollar signing bonus for her album, and had no idea what to do with it. She was going to put it all in the bank. "Let's go out to dinner tonight, and celebrate," he suggested to her.

"I'd love it."

"There's a diner on Tenth Avenue everyone says is great," he said, and she laughed.

"We're going to have to get used to better than diners now, I guess," she said with a dreamy expression. It was all so hard to believe. But it was real.

There were red roses waiting for her at the hotel with a card when she got back there. "Welcome to the family. Love, Clay."

She called Pattie on her cell. She told her she had signed with Clay, but not about the money. She didn't want to make her feel bad. She had already written to Judd to thank him for the phone number that had changed her life. Pattie sounded tired and down.

"What about the contract?" Pattie asked her.

"They're getting me out of it. They said it's no problem. It's not even legal. It violates all the labor laws and our human rights. You can get out of yours too," she reminded her.

"I need the job. I may have to go home for a

while, if he'll let me. My mom is sick. I don't have anyone else to take care of Jimmy."

"How sick?" Iris was worried about her, she knew how Pattie depended on her mother to take care of her son.

"I don't know. Maybe she's just tired. He's a handful for her at her age. He's a lot for me when I'm home. Maybe she'll be okay soon." Iris hoped so for Pattie's sake. They talked for a few minutes and then they hung up. After four years of touring together, Pattie was still her best friend, and now Boy was too. And Clay. But that was different. He was her benefactor, and her boss, not just a friend.

She and Boy went out to dinner that night to celebrate their contracts, and the diner on Tenth Avenue was pretty good. Neither of them could imagine dining in fancier restaurants. The diner was comfortable and familiar and felt like home to them. They walked back to the Plaza, to their new world of luxury and comfort, and security now, thanks to Clay. Boy had called his band to tell them it was official. He was staying in New York, and wasn't coming back to Nashville, maybe for a long time. They were happy for him, and said they missed him. Annie and Sean had been offered a place with another band, and Joe was trying out some new bands before he made a decision. There was plenty of work in Nashville, but they all agreed they would miss Boy, yet were happy for his big break with Clay Maddox. It sounded like a miracle to them and felt like one to Boy.

Iris had just gotten into bed when her cellphone rang. It had been a big day, signing the contract, and it was the first night she had taken off in weeks. She was in a great mood. She looked at her phone, and thought it was Boy. No one else called her except Pattie, and they had spoken earlier. The call was from a blocked number. She answered, and was shocked to hear Glen Hendrix on the other end.

"Where the fuck are you?" were his opening words in a vicious tone.

He couldn't touch her now. She was safe. Clay and the lawyers had told her so. "I'm in New York, and I'm not coming back. Your contract isn't worth a damn. I'm done. You don't scare me anymore."

"Who've you been talking to? Some ambulance chaser? That contract is rock solid, and if you don't get your ass back here, I'll have you put in jail," he threatened her. "You're lucky I'll still take you back."

"You're pathetic, and an affront to the human race. All you do is exploit everyone who works for you. That contract isn't worth the paper it's written on. You're lucky no one puts *you* in jail."

"Get back here, Cooper. I mean it. You'll be

sorry if you don't." She had run away and defied him, and no one did that to him. He had to make an example of her to the others or they'd all be trying to do the same thing, and his profits would go right down the drain.

"Don't call me again," she said, tired of his threats, and hung up. She was shaking when she ended the call, but not like she used to. She had Clay now, and his contract and lawyers to protect her. They had told her that Glen couldn't do anything to her, and she believed them. But he had such an ominous, evil voice. She never wanted to hear it again.

Glen was enraged when she hung up on him. He called Scott Campbell the next day. The scouts hadn't found her, she hadn't turned up in Nashville either. But she had told him she was in New York the night before.

When Scott answered, Glen's voice was taut. "The bitch is in New York. Find her, god damn it. That's what I'm paying you for. It's been two goddamn months."

"I'll see what I can do," Scott said, not happy to hear from him. Scott had decided long since that he didn't want to find her, and from everything he had heard about Hendrix and experienced himself, he was sure she didn't want to be found. He was going to tell Hendrix that he didn't want the job, but he hadn't had the guts to yet. The guy was in a rage all the time, and high on coke.

Against his own better judgment, Scott called a contact he had in New York, who knew everyone and was a genius at accomplishing the impossible. He asked him what he could find out about a singer named Iris Cooper, out of Las Vegas. He said she had walked out on a tour after a concert in Idaho, had been seen in Jackson Hole more than a month ago, and was now in New York. His client wanted to find her.

"I'll see what I can dig up," his contact said. "Is she running from the law? Is there a boyfriend involved?"

"No to the law, and I don't know about a boyfriend. There wasn't one before. I think she's running from a bad manager. The guy's a little crazy, and he wants to hold her to her contract so the rest of his contract players don't do the same."

"It doesn't sound like it's worth the trouble," Mike, his contact, said, unimpressed.

"Probably not."

"I'll see what I can find out."

"Thanks."

Mike called him back three hours later. "I picked up a copy of *Variety*. There's a small notice in it. Just simple publicity stuff. It says that Clay Maddox, the King of Music, just signed two new 'golden voices,' Boy Brady and Iris Cooper. The Brady guy is working on a single and she's recording an album, and 'you'll be hearing more about them soon.' So she's working for Maddox, and she's sure not going to go running back to some two-bit manager in Vegas who wants to kick the shit out of her. And Maddox will protect her. That's his reputation. He's good to his talent. I called around to see if I could find out where she's staying. She's not hiding. She's staying at the Plaza, in a suite booked and paid for by Maddox. And so is the other guy mentioned in the notice, Boy Brady. I don't know if they're together or not. They have separate suites."

"Thanks, Mike. I owe you," Scott said with a heavy heart. He really didn't want the information, or to give it to Glen Hendrix.

"Don't worry about it, it just took a few calls, after I saw the notice. So you've got your girl."

Scott sat staring into space for a few minutes after he hung up, and looked at the photographs he still had on his board. She looked like a sweet girl. He couldn't do it to her. He was sure she didn't deserve whatever Hendrix wanted to do to her, and he was a bastard. Scott called him a few minutes later on his cell, and Glen picked up when he saw it was Scott.

"Yeah? Did you find her?"

"No, I called all my best contacts in New York, and they can't locate her. She's probably staying with a friend. There's no way to trace her, I've tried. The trail is cold on this, Glen. I don't want to waste your money. I'm resigning from the case," Scott said, and felt better as soon as he did. A weight had lifted off his shoulders and his conscience.

"I won't pay you a penny," Hendrix spat at him, "you didn't find her."

"I'm sorry. It works that way sometimes. Good luck," he said, and hung up before Glen Hendrix could say more. He'd heard enough. He looked at Iris's pictures again, and smiled at her. "Take care of yourself, Iris." He felt like she was smiling at him as he took the photographs down and slipped them into a drawer in his desk. It felt good to have done the right thing.

And in his office, Glen had just punched a hole in the wall as he shouted, "You bitch!" His hand was bleeding and he didn't care.

Chapter 9

A week later, Pattie had to call Glen and give him the bad news. Her mother was in the hospital, and there was no one to take care of her son, Jimmy. She had to leave the tour.

"Bullshit!" he shouted at her, and knew immediately why she was doing it. She was following Iris's example and thought she could walk out on her contract because Iris had, but it had nothing to do with it. "I'll have you put in jail if you leave," he threatened her.

"There's nothing I can do," Pattie said. "My mom's in the hospital. She can't take care of my son. He's at a neighbor's and I can't leave him there. You don't pay me enough to hire childcare for him," she said bluntly. "I'll come back when Mom's better, but I've got to leave today. I don't want my son to wind up in foster care."

"I won't pay you a penny while you're gone," he warned her. She knew he wouldn't, and she knew she would have to waitress or work at the 7-Eleven, whatever she had to do for now. Jimmy was the priority for her, not the tour. She was lucky her mom had taken care of him for eleven years. Now it was Pattie's turn to be a mom.

"I just wanted to let you know. I'm not running out on you. I'm giving you notice that I have to go home for a family emergency." She was doing everything by the book, and Glen didn't care. He hung up on her without another word. She took the bus to Biloxi, Mississippi, that night. She sent Iris a text to let her know she had left the tour, and Iris texted back that she hoped her mom would be okay soon.

As soon as Boy's single was released, the publicity office of Maddox Productions booked him onto various radio shows and a couple of TV shows to publicize it. On two of the TV shows, he was booked to perform his single, which was flying up the charts and rapidly becoming a hit. Boy asked the publicity office if they would book Iris on the show with him, so they could do a duet. Iris thought it sounded like fun. The show accepted, and Boy and Iris had been rehearsing one of h songs. It was the one they both liked best, and gave Iris a chance to show her stuff too. Clay thought it was a good idea, and would give the public a glimpse of her, as a teaser for her own album that would be released soon.

They were booked onto a late-night talk show, the most popular one, and their performance was thrilling. Boy's first single was a big hit that week and way up on the charts. They were two beautiful young people performing and the studio audience went crazy. So did the ratings. Their first TV appearance was a huge success. Someone from Glen Hendrix's office called him when they saw it.

"If you're still looking for Iris Cooper, turn your TV on," his booker said. "They're on *Marlon at Midnight*." It was the highest rated late-night talk show, and often featured live talent.

Glen hit the remote. Boy and Iris were halfway through their duet of her song, and they both looked great. As soon as they were finished, he called his booker, who set up all the venues for Glen's tours. Glen sounded tense.

"Find out where she's staying. Is that her boyfriend?" He had missed the introduction, so he didn't know what it had said.

"I don't know," Harvey, the booker, answered, "it looked like it." They had sung a love song and looked like they were in love while they sang.

Glen had to wait until the next morning for the

answer. Harvey walked into his office just after nine o'clock, which was noon in New York.

"I called the station and got some intern on the phone. She said it was her first day and I said I was Iris's long-lost cousin trying to get in touch with her. She's staying at the Plaza in New York City. So is he." Harvey looked pleased with himself, to have made Glen happy. Glen smiled. He picked up the phone on his desk as soon as Harvey left his office. It was a number he had only called a few times before. It was ridiculously cheap, but had been very effective before if anyone needed a little "reminding" or "convincing" or a "wake-up call." In this case it was more about retribution or simple revenge for what he considered an intolerable act of insubordination. His ego couldn't bear it. There was no way he would let Iris get away with what she'd done. He had waited for this moment for more than three months. He gave the person who answered the information they needed, and had an envelope with cash dropped off an hour later. Glen thought it was worth what he had spent. It was only five hundred dollars.

Boy and Iris had taken the day off from the studio after their late night appearance on TV the night before. They'd been basking in glory, and both slept late. She wanted to work on one of her arrangements and was playing pieces of a melody on a keyboard, and Boy was watching TV in his suite, when he heard a knock on the door. He hadn't ordered room service, and figured it was one of the maids or someone to restock the minibar. He opened the door and two enormous men out of a bad movie shoved their way past him into the room. They had tipped a bellboy to get his room number and Iris's and took the elevator upstairs with some of the guests.

"Where is she?" one of them asked Boy, glancing around, and Boy instantly guessed they were looking for Iris, although he couldn't guess why. The other man grabbed Boy by the throat and lifted him off the ground. Boy wasn't a small man, although he was slim.

"You know damn well who I mean. The singer. Your girlfriend."

"I don't know. She doesn't stay with me. This is my room. I think she's out," Boy managed to choke out, as the first of the two thugs delivered a hard punch to Boy's gut. He doubled over, while his attacker punched him squarely in the face when he tried to stand up. Blood gushed from Boy's face as the man hit him again, and the other attacker threw a chair at the wall just for the hell of it. The TV was still on, as the hoodlum who had punched Boy continued to pummel him, until he was on his knees on the carpet, with blood gushing everywhere. He was shouting at Boy to tell him where his girlfriend was, when Iris heard strange noises coming from Boy's room, and assumed it was the TV. Boy looked up with eyes full of blood, with a gash on his forehead, and saw Iris appear in the doorway between their suites.

"What are you watching?" she asked him, and saw Boy crouched on the floor with one man punching him, and the other one kicking him. Boy shouted to her.

"Lock the door!" She froze where she stood and then rushed toward them, as the man kicking Boy slapped her across the face and literally threw her across the room. She hit her head on the dresser and was dazed for a minute. The other man came over and kicked her. She was so small and so light that she flew several feet, and couldn't get up when she landed. He yanked her up by one arm, and slapped her again, as Boy struggled free of his assailant with all his strength to reach her. His attacker landed another punch squarely in Boy's face. He fell back on the floor, his entire head and face covered with blood, as Iris let out a blood-curdling scream. She hit the high notes as never before, and the two men looked at each other uncertainly, while Iris continued screaming. One of them put his hand across her mouth. She bit him hard and screamed again.

The maids were gathering in the hallway by then. They had heard her scream and called security immediately. The two suites had gone silent again, and security was there in less than three minutes, unlocked the outer doors to the suites and saw the carnage inside. The two security men each grabbed one of the stunned assailants. They hadn't expected to get caught. That had never happened to them before. The hotel security guards handcuffed them, and called 911 for the police, and an ambulance for Boy, who was unconscious on the floor.

Iris was kneeling beside him, trying to wipe the blood from his face with a towel one of the maids had come in and handed her. Security had told her not to move him. His nose looked crushed, and the cut on his forehead was still gushing blood into his eyes. The two security men were holding their attackers pinned down in the hall, waiting for the police, and half a dozen more hotel security men had appeared, along with the head of security.

"Do you know the men who attacked you?" one of the security men asked Iris, and she shook her head, crying as she tended to Boy. She could hardly breathe. She was in pain. Her shoes had flown off her feet, and she had blood smeared all over her own body and Boy's. They had cut her cheek when they slapped her, and blood oozed from her nose. "Did they try to rob you?" the head of security asked.

"No, I don't think so. I heard noise so I came into the room. I thought it was the TV, but they were beating him up, and then one of them hit me and kicked me." She wasn't concerned about herself, only Boy.

The two men they were holding handcuffed for the police weren't talking. They hadn't expected it to end this way, with the hallway swarming with security. The police arrived in force a few minutes later, with the paramedics for Boy. They took his vital signs as he lay on the floor.

"Possible head injury," one reported to the other, "get the spinal board. Broken nose." He was trying to assess Boy where he lay, and a third paramedic wanted to check Iris out. The hotel security cleared the room, so they could examine her, and the police took the two thugs away. They were covered in Boy's blood too. It was all over their hands. They looked dangerous even in handcuffs, with two officers with a firm grip on each of them.

As they put Boy on the spinal board, he stirred and groaned, opened his eyes for a minute, and they fluttered closed again. He had looked straight at Iris and asked if she was okay. When she said yes, he closed his eyes again and groaned in pain.

In a moment's lull, Iris called Clay on the cellphone that was still in her pocket, even though she had flown all over the room when she was attacked.

"What? . . . What? . . . Iris . . . talk to me . . ." She was crying and what she said made no sense.

"Two men came into our suites at the hotel. They beat Boy up, and slapped me and kicked me too. The police are here. They're taking Boy to the hospital. They want me to go too. I'll go with him."

"I'll come as fast as I can." He was in a meeting with one of his famous artists, planning his tour, excused himself, grabbed his jacket, and dashed out of the room. He called the head of security at the hotel, who said the police were taking them to NewYork-Presbyterian Hospital by ambulance, and Clay said he'd meet them at the emergency room. He was already there when the ambulance arrived. Boy was conscious by then and he looked terrible, covered with blood. Iris looked dazed with blood all over her clothes and smeared on her face and around her nose.

Clay never left her for a minute, while they took Boy for a number of scans and an MRI to assess the damage. He didn't have a head injury, but he had a broken nose, a fractured cheekbone, four cracked ribs, and trauma to a kidney, and needed stitches for the cut on his forehead. Clay called a plastic surgeon, who came immediately to perform surgery on his nose, and the cut on his forehead. Iris had two bruised ribs, and assorted bumps and bruises. She had a cut on her lip, and her nose had been badly bumped so it had bled but it wasn't broken. Clay was horrified. Who would do such a thing?

A police detective came to talk to them while they waited for Boy to come out of surgery for his nose. There was nothing they could do about their ribs, they would take time to heal. Before he left for surgery, Boy had said he was just glad that Iris hadn't been more severely injured, and she had kissed him on the cheek.

The detective explained that they were pressing charges against the two men who had attacked them. One was on parole, and would be sent straight back to prison, and the other one had a police record an arm long. They had been working for a gangster the police knew, who was recently out of prison and also on parole. The police had already been to see him, and he said that the request had come from someone he barely knew in Las Vegas who had wanted them to "frighten" her, and the two men had gotten carried away. He didn't want to go back to prison to cover for the man in Vegas who'd hired him, so he talked willingly to the police and cooperated with them. They were supposed to just "scare them a little," he said, not beat them to a pulp. The man was being held on charges of assault too, and being an accomplice to the other two causing great bodily harm. The two thugs did what they knew best.

Clay had his suspicions, which he shared with the police. In exchange for charges reduced to a misdemeanor and no parole violation, the gangster who had sent them admitted that he had been contacted by Glen Hendrix, who had paid five hundred dollars for "a little scare" for Iris and what he assumed was her boyfriend. Clay was irate when he heard it, and called Glen himself.

"Let me make it clear. You come within a mile of any of my artists, particularly Iris Cooper, Boy Brady, or anyone else, and I'll see to it that you're behind bars for the rest of your life. You've done enough damage to enough people. No sane human being goes around hiring thugs to rough people up. Don't you dare come near any of my artists again, or I'll personally see to it that you're out of business for good and in prison," and with that, he hung up.

Iris stayed with Boy that night when he came out of surgery, and Clay stayed with both of them. The police took reports from both victims, and Boy was in a lot of pain from his ribs. Iris was too, although less. They had really gone to town on Boy. And both of the men who'd done it were being held and charged, and one of them would go back to prison.

"That son of a bitch is a sick fuck," Clay said about Glen Hendrix. It was the first time Iris had ever heard him swear, and he looked murderous. He took care of both of them as though they were his children, which was how he felt about all his artists. And he wanted Hendrix charged for ordering the assault. They could have been killed, given the force the two thugs had used.

They went back to the hotel the next day, and

there were two security guards posted outside their rooms.

"I'm so sorry," Iris said to Boy, as she helped him settle into bed. Clay had hired a nurse for him, and all Iris had to do was rest, so her ribs could heal. What Hendrix had done was insane. She thanked her lucky stars again that she had met Clay and he had saved her from a disastrous fate at the hands of a lunatic.

The day after they got back from the hospital, Clay called and asked if he could come over. Boy's face was heavily bandaged because of his nose, and Iris had two black eyes from being slapped so hard and the blows to her face. They were sitting in bed side by side, watching TV, and Boy dozed most of the time from the painkillers that the nurse Clay had hired gave him every few hours. Clay's doctor was checking them daily.

Clay came to visit and smiled when he saw them.

"You two look like prizefighters after a heavy-weight bout."

"That's what it feels like," Boy said through his bandages. The doctor had said his nose would look perfect again when it healed, maybe even better than before. They were both wearing pajamas and looked like two kids.

Clay had brought a box with him that he'd left

in Iris's room. When Boy fell asleep, he beckoned her to come with him back to her own room. She tiptoed after him, and she felt better although her ribs hurt when she breathed, and she couldn't imagine singing for a while. It was going to slow her album down for a week at least. Boy had to cancel several TV appearances. The paparazzi had heard that there had been some kind of incident with injuries and were parked outside, but neither of them were going anywhere, so the press vigil outside the Plaza didn't do them any good.

When they got to Iris's room, she sat down on the bed, and Clay put the box next to her. It was a small pink hatbox with roses painted on it.

"You didn't have to get me a present." She smiled at him.

"You deserve a lot more than that," he said, still worried about her. "I hope it fits," he said to mislead her, with a smile. She took the lid off carefully, ready to find a hat. There was a soft pink cashmere blanket inside and a tiny little face too afraid to move peeked out at her. She thought it was a toy at first. She pushed the blanket back and saw a tiny teacup, white, long-haired Chihuahua, who looked straight into her eyes and licked her finger with a tiny pink tongue. Iris's eyes filled with tears as she looked from the puppy to Clay. Nobody had ever done anything that nice for her. She didn't know what to say. Clay leaned over to kiss her on the forehead, and the fluffy white puppy made a snuffling sound. Iris lifted the tiny puppy out of the box, still wrapped in the blanket. She was barely bigger than Iris's cupped hands which held her. She was wearing a little pink collar with rhinestones on it. She looked even smaller when Iris set her down on the bed.

"What's her name?" she whispered, smiling like a kid at Christmas, which was what she felt like.

"That's up to you."

Iris knew instantly what she wanted to call her. "Rosebud," like the flowers on the box. "She looks like a tiny little Rosebud. I can call her Rosie for short. I'm going to take her everywhere with me." She beamed at Clay. "I've never had a dog." She had never had a life before either. Now she was living a dream.

"A whole mountain of stuff goes with her," Clay said, as he sat down on the bed next to her. "Joanne helped me. She's got blankets and sweaters and collars, and bowls and food and toys, and a pink bed. You said you wanted a fluffy, white, long-haired Chihuahua. I thought she might cheer you up."

Iris hadn't stopped smiling since she'd first seen her. She carried her into the next room to show Boy, but he was heavily drugged on the painkillers the nurse had given him, and sound asleep. It was better for him to just sleep away the pain. She went back to her room, and Clay ordered room service dinner for them. He hated to leave her now. He had been so worried about her when she called him two days before.

The New York police had contacted the Las Vegas police department, and Glen was going to be charged with conspiracy to commit assault and battery and inflict great bodily harm. They said he could spend a year in jail for it, but he probably wouldn't. They thought he might serve thirty days or a few months at most. But at least he wouldn't get off scot-free.

While Clay and Iris ate dinner in her room, Rosie slept peacefully on her lap. She looked as though she knew she was home. She was only three months old, and wouldn't weigh more than two or three pounds full-grown. She didn't weigh more than a pound now.

"It's almost worth having gotten beaten up to get her," Iris said to Clay, and he winced.

"I would have gotten her for you anyway. I don't want anything like that to happen to you again. That man is a complete monster. What if he had killed one of you? And all of that because you left the tour, and we broke the contract. He's seriously deranged." She remembered all the times she had seen him berate and verbally abuse the performers on tour. Clay was right. He was insane.

Clay stayed for a long time talking to her that

night. Boy didn't wake up and she closed the door between their suites.

"I was happy to find out that Boy wasn't your boyfriend," he said cautiously after dinner, testing the waters. He was feeling closer and closer to Iris the longer he knew her, and more attracted to her, but he didn't want to make her uncomfortable or risk the relationship they had. She looked up to him, and trusted him, and he didn't want to spoil that. But seeing her injured had made his feelings for her even stronger.

"I've never had a serious boyfriend," she said simply, "for more than a few weeks anyway. Moving every five minutes when I was a kid, and nine years on tour made it impossible to have a real relationship or really get to know someone. Nothing lasts on tour. But I've always had my music." She smiled at him. "That's always been my first love. I want to finish the album soon," she said, angry that it had been interrupted by her injuries.

"You will," he assured her. "I can't wait till we release it. It's going to be a huge hit, Iris. And then we'll go on tour. Not the way you did before. This will be very different." They were going to take care of her like a precious jewel, which was what she was to him. Rosie woke up then, and waved her long fluffy tail like a flag and Iris laughed.

"She's the cutest thing I've ever seen," she said happily.

"So are you." He smiled at her. It was nice having a moment alone with her. That never happened, they were always surrounded by musicians and technicians, or Boy and his backup band. It was nice being alone in a room with her, and if he had dared to, he would have kissed her. But he didn't.

They talked for a long time, and when she looked tired, he left her with her puppy, and went home and thought about her, grateful that she hadn't been more seriously injured.

He had canceled dinner with one of his big stars that night. He still had all his other artists to attend to. But Iris had the priority. And dinner with Iris and her puppy meant more to him than an evening with any star. As his driver took him home, Clay was smiling, remembering the look on her face when she saw the puppy. He was more in love with her than ever, and wanted to be with her to protect her for as long as she would let him, if she ever would.

Chapter 10

The story about Boy and Iris getting attacked at the hotel eventually hit all the tabloids. Bellboys were bribed, maids on their floor, there was always someone willing to talk after an incident. A nurse in the emergency room answered some questions. The name of the hotel was kept out of it, to make sure that no one decided to try it again, or maybe rob them. The hotel kept a security guard outside the door of each of their suites. One of their attackers had gone straight back to prison after a parole hearing, the other was still in jail pending disposition of his case. He had confessed, so he was awaiting sentencing. The man who had sent them had cooperated with the police fully so he was being charged with a misdemeanor, which was reported to his parole officer and would go against him, if he was involved in any other incident in future. And Glen Hendrix had been arrested, posted bail himself, and was being charged with conspiracy to commit aggravated assault and battery. Clay had his lawyers request a restraining order forbidding him to come anywhere near Iris. As far as they were all concerned, she was safe.

After a week, her ribs were feeling better and she could breathe more easily, but she wasn't feeling up to singing yet. Boy was walking around the room, more awake, in less pain, but his broken ribs made it hard to move, and the bandages over his nose, which covered most of his face, drove him crazy.

Clay came to see them every day, and spent most of his time visiting Iris. The first time she sang and held her guitar, she sang a song to him that she had composed while she was recuperating. It was called "Kindness," and had been inspired by him. She'd written a funny song about Rosie, whom she was madly in love with. The tiny puppy kept making her and Boy laugh. It was painful for both of them with their injured ribs. The hotel had cleaned the bloodstains out of the carpets, and covered one with a handsome rug, until the room could be re-carpeted. Iris noticed that a female singer from Boy's backup band had visited him too, and brought him cookies. She

teased him about it when she left. Her name was
Star and she was very sexy. She was tall and slim
like Boy, with bright red hair. Iris thought she
seemed crazy about him.

"No, she's not." He rolled his eyes. "We just
work together."

"Yeah?" Iris grinned at him. "You don't see any
of my backup guys here, do you? No one brought
me cookies," she said and laughed.

"No, he brought you a puppy." He was convinced that Clay was infatuated with her, but Iris
denied it.

"He's our boss. That's different. He's like a father to us."

"He's my boss too, he didn't bring me a puppy."

"Okay, what kind of puppy do you want?" she
asked him, smiling.

"A Great Dane," he said smugly.

"Fine. I'll tell him you want one."

"Why won't you admit that he likes you? Or
more than that?"

"Because he doesn't like me 'that way,' and it's
easier like this," she said shyly. "I don't want to
screw things up. He's been so good to us, and to
me, we're friends." And she didn't want to tell Boy
that she thought Clay was attractive. She was sure
he wasn't interested in her that way. If he had
been, he would have said so before this.

"You're silly, and blind," Boy said to her.

"What about you and Star?" She was curious,

like a sister. He had turned thirty while he was recuperating, and Star had brought him a birthday cake with candles.

"I think she's hot. When I can breathe again without crying, I'm going to take her out for dinner. She can check out my new nose," he said about Star in answer to Iris's questions. The doctor had promised his nose would be even straighter than his old one. The thugs from Brooklyn had done a thorough job of breaking it.

A few days later, Clay called her in the morning to see how she felt, and asked if she was well enough to go out to dinner. She had complained of feeling stir-crazy, stuck in her room at the hotel. The only thing that cheered her up was Rosie, the tiny Chihuahua, and she and Boy played cards and watched old movies. At least they kept each other company, and the prospect of getting out finally for dinner boosted her spirits immediately.

"I'd love it, as long as we don't go dancing." The ribs were taking longer to heal than she'd hoped they would. She wasn't ready to start singing again yet. She was getting impatient about finishing her album.

Clay said he'd pick her up at the hotel at seven-thirty, and they'd go somewhere nearby. The area around the Plaza was full of restaurants. "Perfect, I'll be out front at seven-thirty."

"Have the security outside your room escort you down." He didn't want her to fall or bump herself and get hurt, or anyone to jostle or hassle her, like the paparazzi.

She was dressed and out front promptly at seven-thirty with a security guard, and Clay pulled up in a red Ferrari. He was driving himself. Iris lowered herself gingerly into the car and they took off seconds later.

Iris was wearing a short black leather skirt and a red jacket, with her hair down, and they drove to a bustling, friendly informal Italian restaurant on Second Avenue, uptown. He thought it would be more relaxed than a fancy French restaurant, and they'd be less likely to draw attention. People always recognized him. He was as famous as his artists. They talked for a long time in the restaurant, and he could see she was getting tired. When they left, they were startled to see paparazzi on the sidewalk waiting for them. It was obvious to both of them that someone had tipped them off, otherwise how would they know to find them there, since it wasn't the kind of restaurant that celebrities went to. Clay looked annoyed, and moved swiftly toward the car with her when the valet brought it, and they got several shots of Iris as she got into the Ferrari. They were typical paparazzi shots, and they were on the front page of the *Enquirer* the next day, with a shot of her legs and short skirt as she got into the Ferrari. Clay called Iris immediately to apologize. They'd had a nice time the night before, and he didn't like the tabloids intruding on them.

"I'm sorry, Iris. I didn't think they'd catch us there. Someone at the restaurant must have squealed, probably one of the waiters."

"It's okay, you weren't doing anything wrong. Neither of us is married. We can have dinner with whoever we want."

"I hate being in the tabloids," he said sternly.

"I don't mind," she said. He was as much a celebrity as any of the people he represented, so it seemed inevitable. "I'll bring Rosie next time, in one of her pink sweaters, they can take pictures of her." The tiny puppy followed her everywhere in her hotel suite, and hopped on her lap the minute she sat down. And at night, she slept with her head next to Iris's face on the pillow, and she could feel her soft puppy breaths on her cheek. She was never lonely with Rosie with her, and Clay was thrilled that she loved her.

She had told Pattie all about her, and sent her photos. She had told her too about the attack on her and Boy that Glen had masterminded.

"I hope he goes to prison for it," Pattie said. She was back in Biloxi taking care of her son. Her mother was out of the hospital, but still weak.

"I don't think I'm going to be able to get back to Vegas. I can't take Jimmy with me, and I don't think my mama is going to be well enough to manage him on her own. I'm going to be stuck here waiting tables forever," she said, depressed about it. She didn't want to tour for Glen again, but she didn't want to be stuck in Mississippi forever either. It felt like she had gone back to the beginning, and her dreams hadn't come true.

"Maybe you can get to Nashville eventually, and find some gigs there. It sounds like there's plenty of work in music in Nashville. At least that's what Boy says," Iris told her.

"Maybe," Pattie said, and didn't sound convinced. The world outside her small life in Biloxi seemed like a distant dream to her now. She was going to try to come to New York for a weekend when her mother was feeling better and could take care of Jimmy again, or she said maybe she could leave him with a friend for two days. She was desperate to get away from the drudgery she was living now, although she loved being with her son. But a weekend off, away, sounded like heaven to her. Iris didn't envy her that kind of responsibility at her age. She was thirty-four years old with a child and a sick mother. All Iris had to worry about was herself.

Clay took her to lunch a couple of times, despite his heavy schedule of meetings with his artists. The paparazzi were lying in wait at the hotel every time he took Iris out. They dodged the press by going out the service entrance. When he took her to dinner again, always with the excuse of cheering her up, the paparazzi were outside the restaurant again when they left.

They were becoming an item, while people tried to guess if they were dating or not. Iris always denied it. Clay didn't comment. And Boy insisted to Iris that they were.

Iris had just come back from lunch with him, when the doorbell of her suite rang, and the security hadn't stopped them, so she assumed it was the maid. She opened the door, and found herself staring up at her father. He had gotten past security after he found out her room number from a hotel operator, by claiming it was his own room. It had been more than four years since Iris had seen him, nearly five, and she just stood there and stared and didn't know what to say.

"Aren't you going to invite me into your fancy digs? You got a hug for your old dad?" The dad who hadn't sent her so much as a postcard in nearly five years.

She hesitated and then stood aside so he could come in. She knew Boy was in his suite but the door was closed between them, so he hadn't heard Iris come in. And she thought he might be taking a nap. He still slept in the afternoon, but he was feeling better too.

She noticed that her father looked even seedier than the last time she'd seen him, and his limp was more pronounced. He needed a haircut, and a shave, he was wearing an old Levi's jacket, jeans, and his beaten-up cowboy boots he'd had since his rodeo days. She wondered if he had pawned everything else.

He sat down on the couch, and looked around, as she sat across from him in a chair. It was still hard for her to get off the couch with her bruised ribs.

"To what do I owe the honor?" she said coolly. It was hard to be enthusiastic about seeing him, when he had stayed out of touch for so long. She wondered if he'd ever thought about her, or worried about how she was, or cared. But he was still her father, and she had to fight any kind of expectations about him. He never failed to disappoint.

"I've been seeing a lot of you in the tabloids, with some old guy, and with another one with long hair. You seem to have plenty of men in your life these days. I was in New York, and I thought I'd drop by and see how you're doing. Looks like you got yourself a contract for an album. Hendrix let you out of your touring contract?"

"No, my manager got me out of it. The contract wasn't legal, and he treated us all like dirt."

"That's what I've heard about him," Chip said, making himself comfortable on the couch. She didn't offer him a drink. She didn't want him to hang around long enough to get drunk.

"Funny, you never mentioned that to me before I signed with him."

"I heard it later." He had an answer to everything. "You were already on tour. You got a beer?" The question was inevitable. She got up, got one out of the minibar, and handed it to him.

"So what brings you to New York, Dad?" she asked him. It seemed odd to call him that after he had escaped being one for four years. It didn't surprise her, but it had hurt her feelings anyway.

"I had some business, and I wanted to see you," he said innocently.

"Why now? I wrote to you a few times, the letters always came back."

"I moved around for a while. With you gone, there was nowhere I had to be." He never had to be anywhere for her either. He did whatever he wanted and always had.

"Where are you living now?" She was curious.

"Back in Vegas," he said. "It's good to be back there. I'm staying with a friend," a woman most likely. He was shameless about living off women for free rent and the use of their car. His standard M.O. It was all so familiar. Nothing had changed. She could guess what would come next. She was the business he had in New York. She was sure of it. He looked around the luxurious hotel suite again, and she knew he was impressed, even if he didn't show it. He tried to look as though he took it all in stride, but she knew him better than that. "Looks like you're making some big money these days. That's nice for you," he said, and she waited.

"I don't pay for the hotel, if that's what you mean. My manager does."

"Clay Maddox? Hell, he can afford to. How'd you wind up with him managing you?" As though she didn't have the talent, and wasn't worthy of her good breaks. "I told you to keep hitting those high notes. Looks like it paid off." She didn't answer at first.

"I was lucky to meet him. And I worked my ass off for nine years on tour. That counts for something." He nodded. She could sense that he was looking for a way in. He grinned, and she noticed that he'd lost some teeth. It was sad to see him actually. He was only fifty-nine, but he looked ten or fifteen years older. Like fifty years of bad road. She should have had happy memories, or tender ones, of him, but she didn't. He'd dragged her around to bars, and made her sing for money since she was twelve, and then he took and spent it on booze and women. Stealing from a child. It was hard to feel anything looking at him. She looked at her watch, he'd been there for half an hour. She felt trapped with him as the bad memories came flooding back, the nights she went to bed hungry, or slept in the truck while he slept at some woman's house and left her out in the cold, or in the dead heat. All the times he was never there for her, and acted like she didn't exist and didn't matter, not speaking to her for four years because she wouldn't let him steal her money. He was starting to look as uncomfortable as she felt, as though he could hear her thoughts.

"I know you're busy, Iris, I should get going, I've got some things to do too. I'm going back to Vegas tonight." She doubted that he could afford plane fare, and guessed he was going by bus. He stood up and looked her squarely in the eyes. She hadn't greeted him warmly but his eyes were cold. "I was wondering if you could float me a loan, just to tide me over for a while."

"What did you have in mind?" She was curious to find out just how far he'd go. He had probably come just to see if he could milk her again. He'd seen the tabloids and figured she was good for it.

"I was thinking twenty, twenty-five thousand, maybe fifty. That's probably a drop in the bucket for you. You'll make a fortune on your album," he encouraged her, all for his own gain.

"It's not out yet," she reminded him.

"Maddox must have given you an advance." She didn't answer. She wasn't going to lie to him. It was none of his business. She might have given him five, although she wasn't sure. But twenty, twenty-five, or fifty, just to play her and disappear for another four years, until he wanted more. He'd burn through it quickly on booze and beer, and the blackjack table. She knew why the women he slept with threw him out. They got tired of giving him money, and she was too.

"Sorry, I can't help you, Dad. You always figure

it out somehow. You got the last of my money when you spent everything I earned working for Billy Weston. I decided then that was the end of it. I guess that's why I haven't heard from you for four years."

"Yeah, I guess so." He didn't deny it. He had no regrets and no remorse about any of it. She could see he hadn't missed her, except what he might have taken from her again. "A woman who won't help her father out has no heart," he said coldly, as he ambled toward the door.

"A man who works his child to the bone and takes all her money has no soul. So I guess we're even."

"Guess so." He had reached the door by then. She hadn't been worth the bus fare from Vegas. "You won't be seeing me again," he said. "Enjoy your fancy life, Iris. Keep hitting those high notes. I always said you'd be a star one day. I just figured you'd be a better person when you were, and remember where you came from."

"I try to forget it every day," she said softly. "Take care of yourself, Dad." He opened the door then, didn't acknowledge what she'd said, walked into the hall, closed the door behind him, and he was gone. She suspected he had told the truth. She wouldn't see him again. The sad thing was, she didn't want to. All he'd ever given her was grief and pain, while he profited from her gifts. She stood looking at the door for a minute, feeling like an abandoned child, and then she went to look for Rosie, asleep on her bed. Iris sat down and held her, and the little puppy licked her hand.

Boy came looking for her a few minutes later. He was moving with more ease now, and eager to get back to work on his other single.

"Was someone here?" he asked her, watching her stroke the dog, with a serious look on her face. "I heard voices."

"Yeah," she said with a sad look in her eyes. The reality was ugly, of who her father was, and what he wanted from her. All he wanted was money, wherever he could get it, and she was a convenient source. She had always been profitable for him, ever since she was twelve years old. Without the profit, she was of no interest to him. He was no better than Billy Weston or Glen Hendrix. Blood made no difference to him, she was just another opportunity for money.

"It was my father," she told Boy with a dead look in her eyes, as she kissed the puppy and set her back on the bed.

"Your father? The one you haven't seen in four years?" He looked surprised.

"Yeah, that one."

"What did he want?"

"He'd seen me in the tabloids, and read that Clay signed me, so he came to collect."

"Great guy. Was he nice to you at least?" Boy asked her.

"No. Same guy, different day. Four years later. He disappeared four years ago because I wouldn't sign over my paychecks to him." The truth was the only two men in her life who hadn't wanted anything from her and were good to her were Boy and Clay. The others all used her, and she was well aware of it. She knew it about her father too. It was just depressing to have him show up and do the same thing again.

"You don't need him, Iris. You've done much better without him."

"No, I don't need him," she agreed. "It would have been nice to have had a different father."

"I used to think that, that it would have been nice to have a family, a real one. It would have been nice, but in the end, I did fine without one. We have ourselves, and look at where we are now. Look at Clay, he can't do enough for us. That's just who he is. And shit luck, you wound up with a lousy father. You're going to be fine without him, better in fact. Guys like your dad don't change. They're empty inside. They have nothing to give. They can beat the hell out of us, like the two thugs who showed up here, but they lose in the end. They can't touch us." She hoped it was true. She nodded and he went back to his room to give her some time to think about it. She lay on her bed, holding Rosie, and she let the image of her father drift away until he was gone. She fell asleep with her puppy. Another gift from Clay.

Chapter 11

Boy went back to work a few days after Iris did. Their ribs still ached, but she could sing again, and so could he a few days later. Clay was happy to see them back in their studios. Iris had brought the puppy with her. She was sound asleep in a little pink travel bag, with some toys and one of her pink blankets. The backup band loved her. Iris saw Star and Boy going out to lunch together and she smiled. They looked nice together.

It had been two weeks since her father's visit, and she was in constant rehearsals for her album, and working on her music. She stopped at a newsstand on the way back to the hotel to buy a magazine, and she saw a stack of a popular tabloid with a familiar figure on the front page. The headline read "Chip Cooper—Iris's Dad Tells All." So it had come to that. If she didn't give him money, he would find a way to sell her out anyway. Against her better judgment, she bought a copy. She sat down to read it as soon as she got to her suite, and let Rosie out of her little pink bag. She went to play with one of her toys.

Her father looked like an old craggy-faced cowboy, and had posed in front of a casino in Vegas. He had told a lot of stories of her growing up, singing in bars as a kid. There was a picture of her at about fourteen, in the black velvet dress Sally had made for her. She was surprised he still had the photo. What he didn't realize was that the interview he had given them made him look bad, it didn't make her look like less than she was. It told the story of a heartbreaking childhood, with a father who had exploited his daughter shamelessly. She finished it, and threw it in the wastebasket. She wondered how many more interviews like that he would give before they got tired of him.

Boy knocked on the door and walked in, then saw the tabloid in the garbage.

"You read it?" he asked her, and she nodded.

"You too?"

"It's all crap. It makes him look like an asshole and a shit father. He's a jerk. He's a parasite. People like him can't live unless they're sucking blood from someone else. You really are better off without him."

"I came to that conclusion too." She smiled at him. "You left rehearsal early. Are you feeling okay?" She still felt bad that he had gotten beaten up because of her. But Clay's plastic surgeon had done a good job. The bandages were off his nose and it looked perfect.

He looked sheepish at her question. "I went to look at an apartment."

"For you and Star?" She looked surprised. The romance was still very new.

"No, for myself. In SoHo. It's small, but it's a loft in an old warehouse. I realized that I miss having my own place. I can't live here forever." He glanced around the suite. It suited her. She was used to living in hotels on tour, and this was way better than any she'd ever been in. "I like having my own space." He had been missing his apartment in Nashville. He wondered when he'd get back there. He was too busy in New York, rehearsing and recording, to go anywhere right now.

"Maybe it'll be nice for you," Iris said, but she'd miss him. She was happy at the hotel and had no desire for her own apartment. She loved the service and being able to order something to eat whenever she wanted, and the hotel security right outside her door made her feel safe.

"You can come and visit," he said. He looked happy. Star was only part of it, although he was having fun with her. The recording of his second single was going well and the first one was selling like crazy. People recognized him on the street now. He liked that a lot better than Iris did. She missed her anonymity. She wanted them to love her music. They didn't have to love her, or even see her, just hear her music.

She had dinner with Clay that night. They talked about her album. He was already planning the tour. Most of the time, they talked about business. But other things crept in. She had told him about her father's visit and it made him heartsick for her. He'd seen the interview in the tabloids. It was obvious that Chip would stoop to any level to make a buck, and he didn't care what a lousy father he was. He was the opposite of Clay, who was constantly trying to protect, and willing to spoil his daughters. Iris felt that it was how he treated her, and she was sure that he considered her like another daughter. She told him that Boy was moving out of the hotel. He thought it would be good for him. He was comfortable in New York by then, and felt at home.

It reminded Iris of something she wanted to ask Clay about the tour.

"Have you thought about an opening act yet?"

"I've had some ideas, but nothing definite."

"What about Boy?" She loved the idea of being on tour with him, and having him open for her, and Clay liked the idea too.

"The timing is right, because after he does his own album, he'll be too big to be an opening act.

He can just get away with it now. People are going crazy over his single." Iris was happy for him. There had never been any competitiveness between them. They were always trying to help each other and listening to each other's music, or showing up at rehearsal and making suggestions later.

"I'd love him to tour with us," Iris said.

"I'll talk to him about it." He didn't want to plan it without getting approval from Boy, but he thought he'd like the idea too. "You know, I was thinking about it the other day. Maybe the three of us get along so well because we had tough childhoods, in similar places. Boy was raised by the state in Tennessee, I grew up dirt poor on a farm in Kentucky. I didn't have real shoes until I was ten, and I had to wear them long after I outgrew them. My mother cut holes in the toes. And you grew up being dragged all over Texas, singing in bars. Not one of us had a reasonable childhood. You'll probably be a great mom one day because of it." Just like he tried to be a good dad to his daughters, sometimes too much so. "I was hungry all the time as a kid," Clay admitted to her. He'd never said that to her before. "Sometimes I had to catch something to eat, or eat the scrawny, half-rotten vegetables from our garden."

"I was hungry too," she said softly. "Sometimes my dad handed me a can of beans, and that was it. And it wasn't a big can." She smiled at him, sharing the memory of hardship, although she thought his sounded even worse. "It was great when I started singing in restaurants and bars. They used to feed me in the kitchen sometimes. A waitress called Sally at my first gig used to give me a plate of food to eat in my dad's truck. He'd leave me out there for hours, all night sometimes, no matter how cold or hot it was. Harry said that was why he hired me for my first job, because he felt so sorry for me. Maybe my dad counted on that too. They never wanted me at first because I was so little and so young, but my father always managed to talk them into it, and they hired me."

"It's hard for people who grew up in normal lives to understand childhoods like that. My ex Frances grew up in New York. Her father was a doctor, and she thinks the world owes her whatever she wants. It doesn't work like that. If you grow up that poor, you're grateful for whatever you get later, and you appreciate it." He already knew it was true for Iris too. She was so grateful for everything he did for her, especially the puppy.

They went on talking about the tour, and after that, he took her back to the hotel. Her ribs were still tender, but she sang anyway. She wasn't a diva, and he knew she never could be, she didn't have it in her. She was just a good woman with a heart of gold.

* * *

The next day, Boy told him he'd be thrilled to be on the tour, and was happy Clay had asked him. It was going to be a fast one, five cities in fifteen days. Iris was used to it, and it sounded easy to her. She was already thinking about which songs she wanted to sing, and probably some new ones she hadn't even written yet.

The day Boy moved out of the hotel, Iris went with him to help. He had bought some basic things, like linens and what he needed for the kitchen. He bought four of everything for the kitchen, because the place was small and he couldn't imagine having more people to visit him. They went to Ikea in New Jersey together in Iris's old battered Ford and bought the rest of what he needed. They could barely fit it into her car, but they managed. He even bought a rug that looked like a quilt.

"A touch of home," he said to her, "the women in Tennessee make beautiful quilts." Despite their difficult childhoods, their roots were still strong.

She had almost finished recording her album by then. She only had two songs left to do, and they went quickly. They worked late every night, as they were all eager to finish.

Clay spent a fortune on publicity for the album, and it sailed to the top of the charts. Iris was proud of it, and Boy was too. They both had hit songs on the charts at the same time.

The tour was still two months away, and Clay's publicity department booked her onto a number of television shows, which she found terrifying, but she did them anyway. Clay went with her whenever he could, but sometimes he was too busy, and then she took Boy. Clay was her staunch protector. He'd watch her on the monitor in the greenroom, and hang on her every word. He was surprised by how well she handled it, and she talked about the tour when she was on TV.

Star was going on the tour with them too, since she was in Boy's backup band. She was excited about it. They were openly a couple now. Everything was new in his life, thanks to Iris, who had taken him with her to meet Clay. He never forgot that. He could have still been in Nashville, playing in bars where no one listened to the music. He still talked to Annie and the boys in his band from time to time.

Iris called Pattie. She was having a hard time with her mother still sick, Jimmy to take care of in the daytime, and waitressing at night. Her spirits had been in the tank since she'd gotten home. She couldn't see any way out, to ever leave Biloxi again. She couldn't even get away for a weekend. She kept promising she would, but she had no one reliable to leave Jimmy with. She felt like a prisoner.

Iris was loving the success of her album. It was a tremendous ego boost, and she loved walking into places where they were playing her songs. It made them all so meaningful.

Clay had promised to go on the tour with her. It was two weeks out of his life and he could manage it and stay in touch with his other clients by phone. He wanted to be there for Iris, to make sure nothing went wrong. With him on the tour, everyone would be much more careful, and he wanted it to be perfect for her.

They were going to start in Las Vegas, then head to L.A. He had already invited his daughters to opening night in L.A. and they promised to come. He wanted to introduce them to Iris. Ellen was going to come down from school at Davis for it. From there, they'd head to Houston, Washington, D.C., and their last city was New York. They were already selling tickets, and the advance publicity had been great so far. There was tremendous buildup and excitement, and hype, and because her album was doing so well, ticket sales were increasing exponentially.

Clay had promised to go shopping with her. He wanted her to have all new clothes to wear onstage. He knew she liked wearing simple black when she sang, but he thought that dresses that showed off her figure and were dressier would be appropriate and make the evening seem more special than a black blouse and black jeans, which was what she usually wore.

They spent two weeks just looking for clothes, it was hard finding a middle ground that they both liked. He wanted her in something sexier, and she wanted the simplest lines and plainest dresses. He made her come out and show him each dress so he could vote on it too. In the end, they had found six dresses that they agreed on and both loved, and shoes to go with them. They were in keeping with the image she liked, with the utmost simplicity, but there was just a little more kick to them than what she usually wore. She tried them on for Boy, and he loved them too.

"Now that's what men want to see women in," he informed her. "You always want to look like a nun. You can't sell love dressed like that. There has to be just a little something naughty about what you wear, otherwise it's no fun."

"But I don't want to be naughty," she said, complaining. "I want to be nice."

"Be nice at home. Be naughty onstage. It works better that way." He grinned at her.

She was smiling when she packed her suitcases for the tour. She tried to think of everything, not just her clothes.

She called Pattie before they left. It felt strange going on tour without her.

"I wish I were going with you," Pattie said sadly.

"I hated Glen, but I miss the tours, all the funny little towns we went to, the people who couldn't wait to see us, and this is going to be such a big deal. I never went on a tour like that."

"Neither did I," Iris said, wondering what it would be like to see Clay every day. It would be harder to hide her feelings for him, with so much time together. She was sure that he would never feel about her the way she did for him. He was unattainable. She knew it and respected it. She didn't expect anything other than warm camaraderie while they were on the tour and maybe some fatherly advice thrown in. She had silenced her heart's stirrings right from the beginning, and she intended to keep it that way, no matter how warm, attentive, and handsome he was. There were some men you couldn't have in life. He was one of them, up on a pinnacle somewhere in the sky, so there was no point wishing otherwise. It was just never going to happen. He would always be out of reach. All she had to do now was accept it. Clay was telling himself the same things about her, and had been since he met her.

Chapter 12

They left for Las Vegas from Teterboro Airport in Clay's plane. Iris, Clay, Boy, Star, who was going to sing with Iris's backup band for Boy's opening act, and Iris's backup boys were on board too. Eight of them in total, and the plane could comfortably seat twenty. Iris had never seen such luxury, and gasped when she walked in and looked around. There were two flight attendants to serve them, and everything was upholstered in rich cognac-colored leather.

The pilot and co-pilot came out of the cockpit to greet them. There were two bathrooms, with showers, and a very efficient galley, and there was a bedroom for Clay when he took longer flights, or preferred to spend the night on board instead of checking in to a hotel if he went to a city to see a performer or attended a meeting and didn't stay long. It was supremely luxurious and offered every comfort, and a big screen to watch movies, or individual ones. None of them had ever been on his plane before, or seen anything like it. The seats were large club chairs and there were tables to eat on, or work on.

"Goodbye, Nashville. Hello, Las Vegas!" Boy said in his Tennessee drawl, and the backup boys laughed. Star was too awestruck to say anything, and clung to Boy's hand, and Iris looked at Clay gratefully.

"Thank you. I spent nine years in a van with sweaty guys, crawling over the equipment, traveling for fifteen hours, and going straight into a performance without a rehearsal and taking off again right after we played." This was a whole different experience, just as Clay wanted it to be for her.

"I resisted buying a plane for a long time, but this just makes life so much easier when I'm flying all over the country seeing bands and artists in out-of-the-way places, or have to get to a meeting in another city in a hurry. My girls keep hounding me to borrow it, but I'm pretty strict about only using it for business." He showed her the bedroom then, which was big enough to move around in with a comfortable bed and its own bathroom. It was a four-hour flight from New York, so he didn't plan to use the bedroom, and the flight would go quickly with a meal and a movie. He went to Las Vegas a lot to see performers in nightclubs or concerts. This time he had set up additional security for Iris, just in case Glen Hendrix was on the loose again. They had checked and he was in a halfway house for the remainder of his sentence, which made Clay uneasy. Hendrix could easily slip away and cause trouble for her, if he was crazy enough to do that, which Clay hoped he wasn't. Clay hoped that some jail time had calmed him down a little. Even Glen admitted that he was shocked by how far the two thugs had gone. He said that he had hired them just to "scare them a little." They'd done a lot more than scare them. There was a restraining order still in force to keep Glen well away from Iris. If he violated it, he'd go back to jail.

As they took off smoothly, the others were talking to one another, and Iris sat next to Clay, talking about some details of the performance in Vegas. She wanted to change the order of two songs, which he left up to her. As she looked out the window afterward, she thought about her father, and wondered if he was still in Vegas, hustling odd jobs and willing women, who were foolish enough to let him stay with them and take advantage of them.

She was going to give three performances in Las Vegas. The timing was perfect with her album high up on the charts, along with Boy's singles. Clay had told them both that this was just the beginning, and they were both heading for the stratosphere. They all thought that one of Boy's singles might win him a Grammy. Kids were playing it nonstop all over the country.

They were performing that night, but there would be plenty of time to get ready when they got there. The plane would be following them for the whole tour. Iris had never seen such luxury, or known such comfort. Clay thought of everything to make her happy. She had Rosie in her little pink bag traveling with her. It was the first trip she'd been on. Iris took her out of her bag after they took off, and held her in her lap. Clay smiled watching her with the puppy. Boy called her "Cujo" because she loved to try to "attack" him, despite her tiny size and nearly microscopic teeth. She loved to play with anyone who paid attention to her. She had a bag full of toys, and a wardrobe of little pink coats and sweaters.

The meal they were served on the plane was as lavish as everything else. Joanne had selected the menu for them, with enough steaks for the men, salads for those who wanted them, a vegan plate, and sandwiches for those who only wanted a light meal. Clay had a turkey sandwich, and Iris ate a delicious McCarthy salad, which the flight attendant said was just like the one at the Beverly Hills Hotel. Star had the vegan plate since she was a vegetarian, and Boy and all the band members had steaks.

"I wish it were a longer flight," Boy said to Clay when they were an hour out of Vegas. He hadn't even had time to watch a movie, he was enjoying the plane so much, and chatting with the members of the band.

Iris went over some new songs, and made changes to the sheet music, and then listened to some tracks on her computer, checking out different arrangements she'd recorded. She wanted to polish the material right up to the time of the performance, and they had rehearsal scheduled at five, at the hotel. They were going to play at the MGM Grand, which was a huge venue. The size didn't matter to Iris, just the quality of the performance.

"Do you ever stop working?" Clay asked her when he woke up from a short nap.

"Not if I can help it," she said with a grin. Her drawl always seemed stronger when there were other Southerners around. In this case, Clay, Boy, and two members of the band. There were a lot of soft Southern drawls and mountain twangs in the group, with Tennessee, Kentucky, and Texas represented, which wasn't unusual on the music scene.

An hour later, they all looked excited when they landed in Las Vegas, and shifted into action. Clay and Iris got into an SUV with a driver, and the others got into a van, waiting for them when they landed. They headed for the Wynn hotel, which was at one end of the Strip, but they had the van and SUV to get them anywhere they wanted to go. The boys had all agreed to play a quick hand of poker at the hotel casino when they got there. Iris wanted to do a little shopping, and Clay had a meeting at the MGM Grand. Everything was set up. He just wanted to go over it one more time, and meet the woman who ran it. He had the checklist Joanne had given him, but he knew it by heart anyway. He'd been on countless tours before, and the stage managers and assistant producers would handle everything, and all the technical details. They were using local equipment and technicians, and not bringing their own, which wasn't necessary in a sophisticated location like Las Vegas.

They took off to the heart of town, and then headed toward the hotel to drop their things off.

Once again, Clay and Iris had the two best suites in the group with a view of the city and the desert beyond. And Clay's suite was right next to hers.

"You can call me if you need anything," he offered, "or we can leave the door between the two suites open, and yell if you need help."

"That's what Boy and I did in New York. It felt friendlier and not so lonely." But she wouldn't have time to get lonely here. She'd be too busy, and performing at night. And all the others were staying one floor down. She and Clay were on the club floor with more services, and a butler to wait on them.

"What'll I do with him?" Iris asked Clay in a whisper when they checked their rooms. The butler in full livery was standing by, waiting for them.

"You'll figure out something." Clay grinned at her. "Have him press your dress for tonight."

"It doesn't need it," she said.

"Unpack? Shine your shoes?" She was the least greedy woman he'd ever met. All the other women he'd brought to Vegas on dates had made a beeline to Chanel and every expensive store in the shopping area of their main floor lobby, and charged it to him. Iris was just passing time. All she really wanted to do was see the stage and begin rehearsing. She couldn't wait to get started.

Clay left shortly after they got there, and Iris went out for a walk, the others were all in the casino, having fun before they got to work. For Iris, it felt odd being back here. It had been home for a while. She took a cab to the house where she'd rented a room, picked up the box she'd left there, and took it back to the hotel, to go through it. She still had clothes in her storage unit, but nothing she really wanted, and she didn't have time to go there.

She slit open the small box, and was shocked to see what she had saved. Some pictures of people she had toured with and had forgotten, some sweaters, a pair of shoes that looked out of date now and she wouldn't wear, some letters that had no major meaning to her, two books, and some old notebooks with songs she'd written the music to, but had never developed further. They seemed like such meager bits of a life. She put most of it in the trash in her room, and the butler took it away. In the end, she kept the notebooks, although nothing in them was of much interest, one of the sweaters, and a framed photograph of her dad in his rodeo days, standing near the bullpen. He looked handsome and young, and not dissipated as he had when she'd last seen him. He hadn't looked that good in a long time. It made her wonder again if he was in Las Vegas. But whether he was or not, she doubted she'd see him again. Unless they ran into each other while she was here. If he couldn't get money from her, he had no interest. He'd made that clear.

When Clay got to the MGM Grand, he found everything in good order. The stage manager was efficient and had everything set up for their rehearsal. They were sold out, which was fantastic, and probably due to her album. It was going to be a big night for her, her first as one of Clay's performers, her first tour for him, and also her first in a major venue, carrying the whole weight of the show herself. She kept panicking, thinking about it all afternoon. What if she was terrible, if it was a disaster, if the crowd hated her? She could think of a thousand reasons why everything could go wrong.

By the time Clay got back to the hotel, she looked tense and nervous, having scared herself to death, worrying about all the possible disasters she could think of at the performance that night. He could see how anxious she was, and he noticed her father's photograph lying on the table, and could guess who it was immediately.

"Your father?" She nodded. He picked it up and studied it, looking for a resemblance but didn't see one, except for the blond hair. He looked hard, and like the kind of man who charmed women, but didn't necessarily care about them, including his daughter. She had told him all about her father's visit, once she digested it and it didn't sting quite so much. His total indifference to her well-being had always hurt her. "Good-looking guy," Clay commented.

"He was then. He kind of lost his looks from hard living, booze, and maybe from never giving a damn about anyone." She thought of the missing teeth when she had last seen him. He looked older than he was now. "He used to be able to charm the birds out of the trees, now he just looks sleazy." She was harsh in her judgments of him, but Clay knew he deserved it. He had been nothing but unkind to her for too long. She wasn't a child, and he couldn't con her anymore.

She put the photograph in her suitcase, and ordered a glass of iced tea. Clay went back into his part of the double suite to return some phone calls and check in with his office, and Iris started getting ready for rehearsal. She was going to change and do her makeup at the theater. She planned to leave Rosie at the hotel, so she didn't get lost or scared in the dressing room. She was sound asleep in her little bag. It had been a big day for her with her first plane trip and new surroundings. She looked like a little sleeping mouse when Iris peeked at her.

She knocked on Clay's door when she left, but he didn't answer. She thought maybe he was asleep or in the shower. She met up with Boy, Star, and the band at the van outside the hotel, and they hopped in, which reminded her of her old tour days in what seemed now like another lifetime.

"What did you do today?" Star asked her. She was sweet and seemed very young to Iris, and Boy was crazy about her. She was a gorgeous girl, and thought he walked on water. "I went shopping," she added. She was wearing a hot pink sweater and jeans, and was going to change into a black leather miniskirt and halter-top for the performance.

"I went to pick up some stuff where I used to rent a room. I lived here, between tours. And I went to school here before I started touring," Iris told her.

"That must have been fun," Star said with a sweet smile. There was an almost childlike innocence about her, which was refreshing in the often seamy world they lived in, in spite of Clay's protection. The world of music had a dark underside, which hadn't touched her. Iris could see why Boy loved her, and he had a certain innocence about him too.

"No, actually it wasn't fun. I grew up in Texas before that."

"I grew up in Southern California. In San Diego," Star said, and Iris thought she looked it. She could imagine her on a beach somewhere, with her red hair and freckles.

They chatted on the way to MGM Grand, and Iris could feel the tension mount by several notches when they got there. The moment of truth was coming, if the concert would be a success or not. Clay had poured so much into her and Boy, and had so much faith in them that she didn't want to disappoint him, and was afraid she would. That would be the worst of it for her, letting him down would be even worse than disappointing herself. He had been so good to them. She could see that Boy was feeling that way too. This was their first really big tour, and she was glad they were there together. There were posters of them all over the lobby, and they hurried into the concert hall so they wouldn't be seen in their street clothes.

The stage manager was waiting for them, and had everything ready. Boy was going to rehearse first, and after Iris dropped off her things in the dressing room they'd assigned to her, she slipped into a seat in the auditorium. The band was warming up, and Boy was tuning his guitar. The theater was dark, and five minutes later, they were ready to start. They took off at a rapid rate with a lively country song that Boy did brilliantly and always got the audience going every time they played it. He rehearsed some of his hand-clapping, foot-stomping songs that audiences loved and would loosen them up. Then he slowed things down with a couple of familiar hits, he sang three of Iris's songs, and then he closed with a familiar favorite that everyone knew the words to, and after that he turned the stage over to Iris for her to rehearse. In some ways, he was so good that he set the bar high for her, and she liked that.

She thanked him when he left the stage with Star and told him he was great. She could tell that they were all going to be in high spirits tonight. She started her own rehearsal off with one of her best songs, an old Elvis song that everyone loved, and then she dove into the material at full strength, letting her voice rip and soar, moved into her ballads, and kept going after that. She had had full control of her voice during the entire rehearsal, and left the stage afterward feeling good about how the material worked. It was a strong performance, and she was introducing a new song at the end.

She had an hour to relax before the concert started and went to her dressing room. Boy wandered in a few minutes later.

"You sounded good," he said, letting himself down into a chair. "I stayed to hear the first few songs. You killed it in rehearsal, you'll be even better with the audience," he reassured her, and she hoped he was right.

"I'm so damn nervous." She looked at him sheepishly. More than she'd ever been before. But this was the big time, not some small town where no one would notice if she screwed up.

"Me too," he admitted.

"I don't want to let Clay down," she said softly. "He's done so much for us."

"That's what I've been thinking too. I wish we were onstage together tonight," he said, and she nodded. But they both had to stand on their own, and prove to the people who believed in them that they were right.

"I'll watch your whole performance from the wings," he said, to give her courage.

"I'll watch you too before I go on," she promised. He gave her a hug, and ambled out the door in his cowboy boots that were a part of him.

She did her hair then, brushed it and let it fall straight down her back like a golden curtain. She looked more than ever like Alice in Wonderland. She put on the little makeup she wore, and finally put one of her new black dresses on right before it was time for Boy to perform. The dress had a little sexy kick to it without looking vulgar, which made her look more grown up. There had always been a contradiction between her youthful look and the womanliness of her voice, which spoke of a thousand lifetimes lived, and not easy ones. Her songs said that she knew a lot about life and had learned hard lessons on the way to where she was now. They were songs people could relate to, and addressed the griefs they'd had. What she sang told them that she understood and was still in there fighting, growing, loving, and singing her heart out. She had a special quality as she stood onstage that made people want to embrace her and remember every word she said. She was a wise woman with a miraculous voice, telling their story and her own. There was no question, she had a gift.

She didn't see Clay before she went backstage, and she peeked at the audience through a crack in the curtains. The house was filled, and the crowd sounded boisterous and excited. They were ripe for the plucking, and Boy was just the one to do that. Iris stood quietly hidden when the curtain came up, the stage was dark and then the spotlight shone directly on him, and he reached out and grabbed their hearts with his first song. He talked to them, and warmed them, and seduced them, and opened up to them, and fell in love with them, and they did the same for him. He was perfect, and Iris smiled as she watched him, and listened to his voice. It was strong tonight, and she wiped a tear from her cheek twice when he sang the ballads she had written. The audience shouted when he wanted them to, and clapped and stomped and sang along. He had them in his hand from the moment he started and they first saw him onstage until the very end. He was the best warm-up act they'd ever seen, because he really wasn't one. He was of feature quality himself and it was a gift that he had agreed to be her opening act, and made the concert that much better.

There was a moment's lull as the audience drifted slowly back to earth after his performance, and the stage manager let them cool off while the band took a break. And then the theater went even darker, the curtain came up again, and Iris came out onstage, looking beautiful and just sexy enough. She tried to see Clay in the audience, she knew he was in the front row, but the footlights were too bright to see him. She smiled at the audience, and chatted with them for a few minutes, and told them a little about her life growing up.

"I grew up in Texas, in a lot of little dusty towns. I loved to sing even as a little kid. I had a big voice that didn't fit my body, and the one place I could let it all go was in church. So let's start at the beginning, and I'm going to start with a gospel song. And if you know it, y'all sing along." She had chosen one that everybody knew, started low, and let her voice climb as it did naturally, until she reached the high notes that no one else could reach. The audience was fully engaged by then, singing with her, imagining her childhood, and remembering their own. She had them in the palm of her hand by the time the song ended, differently from the way Boy had. His performance had been wilder and more exuberant. Hers was more carefully thought out, a chronology of her life and everything she'd lived through set to music in a way they understood viscerally. They were in love with her by the time she was halfway through the show. The rest was icing on the cake. She owned them, she loved them, and they loved her. She sang one of her most beautiful ballads at the end, which sang about hopes and dreams, living through the hard parts and coming home at last. When she finished the last song, her voice drifted away and the stage went dark, the audience went insane, standing up and cheering and screaming for more. The spotlight came back on, and she smiled at them, and moved closer to the front of the stage, as though she wanted to be near them, and they belonged to one another now.

"Y'all want more?" She smiled at them. "Okay,

let's have some fun." She sang a wild, happy, un-
bridled song of joy and lust that made them as
happy to listen as she was singing it. And they
went crazy again when it was over. She looked at
them with love in her eyes, took one simple bow,
and spoke from the stage in her distinctive voice.

"See you soon," she said in a tone that was like
a caress, a delicate embrace. "Ya'll take care now,"
she said softly, the stage went dark and she was
off. They were thunderous, hoping she'd come
back for another encore, but she didn't.

They floated out of the theater. Both performances had been superb, complementary in a
way, but sufficiently different to make the audience feel they had been to two extraordinary concerts by two remarkable artists. There had been
greatness on the stage and Iris's voice had been
exquisite, of a purity that even she couldn't always
produce, but she had that night.

She started to walk to her dressing room, and
Boy emerged from the shadows, hugged her and
lifted her off her feet and twirled her around. "You
crushed it," he said, and she was grinning. He was
ecstatic for her.

"So did you! You were fantastic. They loved
us," she said, in awe of what had happened onstage that night. It was the kind of performance
that would have provoked wild abuse from Glen
Hendrix, just to be sure he destroyed their self-
confidence, but she knew better now. What they'd

done that night was molten gold onstage, the music, their voices, their rapport with the audience. When Boy set her back down, she saw Clay a few feet behind him, waiting for her and beaming. She walked toward him, and he looked at her with tears in his eyes.

"I don't know what to say. You were incredible, Iris. And Boy was great too. I was so proud of you, if you were my child, I couldn't have been prouder. You are going to have the most amazing career of any artist I know. Thank you, thank you for tonight." He pulled her gently into his arms and hugged her. Their bodies touched and seemed to fit together. He could feel her heart beating from the excitement of being onstage. He didn't want to let go of her. He just wanted to hold her there forever, he didn't want the moment to end, nor did she. He walked back to her dressing room with her. Her security men followed her closely, but gave her enough space to talk to him without crowding her.

She was excited and elated and exhausted all at the same time. It was a deep emotional experience doing a performance like that. It didn't happen that way every time. But tonight was a special beginning of the rest of her career. She had done it for Clay. She turned to tell him so.

"I did it for you, you know," she said softly.

"I was hanging on your every word. You had them before you finished the first song, and me too." He beamed at her, as she sat down and took off the makeup she wore onstage. She went behind a screen, took her dress off, and hung it on a rack, and came out in a pale blue cowboy shirt, jeans, and little red ballerina flats, and looked like a little girl again with her long golden hair. It was as though she had hung up the womanly side of her with her dress, and she was just a girl again, unmarked by life, full of dreams and happiness. He loved that about her. "What do you want to do?" he asked her. "Celebrate? Party? Go to bed and sleep?"

"I won't be able to sleep for hours after a performance like that. Maybe go somewhere, relax, and have some champagne?"

They rounded up the others, and Clay took them to the main bar at the Bellagio. The headwaiter knew instantly who Clay was, and they gave them a table in the back big enough for all of them. Clay ordered champagne for Star and Iris, and the boys ordered harder liquor, rum, tequila, whiskey. They all needed to unwind after the show, and talked animatedly about it. Clay had just gotten a text that the next two nights were sold out too. Their tour was off to a roaring start. It was everything they had hoped it would be.

They stayed at the Bellagio for two hours, and then went back to their rooms at the Wynn. Iris walked into Clay's living room with him, in the adjoining suites they were in.

"It was just a magical night," he told her again.

"We'll do it for you again tomorrow," she promised with a yawn. She was tired now, but so happy. He kissed her on the cheek, and touched her cheek then for an instant. The evening had bathed everything in beauty and light. He watched her go to her room and softly close the door, as he wished that he was with her, but he knew you couldn't have everything. Just being near her and listening to her sing, with that incredible voice, was enough.

Chapter 13

The rest of their performances in Las Vegas were just as good as the first. In fact, they seemed to get better each night, and the last night she played three encores and Boy came back onstage for the last one with her, and the crowd went crazy. They sang one of her most beautiful love songs and the audience was in love with them. The reviews for all three performances were fabulous. The audience's reaction to them far surpassed anything Clay had hoped for, or that Boy and Iris had dreamed of. They were stars, and Clay wanted to get started on an album for Boy, and a second one for Iris. She wrote such a steady stream of songs that there was no shortage of material for her to sing. They all felt as though the three days in Las Vegas had been a golden moment in their lives, and to top it off, Boy won five thousand dollars at the blackjack table. It was a clean sweep. The three days in Vegas had been perfection in every way.

She wondered if her father had come to see her concert, but it was unlikely. He wouldn't have wanted to spring for a ticket, and their relationship seemed to be over. She realized that she no longer needed his approval, and hadn't in a long time. She hit the high notes just fine without being reminded to.

The approval that meant everything to her was Clay's, and she had that hands down. He was thrilled with how the first stop on the tour had gone. They all felt triumphant and energized as they flew the short distance to L.A. on his plane.

Clay had rented bungalows for all of them at the Beverly Hills Hotel, with its fifties-style Hollywood glamour. Star, Boy, and the band shared one bungalow, and Clay and Iris had a two-bedroom bungalow of their own. They all had dinner at the Polo Lounge that night, and weren't performing until the next day. They had a night off, which was typical of tours for big stars, like the one he had arranged for them. He didn't expect them to play back-to-back performances, night after night. Clay's daughters were due to come to see him in the morning. They were staying at home with their mother, as they always did, but having lunch with him by the pool, and he had told Iris he wanted her to meet them. She was excited about seeing them, and Boy and the others were spending the day at the pool too, until rehearsal at three.

She was working on a sheet of music in her room when she heard the door of the cottage open, and female voices. She wasn't sure who it was, and went on working until Clay showed up in the doorway of her room.

"My girls are here," he said with a broad smile, and she got up to meet them. She was wearing her red ballerina shoes, jeans, and a T-shirt, and walked into the living room of the suite. She wasn't wearing makeup and hadn't combed her hair yet. It was what she called her Raggedy Ann look when she was composing. She saw two very attractive young women standing in the living room. Both tall and slim like their father. Margie had short dark hair, and looked at Iris intently, and the other girl was blond with Clay's green eyes. She had a mane of long blond hair in a messy ponytail, and was wearing a plaid lumberjack shirt and heavy work boots. Iris guessed that the one in the plaid shirt was Ellen, Clay's younger daughter, who wanted to be a vet. And Margie was the elder, who worked for her mother in their catering business. Both were pretty girls, but Margie looked cool and unfriendly.

Ellen apologized immediately as Iris approached them. She looked tiny compared to them, and Rosie was following her closely.

"I'm so sorry," Ellen said to Iris, "I'm volunteering at a rescue shelter for abused horses right now. I didn't have time to change into anything decent." Iris pointed to herself in her T-shirt and jeans and hair in a clip, and laughed.

"I haven't even been taking care of horses. I was working on a new arrangement." Margie gave her a cold look and didn't say anything. Ellen stooped to make friends with the Chihuahua, and Rosie instantly decided she liked her.

"What's her name?" Ellen asked her.

"Rosie."

"She's adorable," Ellen said, trying to make conversation to compensate for her sister's glacial silence.

"It's nice to meet you both," Iris said warmly, "your dad has really been looking forward to seeing you," she said, and got no reaction whatsoever from Margie. "I hear you're coming to the concert tonight," Iris said.

"It was a command performance," Margie said with an angry look at her father. "We don't usually go to his concerts. He said this time we had to, so we could hear you and meet you." Clay looked embarrassed and Iris went on smiling to make the moment easier for him.

"Well, I'm very touched that you made the effort," Iris said warmly. "I hope you enjoy it. The opening act, Boy Brady, is really fantastic."

"I've heard his singles," Ellen volunteered. "He's really good," she agreed.

"Well, have a nice time at the pool," Iris said. "I'd better get back to work." She smiled at them both and went back to her room, and Clay walked in a minute later.

"I'm sorry about Margie. She's a lot like her mother. She's been jealous of every woman I've ever gone out with."

Iris looked surprised. "Did you tell her you're not dating me?"

"I did but she didn't believe me, because I wanted her to see the show. It's not like she has to go a great distance. She came from Bel Air. Ellen's the one who made the effort, as usual. She's got a heavy schedule with school and her volunteer work."

"She's sweet, and I'm sure Margie is too. She's just possessive of you. She has nothing to fear from me. I'm not trying to steal you from her. Maybe she's jealous of your taking talent under your wing who are close to her age."

"Something like that," he said, looking discouraged. "She's so much like her mother. She has something nasty to say about everyone. I think she disapproves of show business in any form." But it had given her a damn nice life, Iris didn't point out to him. She felt sorry for him. Margie had made the introduction an awkward moment.

They left the suite a few minutes later and went out to the pool for lunch. Iris stayed in her room for another hour, working on the bridges in the arrangement she was trying to change for that night. When she finished, she went out to the pool to join Boy and the others. She waved at Clay and his daughters, and went to sit with Boy.

"Did you meet Clay's daughters?" he asked her when she sat down.

"I did," she said softly. "The dark-haired one hates me. The younger one was very nice. She made friends with Rosie. She's going to study to be a vet." Iris had left the puppy in the room, so she wouldn't fall into the pool.

"I'm glad to hear it," Boy said with a look of relief. "She acted like she hates me too. She made some comment about her father forcing her to go to the concert tonight. She wasn't nice to him either. Poor Clay looked embarrassed. The other one has heard my singles and likes them."

"He says the older one is like her mother," she filled him in.

"No wonder they got divorced," he said in a low voice.

The two girls left after lunch and presumably went home, and were coming back for the concert that night. He had given them front row seats to a sold-out concert, which he told them was history-making. He said that Iris and Boy were going to be enormous stars one day, and he wanted them to hear one of their first concerts. But Margie was always systematically critical of everything her father did, just like her mother. It was one of the many things that had destroyed their marriage.

Iris thought that it was a little silly that Margie objected to her, or was jealous, if she thought she and Clay weren't dating. She just seemed like an unusually sour person for someone her age. Iris remembered that she was the one who wanted her father to buy her a house in Malibu and he had refused and thought the idea inappropriate at twenty-two. Ellen seemed much more reasonable and easier to get along with, with simpler tastes. Clay's two girls were very different.

Iris, Boy, and the others left the pool after lunch to get ready for rehearsal. They shared a van to get there and the rehearsal went well. Iris switched one of her songs for the new arrangement she'd been working on. The venue was huge. It was hard to believe that they could fill it, but the concert was sold out for all three days they were playing at the Staples Center.

It was exciting to be in L.A., after playing Vegas. The exhilaration was building again.

L.A. turned out to be an even bigger hit than Vegas had been. Iris felt as though they were developing a cult following, which was going to sell their records even faster. In fact, their record sales, hers and Boy's, had gone through the roof since the concert in Vegas. She had called and told Pattie how fantastic it was, and she was happy for them. She wanted to come and see one of their concerts herself now, and was going to see if she could find someone to keep Jimmy for a day or two, so she could catch the last stop of the tour in New York, and get a little time with Iris, and some time off from her responsibilities in Biloxi.

Iris saw Margie and Ellen backstage with their father after the performance. Ellen was wildly enthusiastic, and mesmerized by Boy and how handsome he was, and Margie remained stone-faced, and had nothing to say to either of them except that she thought the acoustics weren't good, and the music was too loud and drowned out the voices, which wasn't true. It was her way of rejecting everything Iris wrote about, pretending she hadn't heard it. She seemed to have a particularly strong dislike for Iris, but she wasn't warm to her father either.

Ellen was driving back to Berkeley after the performance and she gave Iris a hug before she left, and told her she was terrific. When Iris saw Clay half an hour later when they left the theater, he was alone, and the girls were gone. Iris felt sorry for him. He looked sad and dejected, he obviously didn't have an easy time with his daughters. And if Margie really was like her mother, his marriage must have been a nightmare and it wasn't surprising he hadn't married again. She was a very unpleasant young woman, with a chip on her shoulder and a nasty attitude about everything. Clay had told Iris before that her mother had poisoned her against him, although he did everything he could for them. She hadn't succeeded with his younger daughter. But his relationship with both of them seemed strained. And he was such a nice person, Iris thought. He didn't deserve it.

They had drinks after the performance at the Polo Lounge that night, and Clay seemed subdued when they went back to the cottage. Iris could tell that Margie's attitude had spoiled the evening for him, and he'd been looking forward to it. He had hoped that they would love it. Ellen had, but Margie wouldn't let herself enjoy it, or admit she had. Their performance had been fantastic.

And so were the next two nights. L.A. and Las Vegas were complete triumphs, the press was all over them, and record sales were reflecting their success on the road. The reaction had been immediate. Clay couldn't be happier, as he read the press coverage on their way to Houston.

They were only spending two days there, and Iris had told Clay that she was taking some time off the night they arrived.

"Do you still have family in Texas?" he asked her, and she shook her head.

"Not really. There's just something I have to do, some people I want to see. I called ahead and got a car and driver for tonight," she explained to him. She had a long drive ahead of her when they arrived, but she didn't care. It was important.

She was just leaving the hotel at four o'clock, when she ran into him in the lobby. She was wearing cowboy boots and jeans and a Levi's jacket. She'd had the boots since she was fifteen, and they looked it. They were well worn and battered.

"You look like a real cowgirl," he said to her with a smile. "Will you be okay on your own?" he asked her, always protective of her. She didn't have security with her. They'd had security in L.A., and he had had additional protection for her in Vegas because of Hendrix, but she had said she didn't need any in Houston. She felt safe here, and for the remaining cities.

"I'll be fine," she reassured him, and then hesitated. She wasn't sure why, but she wondered if he'd want to come with her. "Do you want to come? It's a long drive, about three hours from Houston."

"Would I be an intrusion?" he asked cautiously.

"Of course not."

"In that case, maybe I should. I don't like you going that far alone. Does Boy want to go?" he asked.

"I didn't ask him." It was a special mission, and she had planned to go alone. Once they set up the tour to include Houston, she had decided.

"I'm coming," he said simply, and followed her to the SUV and driver she had hired for the night. She had given the limo company the destination, and they said it wasn't a problem.

She'd been in Texas many times over the years when she was on tour for Hendrix and Weston, but it had never felt like a pilgrimage she could make before. She hadn't had the time. It was just another stop on the miserable tours she'd been on, trapped for days on end in a crowded van. This time she had the time to do something she had thought about and wanted to do for years. She had brought three of her CDs with her to give them.

"Am I allowed to ask where we're going?" he asked her gently after an hour. He could sense that it was important to her and he wondered if it was something serious, like the cemetery where her mother was buried. But she didn't even know where her mother was buried.

"We're going to see the only people who were ever nice to me as a kid. They were like my parents, or the ones I wish I had, and never did."

They rode in silence for most of the drive. Clay watched her face and eyes, and was touched that she had let him come with her. When they'd been driving for almost three hours, she told the driver where to get off the highway, and gave him directions after that along some dusty back roads until they were on the edge of a small town.

"Here!" she said. She had seen the sign immediately, and it looked the same. She hadn't called. She wanted to surprise them. She expected them to still be there. It never occurred to her that they might be gone after fifteen years.

"This is it?" Clay asked, looking surprised. "Harry's Bar?" She nodded and looked excited as she jumped out of the SUV. It was a big jump for her, and Clay got out too and followed her to the restaurant-bar with the red neon sign.

She spoke to Clay softly as they approached. "This is the first place I ever sang for money. I was twelve years old. My father ran me in and out. I sang, and then I sat in the truck for hours, sometimes all night. I sang five nights a week, they gave me dinner whenever I did, and one of them made me a dress I wore for years whenever I sang." He realized now how important it was to her, and what it meant. It was the only touchstone she had left of love she had been given as a child. It moved him deeply to be there with her, and he let her walk in first and followed her. There was an older man behind the bar, cleaning it with a wet rag. There were half a dozen tables with people eating dinner, and two men who looked like ranch hands at the bar. She stared at the back of the room, and the stage was still there. She stopped and gazed at it, and noticed a young waitress serving dinner. There was no sign of Sally or Pearl. He seemed much older, but the man at the bar was Harry. She stood watching him, as tears filled her eyes and she approached the bar.

"Harry?" she said in barely more than a whisper, and he stared at her, as though she was familiar. Clay kept his distance and watched with tears in his eyes too. It was a defining moment for everyone involved. "I'm Iris Cooper," she said, and he reached out and touched her face with a gentle hand.

"Oh my God . . . it's you." He started to cry and came rapidly from behind the bar to hug her. "Oh my God, you're so grown up and so beautiful. We've been hearing about you, and listening to your songs." All the way here, they had heard about her.

"I'm singing in Houston tomorrow night. I had to come and see you," she said, clutched in his bear hug, and then he released her to look at her again. They were both crying. "We never forgot you. How could we? You were our little girl."

"Where are Sally and Pearl?" she asked. There was no sign of either of them. Maybe they had retired or moved away.

He went to the kitchen door then and bellowed for Pearl. She came out a minute later, wiping her hands. She had gotten older too, but she hadn't changed.

"Do you know who this is?" Harry said to her, his voice shaking, and she let out a scream and flew into Iris's arms and held on to her for dear life. She kept stroking her face and kissing her and hugging her again, and Iris couldn't stop crying.

"I always wanted to come back to you. You were always so good to me. I don't think I ever had a decent meal after I left here. We moved to Houston, and then Austin, and all over Nevada, and finally Vegas. But I always wanted to come back and see you. Where's Sally?" she asked Pearl then, and she wiped her eyes.

"She died, about ten years ago. Breast cancer."

"And you came back just in time," Harry told her. "I just turned sixty-five. I'm retiring. I sold the bar. I'm leaving in a month. My brother has a place in Montana, and he lost his wife last year, so I'm going to live with him."

"I'm staying," Pearl said staunchly. Harry handed a fresh beer to each of the ranch hands, and sat down at a table with Pearl and Iris, and she introduced them to Clay and explained that he was her manager and had organized the tour, and the album.

"You're a big star now," Pearl said proudly, "and so pretty. You can still hit those high notes," she said, and they all laughed, and Iris took the CDs out of her purse, and handed them to her and Harry. "I brought you my album. I wore the dress

Sally made me till it nearly fell off my back." She grinned at them.

"Your dad?" Harry asked with a stern look.

"He's about the same. We had a falling out about five years ago. I saw him a few months ago in New York. I don't think we'll see each other again," she said quietly.

"What'd he do, show up to ask you for money?" Harry hit the nail squarely on the head. "Forgive me, but that son of a bitch left you freezing out in the truck, or boiling in the sun. He wouldn't have fed you if we didn't here. We were all worried sick when you left."

"I survived it." She smiled at them. None of that mattered now. She had found them again. She was sorry about Sally, but so grateful to have found the two of them. It really was like coming home. She was so glad she had come before Harry left.

"You're not married? You don't have kids?" Pearl asked her, with a sideways glance at Clay.

"No, I've been touring for nine years. And I've just been singing."

"Thank God you're okay. We never forgot you, Iris," Pearl said, staring at her and looking at every detail.

"I never forgot you either. You're the only family I ever had."

"Sally and I cried for weeks when you left. We were scared of what he'd do with you. Just leave you to starve somewhere, or work you to death," Pearl said.

"I'm fine," she said, and she was. Now. But those had been hard years. She had come through them, and had come back to them.

They sat and talked for an hour, and then Iris stood up slowly. She hated to leave, but they had a long drive back to Houston. Clay stood up and took two of his business cards out of his wallet.

"If you want to find Iris, just get in touch with me. I'll find her for you." They both thanked him, and put the cards in their pockets.

"We have to get back to Houston," Iris said regretfully, sorry to leave them.

"Do you want something for the road?" Pearl offered. "We've got that peach pie you love." Iris smiled at the memory.

"We're okay. All I needed was to see you." She hugged them both tight, and they walked outside with her and she hugged them again. "Take care of yourselves. I love you guys."

"We love you too." Pearl spoke for both of them. "Keep in touch."

"I'll come back," Iris promised, even though she didn't know when. Clay took a picture with his phone of the three of them standing together. She couldn't take her eyes off them, filling her heart with their image, standing outside the bar. She got into the SUV with Clay and waved to them as long as she could see them, and she sobbed when they were finally out of sight, and Clay took her in his arms and held her.

"Oh, baby, I'm so sorry for that hard road you traveled for all these years." He could see how much Harry and Pearl meant to her, and how much they had cared about her.

"You had a hard road too," she said as he held her, "and so did Boy. We all did. You don't get where we are now on an easy road. It makes it that much sweeter when you get here." She smiled up at him through her tears. "I'm so glad I saw them again. I really loved them. They were the best people I ever knew. My father was such a shit, but they were like guardian angels for me when I was here. We only stayed for six or eight months, which was a long time for my dad. But they were so good to me, I never forgot them, and Sally was sweet too."

Clay held Iris close to him on the trip back to Houston, and halfway there, she fell asleep. He knew he had made a special journey with her that night, to a place back in time which was a sweet spot for her, maybe the only one, and she had let him share it with her. It meant the world to him. He was gently stroking her hair when she woke up and looked at him.

"It was nice, wasn't it, seeing them?" she said.

"Thank you for letting me come," he whispered in the darkness, and she sat up next to him. Her heart felt lighter, and she smiled at Clay. And as though it was the most natural thing in the world, he kissed her. He felt as though she had bared her soul to him that night and he couldn't hold back anymore. He had felt too much for her for too long. "I love you, Iris," he said simply.

She nodded, she loved him too. "I've been in love with you all this time," she admitted to him.

"Me too." He smiled. "I thought you'd think I was too old."

"I thought you were too important to ever look at me that way."

"Now that is the *only* dumb thing you ever said to me. You're just as important as I am, and probably a better person."

"What are your girls going to say?" She was worried about it, but he wasn't.

"They'll say whatever they want to. Ellen will be nice about it. Margie won't. And then they'll get used to it. This is my life, Iris. They're grown-ups now. You and I have traveled a long hard road to find each other, and we're lucky we did. I'm not giving that up now, for anyone or anything. Now hush, woman," he said, sounding like the depths of Kentucky, and she laughed.

"I had to come all the way home to Texas to find you," she said, smiling. She felt as though she had come home that night. To Harry, to Pearl, and now to Clay. And he was right. It had been a long hard road, but was worth it. Now neither of them would be alone anymore, and the rest of the way would be easier. They sat holding each other all the way back to Houston, and she slept in his room that night.

They didn't say anything to anyone, and figured they didn't owe anyone any explanations.

Both concerts in Houston were an amazing success, and their nights together afterward were even better. They had found what they both needed in Houston. It was as though they had her parents' blessing. He had met Harry and Pearl, and now she had Clay to watch over her. He was everything she had never had. He guarded her like a treasure and when his plane took off for Washington, D.C., there was no doubt in their minds. They belonged together. She had come home to Texas, and her dreams had finally come true.

Chapter 14

The concert in Washington went well and was exciting, but it wasn't quite as special as Vegas, L.A., and Houston had been. Iris felt as though she had wings onstage now that she and Clay had admitted that they loved each other. She couldn't believe how foolish they had been, each one thinking that the other would never want them. They'd been in love almost since the first day. They fit together perfectly.

She called Pattie and admitted it to her. And Boy asked her point-blank after Houston. Everything about their energy had changed, and they were totally focused on each other. He was happy for her.

Washington was fun, but they were all excited about the concert in New York. They were booked into Madison Square Garden right in the city. It was going to be a fantastic venue for them. And after the concert, Clay wanted Iris to move in with him. She said she would, after he told his daughters. She didn't want to cause a rift between them. He insisted he wouldn't let that happen. They had to accept that he had a right to a life too, whether they approved or not. And there was nothing for them to disapprove of, in his opinion. Iris was sure that Margie at least would disagree.

Iris was going to introduce two new songs at Madison Square Garden, one of them written about him. It was the most beautiful love song she'd ever written, and it made him cry the first time she sang it to him. It talked about how they had come from Kentucky and Texas to find each other, and they would travel the rest of their road together, and there would be no more hard times. She was going to close the show at the Garden with it, and couldn't wait for the audience to hear it. She called it "No More Hard Times," and hoped it would be true.

She picked up some of her things at the Plaza when they got back to New York, and took them to his apartment. And they left for Madison Square Garden together. She saw Boy and the others when they got there. Boy kept teasing her that she smiled all the time now. She had good reason to.

Like the other concerts on the tour, they were sold out. The most exciting thing for Iris was that Pattie had found a babysitter to stay with Jimmy and her mother, and she was coming to the concert that night.

Her plane was landing just in time for her to catch a cab and be there before it started, and she had promised to come backstage right before Iris went on. They hadn't seen each other since Iris had left the tour nearly a year before, and Iris couldn't wait to see her.

Pattie arrived breathless five minutes before Iris went on. She gave her an enormous hug and Iris asked one of the stagehands to take her to Clay in the front row. He had a seat waiting for her.

Boy had just finished his opening act, and Iris waited for the applause to die down. The stage was dark, and then Iris appeared as the spotlight followed her across the stage.

She chatted with the audience for a few minutes, as she liked to do. She told them it was a special night, and her best friend, a talented singer called Pattie Dixon, had come all the way from Biloxi, Mississippi, to be at the concert. "There's nothing like a good friend," she said with a warm smile, and opened with a song that paid tribute to it. Pattie squirmed in her seat and smiled at Clay. She was surprised by how handsome he was, and didn't look his age. Then she got lost in the show. Iris was fantastic and ripped the audience's heart out again and again, and Iris soared into the high notes the way she always had, with ease.

She was well into her fourth song, and hitting her stride, when she heard an unfamiliar sound, like an explosion, followed by a series of them. The sound cut right across her song and she had no idea what it was as she tried to keep on singing, and suddenly people were screaming. A man with automatic weapons slung across his body ran up onto the stage. He shot at someone in the wings. Powerful hands pulled Iris off the stage, and she flew onto the floor below and saw Clay's face, as the gunman started shooting wildly into the crowd. People were falling. Someone turned the lights up. Iris heard more screaming, and everywhere on the audience around her, she saw blood. People tried to take refuge under the seats, and run out of the arena, and the gunman kept shooting. Iris saw Pattie fall off her seat in the front row and slip onto the floor. Iris tried to get to her, but the bullets were flying too wildly, and Clay was pulling her away. They both stopped behind an alcove, and looked at each other.

"Oh my God, Clay, what happened?" Iris was breathless and pale.

"I don't know. The guy just came out of nowhere and started gunning people down." They could hear screaming all around them, and they were crouched on the ground. "Do you have your cellphone?" he asked, and she handed it to him.

His had disappeared while he was running. He dialed 911 to tell them what had happened.

"We know," the dispatcher told him immediately. "Are you in a safe place?" he asked hurriedly.

"No, but we have cover right now."

"Stay low, stay out of sight if you can. Try to find cover and get out of the building if you're able to. We have SWAT teams on the way," they told him, and Clay hung up.

"I saw Pattie fall," Iris said urgently to Clay. "I have to get back to her." She was desperate to go to her.

"You can't." Clay grabbed her arm. "The shooter is still on the stage," and he was still firing an automatic rifle into the crowd. "I want to get you out of here." He pulled her in the direction of an exit he had seen people running toward, and she wouldn't go.

"There are injured and dying people back there. We have to help them." She tried to pull free of him, but Clay had a grip on her arm, and wouldn't let her go.

"You're not going back," he said fiercely. "I'm getting you out of here." He almost dragged her toward the exit, just as the SWAT teams arrived with bulletproof suits and shields, helmets and masks, carrying weapons of their own.

"Go, go, go, go!" one of them said to them, and Iris finally dashed to safety with Clay's body shielding her. She realized with shaking legs that he could have been shot trying to save her, and if he hadn't yanked her off the stage, she would be dead by now. She had never seen anything so horrible and terrifying. Once outside, they could still hear gunshots from inside the Garden, as several more people came through the same exit they had. Some of them were bleeding, and one man was carrying a young girl. She had a wound on her neck and another in her chest and Iris thought she looked dead. The man was crying as he laid her on the pavement and paramedics rushed toward her, and then shook their heads as the man lay on the ground holding her and sobbed.

It was over in another ten minutes. The marksmen from the SWAT team killed the gunman, and then teams of police and paramedics swarmed the building to assist the wounded, and lead others out. Iris rushed back in to find Pattie, she found her where she had seen her fall. She was lying facedown, and Iris gently turned her over. She was dead. Iris looked at her in shock and horror and then lay her down gently and went down the rows of seats, looking for people who needed help. Clay was in another row helping anyone he could. The auditorium was littered with bodies, and other people crying, calling out for help, and waving an arm to catch someone's attention. Iris went from one person to the next, stepping over bodies of young people. She saw Clay in another aisle holding a woman who was covered with blood, and the band members were standing on the stage, and she didn't see Boy among them. She saw that Star was crying, and as soon as she could hand over the person she was helping to the police, she ran to the steps at the edge of the stage, and dashed up them. The body of the gunman still lay on the stage, peppered with bullets. She asked Star first, "Where's Boy?" She pointed to the wings and couldn't speak. Iris ran in the direction she pointed and found Boy lying on the ground, drenched in blood, with two police paramedics, and a member of the SWAT team working on him. She could see that he had a wound on the side of his chest, and she knelt down next to them.

"Who are you?" one of the paramedics asked her.

"Iris Cooper. This was my concert, his too. He's my friend." They were packing the wound, and had run an IV line into his arm, and one of them had a defibrillator in his hand. All she could think was that she couldn't lose him too. They put Boy on a gurney and rushed him outside, and Iris went with him. Clay saw her go and followed them out. They were loading Boy into an ambulance when he got to them.

There were emergency vehicles everywhere with sirens blaring. The news trucks had arrived by then, and there was a steady stream of blood-covered victims being removed from the building on stretchers and gurneys and in wheelchairs. Inside, they were covering the bodies with tarps. It looked like a sea of them to Iris when she glanced inside.

"Pattie . . ." she said to Clay. He had seen it happen, and he knew. She'd been shot in the chest, straight to the heart. The gunman had known what he was doing. She went back inside then to wait with Pattie so she could identify her, and Clay went to speak to the chief of police to see what they could do to help.

The police chief was grim, once he knew who Clay was. "We don't know how he got in. Maybe through an underground passage he knew about. He couldn't have gotten past the metal detectors with those weapons. We've got forty-two victims so far, and thirty-four critically injured at first count, and two dozen others who are injured but ambulatory," the police chief said unhappily. It was a massive tragedy, and most of them young people.

"One of my singers was shot," Clay said. He looked gray after what he'd just seen, and Iris had narrowly missed being shot. "What can we do to help?"

"Nothing," the chief of police said. "Change this crazy sick world where people do things like this." A reporter spotted Clay then, and interviewed him as the organizer of the event. "We're devastated," Clay said, visibly about to cry, and deeply moved by what he'd been seeing, so many young lives wasted, so many people dead.

None of the other members of the band had been hurt, and they left with Star to wait at the hospital where they'd been told the victims had been taken.

Clay and Iris left a short time later too, to wait with the others for news of Boy. They were told that he was in surgery when they got there, and two hours later, the surgeon came to see them all in the waiting room.

"Your friend is one lucky guy," the doctor told them. He looked like a butcher, smeared with blood. "He was grazed by a bullet, it did some minor damage. It entered and exited his chest without injuring any vital organs. We did some minor repair work and he lost a lot of blood, but he'll be okay." He was the person the gunman had been aiming at in the wings, because one of the boys said the gunman had spotted them and Boy shouted to try and stop him, and the shooter had gunned him down. Star sobbed in Iris's arms. Boy was in the recovery room, but they said he was stable and would be in a room in a few hours. The surgeon was right. He had been lucky. Others weren't. And Iris kept thinking of Pattie. What was Jimmy going to do? And how would they tell her mother what had happened? She was in no condition to take care of her grandson and step into her daughter's shoes. She couldn't even take care of herself. Iris called Pattie's home number, and spoke to the sitter, who was a neighbor, and told her what had happened. She sobbed when Iris told her the terrible news.

"What do we do about her mother?" Iris asked her.

"I'll tell her," the sitter said.

"I gave the police Pattie's home number," Iris told her. "What's going to happen to Jimmy?" She knew Pattie had no relatives, other than her mother.

"He'll have to go into foster care, and her mother will have to go into hospice. She's in the final stages. I'll do what I can from here, but I can't take Jimmy. I'm seventy years old, I work, and I can't take on a child his age. I'll take a week off from work. But after that, they'll have to take him. Do you know when they'll send the body home? Will they?"

"I don't know," Iris said, choking on tears. "I'll try to find out," she said, and went to tell Clay what the neighbor had told her.

"There will be other cases like that," he said sadly. They were both haunted by everything they'd seen that night.

They went to Clay's apartment then, and sat in the kitchen in their bloodstained clothes.

"I'll call the police about Pattie tomorrow," he promised. "I'll take care of it. It doesn't sound like they're in a position to pay for sending her home."

She nodded, and as she fell asleep next to him an hour later, huddled close, she looked at him with an idea.

"I want to do a memorial concert, to benefit all the people who were injured or killed, to start a fund for them." He nodded, and then they both drifted off, trying not to think of the nightmare. He kept dreaming of seeing Iris at the edge of the stage when he grabbed her. And then he woke up, and was up for the rest of the night.

By morning they knew that the shooter was an ex-marine who had a long history of psychiatric problems. There was no particular reason anyone knew of as to why he had done what he did, but he had a history of violence, and a collection of automatic rifles. He had worked at the Garden briefly as a janitor and knew the underground passages that had given him access into the auditorium. Two more people had died during the night, so he had taken forty-four lives, and lost his own. It was a major tragedy, and photographs of the victims were being shown on TV.

Clay called the number he had for the police and they told him Pattie was at the morgue, waiting for family arrangements. He promised to call back, and called a reputable funeral home to have her body sent to Biloxi for burial. And then Iris called Pattie's neighbor again. She said that she had told Jimmy and Pattie's mother about the shooting. Jimmy was devastated, and her mother was despondent. They were waiting for the hospice people to come for her that afternoon, and Jimmy was going to stay at the neighbor's for a week. She said she'd call the local funeral home to arrange the funeral when they knew when the body would arrive. Clay called to inform the New York mortuary about where to deliver the body. It was gruesome, and Iris couldn't believe they were talking about Pattie, who hadn't been able to arrange for a weekend away since she'd been home and got killed the first time she did. And she knew how much Pattie loved her son. She would have died to think of him in foster care with families who might not care about him or treat him well. She thought of all of Boy's stories about how badly he'd been treated in foster homes until he was sixteen. Jimmy was eleven, nearly twelve, and still a child, who had been lovingly cared for all his life, and now his grandmother was dying and his mother was gone.

It was overwhelming, and she was shocked to see footage of herself and Clay in film clips from the night before on the news, helping people out of the building. They were referred to as heroes, which didn't seem like the case to her. They hadn't saved a single person, only assisted the injured, and consoled them.

They went to see Boy that morning, and he

looked much better than they had feared. He'd had two transfusions, and the wound wasn't too deep. He looked at Iris and shook his head.

"I am one lucky guy," he said. Star sat by his bed, looking worse than he did. "He could have killed me." Clay was equally unnerved by Iris almost getting shot.

"I want to do a memorial concert," Iris said somberly, "in the same place, to raise money for the victims and their families and honor the dead."

"I'll organize that," Clay volunteered. "Or my office will. Let's get a star-studded lineup, more than just you two." They liked that idea, and Clay could already think of at least twenty major performers who would sign on to do it, who were generous with their time for good causes. It was one thing he could do. And he decided to pay for the venue as his contribution if they wouldn't donate it. He thought of that, as they talked about it. Iris had told Boy about her friend Pattie. She was still in shock over it, and could just imagine how her mother and Jimmy felt.

It was a terrible end to their successful, joyful concert tour.

Why the gunman had gone berserk at the concert remained a mystery. He had no close friends, no family, no one to shed light on the reasons. It was senseless and heartbreaking. Boy was released from the hospital on Sunday, and by then they had been told that Pattie's body would be in

Biloxi on Tuesday night. Mrs. Maybeck, Pattie's neighbor whom Iris had spoken to, had made arrangements for the funeral on Friday, and had put a notice in the paper.

"I want to be there," Iris told Clay. He helped her move her things from the Plaza to his apartment. He was surprised by how little she had. She had none of the trappings and accumulations that most people had when they moved. She was grateful that she had left Rosie at the hotel the night of the shooting.

Clay volunteered his plane to take Iris to Biloxi. He had important meetings on Friday, and couldn't go himself.

He was continuing to see her album and Boy's singles climb the charts, but the tragedy at Madison Square Garden overshadowed the news for them all. Iris didn't want to think about it. She called Harry and Pearl to tell them she was all right. They had seen it on the news and were grateful she hadn't been shot. She didn't tell them how close she had come.

She stayed home and was quiet and subdued until she left for Biloxi. She went down on Thursday night so she could visit Pattie's mother and Jimmy. Pattie's mother was already in the hospice facility, and Mrs. Maybeck said that Pattie's mother wasn't up to attending the funeral. It was just as well. Jimmy was staying at Mrs. Maybeck's. It was too depressing to be in the empty house now without his mother, and there was no one to care for him there.

"A social worker came yesterday," she told Iris. "They'll let him stay with me till Sunday. And they'll take him on Monday. One of their regular foster homes has agreed to take him. They have another boy his age." Iris felt sick when she heard it, but there was nothing she could do or say. He was starting a hard journey, and already had. Pattie had enough money saved to pay for the funeral, but there wasn't enough to provide for Jimmy and a caretaker, and she rented her small house, she didn't own it. They needed to empty it as soon as possible.

Iris checked in to a hotel not far from Pattie's home when she got to Biloxi, and then she went to see Jimmy at Mrs. Maybeck's. He came downstairs, looking very small and pale. He was blond with big blue eyes, and Iris told him that she and his mom had been best friends.

"I know, she talked about you a lot," he said, looking at her with serious eyes. Mrs. Maybeck had told him that he was going to live with a new family on Monday. Neither of them knew if he understood all the changes he was about to go through. His life would be altered forever. She said she heard him crying every night, and he'd had nightmares since his mother's death.

After she saw him, Iris went to the funeral home where Pattie was, in a coffin Mrs. Maybeck had picked out. It was a simple pine casket, and it was closed. She was too damaged for a viewing, and there was a guest book several people had signed, and a few arrangements of flowers people had sent. She led a small life in Biloxi and had few friends. She spent all her time with her mother and Jimmy when she wasn't working.

Iris sat quietly in a pew and thought about her and the years they'd been friends while they toured. She would have been lost without Pattie. Everything she did or thought about or earned was always for Jimmy, and now he had no mother or father and no one to look after him. Pattie didn't even know how to contact Jimmy's father, he had given up his parental rights years before and had no interest in him. He'd never even seen the boy, and wanted no contact.

Iris lay awake all that night in her hotel room, thinking about Pattie, and Jimmy.

Clay called her, and she barely had the energy to talk to him. He said they were making progress on the memorial concert, and Boy was helping too. Half of Nashville wanted to come. Clay already had seven major stars lined up. He told Iris the names, and she was impressed. They were huge names, and had said yes immediately. Clay had set up an entire staff and dedicated an office to the memorial concert, and the finest gospel choir in New York had signed up.

"If I hadn't begged her to come, she'd be alive

today," Iris said to Clay, "and now her son has no mother. I wanted her to hear me in a real concert." She felt acutely guilty and had agonized about it ever since the concert. A week after Pattie had come to New York, Iris was going to her funeral. Everything about it was so wrong.

On the morning of the funeral, Iris got up early and dressed in the simple black dress she'd brought, and black stockings to go with it. She went to the Maybeck house to help Jimmy get ready. She made breakfast while Mrs. Maybeck dressed.

The funeral was being held at the church Pattie attended irregularly. All of her coworkers came from the restaurant where she worked as a waitress, and several neighbors. There had been a photograph of Pattie on the front page of the paper, so word had traveled quickly within her small circle.

It was a somber, respectful service, with a soloist from the church choir singing "Amazing Grace," and an elderly man playing the organ. Iris had wanted to sing for her, but didn't think she could get through it. So she stayed with Jimmy and held his hand through the service. He sat bravely the whole time, with a devastated look. Mrs. Maybeck sat on his other side. Iris was flying out that night on Clay's plane. She spoke to a number of people after the service, and everyone looked shocked.

And then Iris went to the hospice facility to pay a respectful visit to Pattie's mother, and was told that she was sleeping, and that she was awake only for short times now, and didn't recognize most visitors. They said it would only be a matter of a few days now, so Jimmy would lose his grandmother too. A clean slate for him, of everyone he had ever known and loved, and who loved him.

Iris had an idea as she was driving back to see him again, and pulled over in the car she had rented to call Mrs. Maybeck.

"Could you give me the social worker's number?"

"Of course." Pattie's neighbor was impressed by what a dedicated friend Iris was. She was back on the line in a minute with the number. Iris called her and asked if she could come in immediately, she was leaving for New York in a few hours. She had no idea what she would say, but it was worth a try. The social worker, Jennifer Paley, said she could see her in half an hour.

Iris arrived ten minutes early, and Ms. Paley was free to see her. She was in her early forties, and saw a lot of sad cases, some like Jimmy's, of children with no relatives who had been orphaned, and foster care was the only option, others who had been mistreated or abandoned by their parents.

Iris explained that she was a longtime friend of Jimmy's mother, and started to explain that they had toured together, and the social worker smiled and said, "I know who you are, Ms. Cooper. So does the whole country by now. I downloaded your album, it's great."

"Pattie Dixon and I toured together for four years, and we stayed close. She was visiting me in New York last weekend."

"I know. Mrs. Maybeck told me. It's a very unfortunate situation."

"That's why I'm here. What are my chances of taking Jimmy to New York with me, to foster him there?"

"It would be very unusual to let him leave the state, but there are no relatives to object," she admitted. "My supervisor would have to approve it. We would have to say it's a visit. If you would want to prolong it, we would have to have a judge sign a court order, if we had no objections. And we would have to refer it to the appropriate office in New York, for them to do a home study, if you would like to keep him with you there. It sounds more complicated than it is. You're not married?"

"No, I'm not."

"We'd need proof of employment, with personal references. In your case, employment wouldn't be an issue."

"Clay Maddox is my manager. He could vouch for me."

"I'm sure that wouldn't be a problem. Would

this just be foster care, or are you thinking of adopting him?"

"I don't know," she said. "I guess we'd have to see how it works out, for him too."

"When were you thinking of taking him? We've made arrangements for him on Monday. He'll be at the neighbor's until then."

"I could take him with me tonight, if you let me."

The social worker asked Iris to wait in her office, and she went to speak to her supervisor. It was an unusual request, but it was an unusual situation. She was back fifteen minutes later, while Iris thought about what she was doing. She'd never even thought of having a child before, and she and Clay were brand new. But she couldn't let Pattie down, or Jimmy. She knew what the life of an unwanted child was like, with no roots, and no real parents. And he had no parents, the mother who loved him was gone, his grandmother would be soon, in a matter of days. He was virtually alone in the world.

Ms. Paley came back, and she was smiling.

"We're going to call it a visit to a close family friend, and give you six weeks. We'll get a home study done out of the New York Department of Social Services, while you send me your references and paperwork. If it's working out and you want to pursue it, we'll set up a hearing, and you'll have to come back for that, or you can set one up in

New York, if we contact them for you. After you foster him, with no living relatives, adoption is fairly simple, if everything else checks out. If you can't manage it, then you can send him back to us to have him fostered here. And you'll have to enroll him in school in September if he stays with you," she reminded her. It all sounded sensible and reasonable, and Iris thanked her. She was shocked at what she'd just done, but it was the right thing to do, she knew it. She had no idea what Clay would say. But even if he wanted no part of it, she owed this to Pattie, and she could afford to now, even if she had to get her own apartment for her and Jimmy.

She called Clay on her way back to the Maybeck home.

"I have something to tell you," she said in a strangled voice.

"It's too soon for you to know you're pregnant," he said, trying to lighten the moment.

"Well, not exactly too soon," she said, and there was no way around the truth. "I'm going to foster Pattie's son for six weeks and see how it works out." Clay was shocked into silence, and she didn't think it was a good sign, or boded well for the future. He wanted an adult relationship, not an almost twelve-year-old as part of the deal.

"And then you're going to keep him and adopt him after you foster him?" Clay asked her.

"I don't know yet."

"That's a big responsibility. Are you ready for that?" She was young to take it on, but Pattie had been four years younger than she was when Jimmy was born. Others did it. And she could afford to take care of him.

"I don't know that either. But Pattie loved that boy more than anything in life. He has no one, just like Boy didn't. I don't want him to have a childhood like ours. It would have killed her. His father vanished years ago, and has never even seen him. He was no good. His mother's dead and his grandmother's dying. So that leaves me. I'll get an apartment," she said quietly. "I'm not asking you to do this. But I had to tell you what I'm doing. Is it okay if we stay with you till I get organized?"

"When is he arriving?" Clay's tone was even. He didn't sound angry or upset. He was just asking questions and he sounded serious. He knew more about children than she did, and what it took.

He laughed then, which she didn't expect. "You're not moving out and leaving me so soon. You just got here. Three weeks ago, I was a lonely bachelor. Now I've met the love of my life, and I have a dog and an eleven-year-old son. Instant family. Come on home, Iris Cooper. I'm ready for you. You don't mess around, do you? I have a guest room I use as a storeroom. I'll get it ready for him." He was still laughing when he hung up. Iris was smiling. She was as shocked as he was at what she'd done. He had taken the news better than she'd expected. Not many men would have.

When she got to the house, she told Mrs. Maybeck. She looked stunned too, and then Iris sat down and explained it to Jimmy. He was coming to New York for a visit, and if everything went okay, he could stay. And he was going to meet her friend called Clay, and they would stay at his apartment.

Jimmy sat silent, and nodded, thinking about what she'd said. "Can we go to the top of the Empire State Building?" he asked her quietly. "A boy in my class went to visit his grandma in New York, and that's what he did." He was still in shock over losing his mother, but going to New York was a good distraction. He was a sweet boy, and reminded her so much of Pattie.

"Definitely."

"Can I bring some of my videogames?" he asked. They went to Pattie's house a little while later to get them. She could see tears in his eyes when they walked into his house. He had a carrying case for his games and PlayStation, and put a battered teddy bear on top. Iris took some photographs of Pattie to take with her. And they packed a suitcase of his favorite things, and Iris packed his clothes in another suitcase. They could take everything he needed on Clay's plane. They were ready by six, and she had to be at the airport at seven. They said goodbye to Mrs. Maybeck. She hugged Iris and thanked her for what she was doing. They had discussed the house quietly. Pattie hadn't left a will. Iris told Mrs. Maybeck to sell the contents of the house, to keep some token for herself, and sell the rest, and put it in an account for Jimmy and then relinquish the rental. And to save all the sentimental items for Jimmy. He had been very somber and serious since it happened. And he and Iris had a long talk about what it would be like for him in New York. She didn't want to push him, but he was relieved to leave with her. Foster care had been a daunting prospect, although he was trying to be brave, but he was only eleven. They didn't go to see his grandmother, it would have been too upsetting to see her as she was, and not recognize him.

Clay's flight attendants helped her with Jimmy's belongings, and she returned the rented car at the airport. Jimmy was stunned when he saw the plane and boarded. They took off on time for New York, with Jimmy's eyes wide. He'd never been on a plane before. They had a car and driver waiting for her at Teterboro. When she got home, Clay had spaghetti and meatballs prepared for them, and he had set up the room as promised, and had bought some magazines, and more videogames for Jimmy. Rosebud was intrigued by him and she followed him around. Jimmy liked her and she made him smile.

It was late when Iris put him to bed in his new

room. She left the light on and he called her Aunt
Iris when he said good night. Clay put his arms
around her when she came out of Jimmy's room.

"Welcome home," he said to her and kissed her.

"Are you sure you don't want me to get my own
place?" she asked him, as she helped him clean up
the kitchen.

"Not a chance. I had no idea how dull my life
was before you got here. This is going to be fun."
They both knew it might be hard too, but they also
knew what it was like to be robbed of your childhood, and they didn't want it to happen to Jimmy.
Clay felt the same way about it that she did, as he
kissed her, pulled her into his arms, and held her
tight.

Fate had dealt them a very full hand, and they
were going to play it as best they could.

Chapter 15

Plans for the memorial concert were going ahead full steam. Iris was in rehearsal for her next album, and Boy was working on another single.

Iris had hired a full-time babysitter to take care of Jimmy, but she spent as much time with him as she could. His grandmother had passed away two days after they left Biloxi, and Iris told him as gently as she could. He cried, but Pattie had prepared him for it. It wasn't the shock that losing his mother had been. That still didn't seem real.

Iris took him to the top of the Empire State Building, as promised, and he had loved flying on Clay's plane and thought it was cool. Clay was still startled to come home to a child, when he returned from work, but he was a sweet boy and good company, and Iris discovered that Pattie had taught him to play the piano and he liked to sing. She was teaching him to play the guitar.

Iris arranged for a home visit by the social work office, in case he stayed. She hadn't explored schools for him since she didn't know if he would stay, and the social work office told her that any of the public schools in the district would be acceptable until she could make other arrangements if she wished.

The memorial concert was set for one month after the tragic concert at Madison Square Garden. The management offered half the fee as a donation, and Clay paid the rest. The death toll was forty-eight by then, and Boy recovered very quickly. He took Jimmy to the studio with him and Jimmy loved it. He liked all of his new friends. He thought Boy's name was funny. And he called Clay "Uncle," which touched him.

Clay invited his daughters to the event. They had nineteen major stars signed up, and both Iris and Boy would be featured. She would perform a full concert, and the others would each do one song. The choir that had volunteered would close the show, with the last song being sung by everyone who had performed, plus the choir. Victims of the event, their families, and everyone who had been there that needed them got free tickets.

Clay described it to both his daughters on a

conference call and said he hoped they would come, and he'd send the plane for them. And then he added the rest.

"I want you both to know before you come that Iris is living with me. Things have changed since you met her in L.A."

"I knew she was your girlfriend," Margie said. "You lied to us."

"No, I didn't. It started after that, in Houston. Neither of us realized before that, that it was what we wanted. It just kind of landed on us, along with some other things."

"Like what?" Margie asked suspiciously, and Ellen groaned.

"Lighten up, Margie. What's up, Dad?" Ellen asked more pleasantly.

"Is she pregnant?" Margie wanted to know.

"No, she's not. She's living with me, and we have an eleven-year-old boy living with us."

"She has an eleven-year-old?" Margie nearly shrieked. "She had him at seventeen?"

"No. Her best friend was one of the victims at the Garden. It's her son. And for now, we both have him. Her friend was at the concert that night, and was killed by the shooter. Her son now has no living relatives, so he's staying with us. We'll see what happens. Iris is fostering him."

"You don't need to put up with that, Dad," Margie said cynically.

"No, but I want to. I didn't have such a great

childhood myself. Neither did Iris. It's our way of giving someone else a better childhood than we had."

"That's beautiful, Dad," Ellen said kindly, moved by what he'd said to them and what he was doing.

"He's a sweet kid, and he'll have a rough ride if he winds up in foster care in Mississippi, or anywhere. We'd like to make things better for him than that."

"So now you have a girlfriend and an eleven-year-old," Margie summed up and sounded disgusted. "Thanks for warning us. I can't come to the concert anyway. Mom and I are doing a wedding that weekend, and she needs me. We've had it on the books for a year, and I can't let her down." She sounded happy to refuse.

"That's fine," he said evenly. "I just wanted you both to know that you're invited, and I'd love for you to be there."

"It sounds like a glittering cast, Dad. For a good cause. I'll be there," Ellen said, happy to be invited, and wanting to support him for what he was doing after a tragic event. And it sounded like an incredible evening. Some of his biggest artists were going to be performing. "And you don't have to send the plane for me," she added, "I'll fly commercial." Ellen was much more modest than her sister, and rarely asked for anything.

"I'll have Joanne get your ticket," he said to

Ellen. "And, Margie, if you change your mind, you're welcome."

"It sounds like you have a full house," she said, miffed.

"There's always room for you." He didn't make an issue of her not coming, thanked Ellen again, and they hung up. Margie was so shocked about Jimmy that she didn't object to Iris as much as he expected. It was actually working out surprisingly well. Jimmy had been there for three weeks, and was happy and liked Zoe, the sitter, who was a sweet graduate student, going to law school at NYU at night. She kept Jimmy entertained by day and she babysat on some nights too. And Iris tried to be home for him as much as she could. He seemed to be thriving. They were still waiting for the home visit, which hadn't happened yet, but was due any day.

The day of the memorial concert, Clay and Iris had a thousand things to think of. Boy had volunteered to keep the players straight when he wasn't singing, and he and Iris were doing three duets, and he was singing four more songs on his own. Clay helped them with the order of appearances, determined by who the biggest stars were. Some were more easygoing than others. Even for charity events, there were rivalries. The press had been notified and were being given access for free.

They were making it casual, and Iris was planning to wear a denim miniskirt, within reason, red cowboy boots, and a rhinestone Levi's jacket that was fabulous. She wanted the evening to be upbeat and made a point of not wearing black, as she usually did onstage.

Ellen arrived the night before, and stayed in the room she always did. She and Margie both had their own bedrooms at their father's. The room Jimmy was sleeping in was a fourth bedroom Clay never used. Jimmy was right at home there. And Iris had put a framed photo of Pattie in his room. Ellen was very friendly with Jimmy, and played card games with him she had loved as a kid. She was respectful and kind with Iris, and Iris liked her. She was a straight-shooting, warm, open, nice young woman, with a passion for animals. Rosie loved her, and Jimmy too. He loved having a dog now. His mom had never let him.

Most of the stars who were signed up were too busy for rehearsals, so they were going to wing it. Boy tried to get them to say what they were going to perform, but many of them still didn't know even the day before. He was resigned to the fact that with that many stars lined up, there was going to be a certain amount of chaos, but it was all for a good cause.

There had been a lot of press about the event, and Clay was having it filmed. It was going to be unforgettable. They were all proud of what they were doing, and everyone had pitched in. But Boy and Iris had worked the hardest on it, and they made a point of having rehearsals. They didn't want their performance to be less professional than those by the more established stars.

T-shirts had been donated to be given away free, with the slogan "Never Forget Madison Square" and the date.

Boy and Iris got there three hours before the event to check everything. Clay would come a little later with Ellen, and Jimmy was coming with Zoe, his sitter, in case he got restless if it went on for too long. Clay's group had front row seats. They all knew it was going to be very emotional, especially for the families of the victims.

Iris was looking frazzled when Clay arrived with Ellen, Jimmy, and Zoe. They had set up trailers outside Madison Square Garden to provide enough dressing rooms for all their stars, and there were a million assistants and technicians everywhere. They had a commissary truck for them if they got hungry. Clay was used to catering to them, and knew how to keep them happy, and make each of them feel important and special, whatever it took.

The final countdown had started an hour before the event, when Margie walked in, and Clay was stunned.

"What are you doing here? I thought you were

doing a wedding." He was truly shocked and didn't expect her, but he was very touched.

"Mom said she could manage without me." She tried to sound casual and disengaged. "And I figured I would never hear the end of it if I didn't come."

"What she's trying to say"—Ellen rolled her eyes at her sister—"is that she wanted to come, but doesn't want to give you the satisfaction of saying so. Why don't you just admit it?" Ellen goaded her. She hated the way Margie treated their father, as though he was always at fault and guilty of something.

"I'm glad you came," Clay said warmly, and hugged her, and then introduced her to Jimmy.

"Hi," she said coolly.

"I'm happy to meet you," he said politely, and shook her hand the way Pattie had taught him. He was a very well-mannered child, and so far no trouble at all. He was sweet and sometimes very funny, without meaning to be, with his thick Mississippi drawl, which brought out the Texas in Iris. Iris was getting a crash course in parenting, and was surprised that she liked it.

The show started half an hour late, but no one seemed to mind. There were two people assigned to get the stars out of their trailers in time to go on. The police had cordoned off two blocks of the street to make room for their trailers. They were doing all they could to make the event go smoothly.

Iris and Boy looked at each other right before he went on as the opening act, and gave each other a hug for good luck.

He walked out on the stage with a list in his hands, so he wouldn't forget anyone.

He stood very quiet for a moment, and smiled at the audience. And then he spoke in his Tennessee drawl, which made him even more appealing.

"We're here to honor the people we love tonight, the people we lost, the people who got hurt, the people who matter to us because we're grateful they're alive." He glanced at Star in the backup band and she smiled at him. "We're here so we never forget how much we loved those people, and love each other. And we're here to have *fun* tonight too, and celebrate! I can't believe the stars who are here tonight. And you are *never* going to forget this concert. I'm going to read off a list. You know who they are and what happened to them." And then he began reading the names of the forty-eight people who died and the thirty-eight who had been injured, and when he got to his own name on the second list, he said "that's me!" And as soon as he finished the list, he opened with his first song, which was mind blowing. His biggest and best and loudest. His own Nashville band was there too, to pay tribute to him, and they joined in. The sound was amazing, and rocked Madison Square Garden. It was a great beginning. He ran through his entire repertoire and ended with a

duet with Iris, and he was followed almost immediately by one of their biggest stars, who gave a
dazzling performance. The audience was going
crazy. Another big name followed. And then Iris,
who ripped everyone's heart out, and brought Boy
back for two duets. Her final song was about the
people they had loved and lost, and was dedicated
to Pattie. And before anyone could sink into too
much sorrow, a huge headliner from Vegas took
over and rocked them to their core.

There were rhinestones and sequins and every
kind of bling and glitz onstage. Some of the sexiest
stars in the business performed that night. The entire concert was three hours long without an inter-
mission, and no one was bored for a minute. There
were screams of ecstasy from the crowd every
time a bigger star than the last one came onstage.
Then the choir performed the best gospel they'd
ever heard, and Iris sang with them, and hit all the
high notes. The crowd yelled and cheered her and
shouted Iris's name, and then the entire cast came
out to sing the finale of "Amazing Grace," and invited the audience to sing with them. There was
hardly enough room for all of them, and they were
waving to the audience and dancing onstage. They
played five encores, and by the time it was over,
the entire audience had had an experience never to
be matched and that they would never forget. Clay
had brought Jimmy onto the stage at the very end
and he was singing his heart out too, holding

Clay's and Iris's hands, and she beckoned Ellen and Margie to come up too, and much to Clay's amazement, they came up and joined them. Even Margie was singing, and had tears in her eyes as she held her father's hand.

No one wanted to leave the theater when it was over. People were hugging and dancing and laughing and some were crying, but they were tears of release and joyful remembrance. Boy could hardly get the big stars off the stage, they were having so much fun with one another, and they jumped down and mingled with the audience and posed for pictures. It was a very different scene from the night a month before. Clay, Iris, and Boy had pulled off a historic event. It took two hours to get everyone off the stage and out of the auditorium. And when the last limo had finally pulled away, and the trailers were being towed away, Clay looked at Iris and Boy and his daughters, and smiled from ear to ear.

"You guys pulled off a miracle tonight. I've never seen anything like it, and I doubt we will again."

"They did it for you, Clay," Iris said gently. His name worked magic, and who he was, and she was glad his daughters had seen it. She thought he was too modest with them, and they needed to see what a great man he was, and how greatly loved and respected.

"It was fantastic," Ellen said to all three of

them, and Margie was glowing. She had had a ball. They all had. Iris had sent Jimmy home with the sitter an hour before, he was falling asleep on his feet. He didn't want to leave, but Iris convinced him that he needed to go home and check on Rosie because she'd be so lonely, so he went.

Clay, Iris, Boy, Star, Ellen, and Margie all went to Clay's favorite diner afterward, and they were ravenously hungry. They'd all been so nervous and worked so hard that they'd hardly eaten all day, except for Margie and Ellen. It was a relief to have the event behind them, and a night filled with love and caring for others.

"What are you going to do about Jimmy?" Boy asked her quietly at the end of dinner. Clay was talking to his daughters, and Star and Ellen hit it off. They were almost the same age. Iris seemed considerably older than all three younger women. She looked younger than they did, but there was something more mature about her, particularly lately with an almost twelve-year-old child to take care of.

"I don't know," she said to Boy. "We have to have a hearing in two weeks, if we want to foster him officially. He's an easy kid, and we love him. If he stays, I've got to get him signed up for school." One of the best schools in New York was a few blocks from Clay's apartment and they'd discussed it. She was going to put him in public school until she could get him a place in a private school. They were living the experience day to day, not trying to force a decision, and letting it come naturally.

"I admire what you're doing. I've thought about doing that one day. Adopt a kid, to spare him a life like the one I grew up with," Boy said.

"There's a little bit of that for us too. Neither of us had even halfway decent childhoods," Iris said. She hadn't heard from her father and didn't want to, and she had made her peace with it. Jimmy had put balm on that wound too. She no longer had a father, but now she had a child. Pattie had left her an incredible gift.

"Do you think you'll adopt him?" Boy asked her.

"Maybe. We're figuring it out."

"How are you and Clay doing?" He didn't need to ask. He could see it. She was glowing.

"He's an amazing human being. I don't know how I got so lucky."

"Are you kidding? I meant it when I told you that you paid your dues. We all did."

"Maybe so, but I'm grateful every day. And he's been great about Jimmy. I think he enjoys it. He didn't get a lot of time with Margie and Ellen when they were kids."

"Maybe you two will have more kids," he said, and she laughed and shrugged.

"I've got songs to do, and albums to make, and tours to do."

"You can do both. We all know people who do."

"I don't know how they do it. I've got one kid with a full-time babysitter, and I haven't had time for a manicure in a month. Being a mom is a lot of work. And I've got music, I'm not sure I need kids, other than Jimmy."

"What are you two talking about?" Clay asked, as he horned in, and let the three girls talk amongst themselves.

"We were talking about careers versus kids," she said blithely.

"I vote for kids," Clay said without hesitating. "The careers take care of themselves. More or less. Kids are forever, like nothing else in life. Look at Jimmy, what a great kid he is." As he said it, Boy looked at Iris and raised an eyebrow.

"There's your answer," Boy said to Iris, and she smiled.

Two weeks later, Clay flew to Biloxi with Iris for a hearing in front of a judge. Jimmy went with them, and Ms. Paley, the social worker, spoke to him in private. He told her he loved New York and they had a dog named Rosie, and Clay was the best dad in the world, even though he called him "Uncle," and Iris was a terrific aunt. He hadn't let go of his mom, and Iris didn't want him to. She wanted Jimmy to remember her, and intended to keep her memory alive.

They had had their home study by then, and passed with flying colors.

The judge asked them if they intended to get married, and Clay said they had no firm plans at the moment, but it was an option. The home study had reported that they had a warm, loving, stable relationship, and they had a beautiful home which was an excellent environment for a child.

The judge set his stamp on their papers, which gave them permission to officially be Jimmy's foster parents, unless anything changed in the future, which no one could predict.

Jimmy wanted to see his old house. It was empty now, and there was a FOR RENT sign out front. Jimmy looked sad when he saw it. They visited Mrs. Maybeck for a few minutes, and he told her about his new home in New York. And then they went back to the airport, and flew back to New York. The pilot let Jimmy sit in the cockpit, with his seatbelt on so he couldn't wander around, and he showed him how he flew the plane. Jimmy thought just about everything about his life with Iris and Clay was cool. He said his mom would have loved it too.

With the memorial concert behind them, and the decision to foster Jimmy, Iris got to work in earnest rehearsing and writing for a new album. Boy was working on one too.

It was released after Jimmy was settled in his

new school. They had gotten him a place in the private school near them. Clay was working on a new tour he was thinking of organizing to Boston, Chicago, Denver, San Francisco, Dallas, and Atlanta this time, all the cities they hadn't done last time, and maybe the U.K. and Japan and Hong Kong in the next year or two. It was an ongoing rotation. He was always thinking about what would be good for her career, and that of his other major clients. He had just finished organizing tours for two of his other big stars. He was sure Iris was going to be nominated for a Grammy, and thought Boy might be too. She thought Clay was crazy when he said it. She was hitting the high notes better than ever. But she didn't expect to win any awards. She was just grateful for everything that had happened, and all that Clay had done for her. And Jimmy was an unexpected blessing.

He got to work on her tour a few weeks later, and was scheduling it to start just after the release of her next album. He needed to find her a new opening act. Boy was too big for that now, as Clay knew he would be. It was their last chance for that on the previous tour.

He wanted to start the tour in December and be home for Christmas. The timing was perfect. They would start right after Thanksgiving and be home before Christmas, to spend it with Jimmy. He was part of their life now. Once he'd been with them for six months, they could adopt him whenever they wanted. Ms. Paley had told them that, but Iris said they weren't ready to make that decision and there was no rush. She was twenty-eight years old, and she had time to do lots of things. None of it was pressing, except her next album.

Jimmy loved visiting her at the sound studio when she was working. He'd listen to her quietly for a while, visit Boy, and then he'd help Joanne in Clay's office. He called him Dad now, which Clay liked. He still called her Aunt Iris, which she preferred out of respect for Pattie, who would always be his mother. Iris had explained to him that she and Clay weren't married, even though they felt like they were.

"Why do some people get married and some don't?" he asked her.

"That's a good question, I don't know. Maybe they haven't met the right person."

"Isn't Clay the right person for you?" He looked puzzled. "My mom said she never met the right person either, so we didn't have a dad. Clay is a good dad."

"He sure is the right person," she corrected him. "He's the only man I've ever loved."

"So why don't you get married?" he asked, with the logic of children, and she was stumped. Clay walked into the room when he asked her, and stopped to hear what she said.

"He may have a point," Clay said, smiling at

her. "I've wondered about that myself," he said, and she smiled. She knew he was in no rush to get married. He'd had two disasters and didn't want another one, but Iris was the best thing that had ever happened to him.

Two weeks later, he came home with a mischievous look. He had a lump in his jacket pocket, which she didn't notice. She was writing lyrics on their bed. Rosie was asleep next to her, and Jimmy was out with Zoe. Clay got down on his knees next to her, and she ignored him while she was finishing the lyric, and when she looked at him, his face was next to hers.

"Iris Cooper, will you marry me?"

"What? Are you serious? Why now?" She was stunned.

"I think Jimmy has a point. If we're not getting married, we should at least get engaged, we have a twelve-year-old son after all. What do you think?"

"I think you're crazy and I love you," she said, and kissed him. He had done it so casually, she hadn't suspected what was coming.

"Is that a yes?" She nodded, feeling shy for a minute, and he took the box out of his pocket, opened it, and put a staggeringly beautiful diamond ring on her finger. She stared at it, awestruck. She forgot who he was sometimes, and what he was able to do.

"My God, that's gorgeous. Clay, it's huge." She smiled at him.

"You deserve it. You deserve even bigger." It was a fifteen-carat solitaire, which was more than big enough, but Clay never did things on a small scale.

Jimmy noticed it on her hand as soon as he came home from the park with Zoe. He stared at it for a minute and asked her what it was.

"It's a diamond. Clay and I just got engaged."

"Does that mean you're getting married?" He looked hopeful, and she wondered why it mattered to him so much.

"Not yet." She said something about it to Clay later.

"That's easy, he just wants to be sure we're staying together and he's safe."

"And he thinks that's a sure thing?"

"I guess so," Clay said quietly. "You know, if you ever do want to get married, I'd be willing. I'd like that very much. I just figured you weren't ready."

"I'm not. I feel too young to get married." He respected what she said and didn't press her.

"Then we'll just stay engaged for as long as you want. After our fourth or fifth child, we'll go down to city hall and get married," he teased her.

"I'm really not ready for kids," she said, but he knew that too.

"Even though you have a twelve-year-old kid?"

"He's not mine. That's different."

"I'm not sure it is," he said. "I love Jimmy almost as much as my daughters. In time, I'll bet it will be the same."

"Let's not test the theory for a while. Let's celebrate our engagement first," she said, and they locked the door to their bedroom and did.

Chapter 16

Iris's new album came out in November, and was a smash hit. They went on tour the day after Thanksgiving and she played her first concert of the tour on December 1 in Boston. Clay had gotten her a great opening band, which warmed the audiences perfectly. They were new talent he'd recently discovered.

They played Boston and Chicago, and then went to Denver. Her second tour was even more successful than the first one, and Clay stayed with her for the whole three weeks, making sure that everything went smoothly. The hard part this time was leaving Jimmy. She missed him, and they FaceTimed with him at breakfast and dinner.

She got food poisoning in San Francisco, but went on anyway, and in Dallas, it turned out to be the flu. She had no trouble singing and hitting the high notes. She just couldn't eat. Clay was worried about her. She'd been working too hard for months, and she was sick for the rest of the tour but performed anyway. She'd been well trained to do that on her earlier tours for Weston and Hendrix.

She fainted in Atlanta before she went on, and realized it was because she hadn't eaten, and when they got back to New York, he insisted she go to the doctor.

"I'm fine," she dismissed it, but he could see that she had lost weight. She was exhausted. She was busy getting ready for Christmas since they'd been away for three weeks, and she'd been too sick to go shopping for most of the trip.

He came home early from work one afternoon, and found her asleep on their bed. She hadn't been to the studio to rehearse in several days, he discovered when he checked, which was unlike her.

"What are you doing home so early?" she asked him sleepily, and he looked serious.

"We're going to the doctor."

"That's ridiculous, I'm not sick."

"I hope not. You felt lousy for most of the tour. You had food poisoning in San Francisco, the flu in Dallas, and you fainted in Atlanta. That doesn't sound good to me. You've been working too hard.

We have a four o'clock appointment with my internist. I can't have my biggest star out of commission."

"I have too much to do. I promised Jimmy I'd take him to get a new action figure that just came out, before it sells out."

"Nope." He sat down on the edge of the bed then. "Iris, I love you, you're scaring me. Let's find out what you've got and fix it. Please." There were tears in his eyes, and she nodded and got up. She felt silly being taken to the doctor by him, but she didn't like going to doctors, and he knew she wouldn't go on her own. Her father had never taken her when she was a kid. She just kept going till she got over it.

"I promise, I'm not sick. I'm just tired after the tour."

"You were tired before the tour," he reminded her.

"I was recording the album then. I worked late every night."

"Shut up and be good. Would you take Jimmy to the doctor?" She nodded and she could see that she wasn't going to talk him out of it. He had his car and driver downstairs, and twenty minutes later, they were at his doctor's Park Avenue address. She didn't have one of her own.

He walked into the waiting room with her, and sat down. "You can take it from here," he said. He wasn't going to go in with her. He just wanted to get her there. After that, it was up to her. She sat down next to him and read a magazine, and they called her name five minutes later and she disappeared. She was gone for half an hour, and came out looking dazed. Clay didn't like the way she looked, but didn't want to ask her with other people around.

"Are you okay?" he whispered to her when they left the office.

"I'm fine," she said. She looked shell-shocked.

"Did he run tests?"

"Yes."

"Is it serious?"

"Very." He looked panicked when she said it, and wanted to cry. He didn't want to lose her. He had waited for her all his life. He stopped walking before they got to the car, and he pulled her into his arms.

"Whatever it is, we can deal with it. I love you. What did he say?"

She clung to him and it started to snow. She felt as though the world was spinning around her, and she pulled away to look at him and burst into tears.

"I'm four months pregnant, and I didn't even know," she said, and he stared at her. It hadn't occurred to him either, since they were usually careful, but not always.

She was crying and it was snowing, and he started to laugh. "That's it? You're pregnant?" He hugged her tightly again. "I thought you were dying."

"I'm scared," she cried into his shoulder, as he held her. "I don't know how to be a mother. I never had one. I didn't want a baby, and it's already four months."

"You're a great mom to Jimmy. You don't have to have a mom to be one."

"Yes, you do. I don't know any of that stuff. I love you, but I'll be a terrible mother."

"No, you won't. You'll be a fantastic, loving, talented superstar mom."

"All I can do is sing. That's all I've ever known. How to hit the high notes."

"You'll be great. We'll do it together." He walked her to the car then, before she froze. She was shivering in the cold. They got into the car and she blew her nose. She couldn't stop crying and he was beaming and then he thought of something. "Do you think we should get married?" he whispered to her, and she looked surprised.

"Why?"

"Because that's what people do. Usually, at least."

"But you hated being married," she reminded him.

"To Frances. Not to you. I'd love being married to you. I feel like we already are."

"What if it spoils everything and you hate being married to me?"

"I won't," he promised her. "I just think it would be nice to be married if we have a baby," he whispered so his driver didn't hear him.

"I'll think about it."

"Do you want to be married?" he asked her.

"Not really, I'm happy the way we are."

"Then we won't," he said. She was too upset to make sense.

"Do you want to be married?" she asked him.

"To you, yes." She nodded, and continued crying until they got home. He was trying to remember what Frances was like when she was pregnant, but it was too long ago. All he could remember now was how mean she was during the divorce and ever since. He couldn't remember anything pleasant before.

Jimmy was upset when they got home.

"You said you'd take me to get the new action figure," he said to Iris.

"We'll go tomorrow. I promise," she said, and Jimmy slunk off to his room like any twelve-year-old.

The three of them had dinner together in the kitchen, and Iris went to bed right afterward. Clay came to find her a little while later and lay down next to her, and held her.

"I'm sorry you're upset," he whispered to her and stroked her silky blond hair. "I should have been more careful."

"Maybe I wanted it to happen," she said, and

turned to look at him. She had been thinking about that for the last hour. She kissed him then. "I think I want to get married," she said with a sigh. "I was just so shocked when the doctor told me. Maybe we should adopt Jimmy so he doesn't feel left out."

He was smiling at her. She made him so happy. "It sounds like a plan," he said and kissed her. She thought that maybe everything would be all right.

They got married between Christmas and New Year at a little church she'd seen before and liked in the East Seventies. Boy and Star were their witnesses, and Jimmy held their rings. He was beaming, and they had asked him if he'd like to be adopted and he said yes, right away. He didn't know about the baby yet. There was time. They wanted to adopt him first. He was their first child. The baby would be second. When they left the church there was snow on the ground. They had a snowball fight, and then the five of them went to lunch at a little Italian restaurant, and ate pasta. Boy was happy for them.

It wasn't the way Iris had imagined she would get married one day. It was better, because she married the right man.

Chapter 17

Clay was right. Both Iris and Boy were nominated for Grammys. She for her first album, and he for his most recent single. Iris had written the song for him and it was a huge success. Clay went to the Grammys every year. It was old hat to him, although it was always exciting when his artists were nominated. He represented two of the other artists who were nominated that night, but he wanted Boy and Iris to win.

Clay and Boy wore tuxedos, and Star was wearing a sexy black dress that clung to every inch of her and was very glamorous. Iris wore a deep blue dress the color of her eyes that floated around her. You could see that she was pregnant, but not as much as she was. She was six months pregnant. They had adopted Jimmy in January and had a party afterward to celebrate. He had taken Clay's name, but they kept his old last name as a middle name, to honor Pattie, since she had given him her last name and not his father's. He left the courtroom as James Dixon Maddox. It sounded very distinguished.

"He'll have to be an attorney one day with that name," Iris said.

"Or run my business," Clay said proudly. They didn't know what sex the baby was yet and wanted to be surprised. Iris felt better than she had in the beginning. The baby was due in May. She wasn't tired and didn't feel sick anymore. She was writing a lot these days. She couldn't believe it when she found out that she'd been nominated for a Grammy. She and Boy were both wildly excited, but he was sure he wouldn't win. Just being nominated seemed like enough. Iris was sure she wouldn't win either, and didn't bother to write an acceptance speech she'd never use.

There were half a dozen parties that week, in anticipation of the awards. And they'd been invited to several after-parties, which sounded more appealing. The tension at award ceremonies was always tremendous, in every category. Nominees sat at the edge of their seats looking intense and nervous as the evening droned on.

Clay was surprised that Iris looked as relaxed

as she did, when they left for the ceremony, and picked up Boy and Star on the way. Boy joked in the car, and they walked the red carpet as photographers snapped their pictures and had them pose looking very elegant. Every TV network had cameramen and reporters there, every newspaper from around the world.

Iris had been asked to perform one of her songs at the ceremony, which she didn't want to do six months pregnant, so she had declined.

Boy's category came first, and they had a film clip of each artist's performance, which they played one by one. Boy looked tense for a moment, and looked over at Iris, and thought of when they'd met in Jackson Hole, Wyoming, and sang at the Elk. It was a lifetime ago, and had changed both their lives. But they both remembered back to the beginning, when they were no one, and now, thanks to Clay, they were both stars. That alone seemed like enough to Boy. In everything that mattered, he had already won his prize.

Iris held her breath when they called out the names in Boy's category, and closed her eyes when they fumbled with the envelope. She was hoping that he'd win. It would be a big step up in his career, but Boy was already hurtling through the skies of fame at lightning speed, and had already come far since his first appearance on the scene in what seemed so long ago now, when Iris had taken him with her to meet Clay.

It had all begun then, thanks to Clay's incredible vision and foresight, and ability to discover talent that no one else had recognized before or in quite the same way.

The winner's name was finally announced, and Boy didn't win this time, but Iris was absolutely certain that next time or the time after, or in a not-too-distant future, he would be standing on the stage holding the trophy. She met his eyes and they both smiled. He felt like a winner no matter what name the envelope had held. He wasn't even disappointed, just grateful to have been nominated, and to have been there for the experience.

He leaned over and kissed Star's cheek, and she nestled closer to him. As she did, he remembered the bullet that had only grazed him at Madison Square Garden, and felt lucky all over again. He was well aware that with the encounters he'd had, and the opportunities, he led a charmed life. He would have felt greedy wishing for more.

Iris was talking to Clay, whispering intensely, when they read off the names in her category. Then they showed the film clips and heard each song. She was intensely relieved that she had declined to perform hers onstage that night. She would have felt like a large helium balloon drifting off the stage.

She glanced at her fellow nominees, so obviously desperate, while trying to look glamorous, and not to show how badly they wanted it. It was a game changer to walk away with a Grammy. Iris knew others who had done it, but could not imagine it happening to her. Her mind drifted as they called the names again, after the film clips, and cameras panned their faces, and showed hands clenched, teeth gritted. You could almost hear their hearts beating like metronomes. Her competitors looked like they would have killed someone to grab the little statuette and run. Like Boy, she thought back to the beginning, the beginning of her time with Clay and everything that had come before. It was all held together, one long chain from beginning to end, and the people who belonged to the chapters in her life. Her father, Harry, Sally, Pearl, Pattie, Boy, Billy Weston, and Glen Hendrix, and then finally Clay, who had been the guardian angel who had brought her to where she was now, sitting here next to him, waiting to hear if she would win the coveted award. Her mind was drifting and she paid no attention, as she held Clay's hand. Somewhere in the distance, she heard someone say her name.

She was still daydreaming, thinking about her husband, when he nudged her. She smiled at him and he whispered to her.

"Stand up, you won! Go up on the stage."

"What?" He'd broken into her reverie. For an instant she didn't remember where she was.

"Go up onstage," he whispered to her again,

and Boy was staring at her, and reached over Star to touch her hand. Sweet victory was hers. She fumbled with her dress and stood up, feeling disoriented, and then ran lightly down the aisle to the stage, as someone lent her a hand up the steps so she didn't trip on her dress or fall. Then suddenly she was standing on the stage, staring into the audience, as they all waited for a speech she hadn't prepared. All she could do was speak from her heart, just like her songs.

She walked slowly to the mike, trying to regain her composure. "I'd like to thank my wonderful husband, Clay, and my son, Jimmy, for giving me the amazing life I lead today. When I met Clay, I knew him only as the remarkable impresario who has given all or most of you work. To all of you in my life, I thank you, for the good times and hard times you gave me, for the lessons that I learned from you or because of you. For those of you who loved and respected me, I thank you. To those of you who hurt me and made the dark days longer, I forgive you. To my husband, Clay, I owe you my life, and this life," she said, lightly touching her belly, "thank you for my incredible career, and helping me hit the high notes. I will love and be grateful to you till the end of my days, and for my peers and colleagues"—she held the Grammy high—"thank you for this."

* * *

The after-parties were fun for a while, when she went with Clay and Boy and Star, looking awe-struck and clinging to Boy. But Iris knew the best of it, the long hard road she'd traveled to reach where she stood now, with the Grammy in her hand. The life she'd led had given her something to write and sing about. Everything she'd done and lived and suffered and hoped, and the love and joy she and Clay shared now, was in her songs.

About the Author

DANIELLE STEEL has been hailed as one of the world's bestselling authors, with a billion copies of her novels sold. Her many international bestsellers include *Palazzo, The Wedding Planner, Worthy Opponents, Without a Trace, The Whittiers, The High Notes, The Challenge, Suspects,* and other highly acclaimed novels. She is also the author of *His Bright Light,* the story of her son Nick Traina's life and death; *A Gift of Hope,* a memoir of her work with the homeless; *Expect a Miracle,* a book of her favorite quotations for inspiration and comfort; *Pure Joy,* about the dogs she and her family have loved; and the children's books *Pretty Minnie in Paris* and *Pretty Minnie in Hollywood.*

daniellesteel.com
Facebook.com/DanielleSteelOfficial
Twitter: @daniellesteel
Instagram: @officialdaniellesteel

Look for *Happiness,*
coming soon in hardcover

From #1 *New York Times* bestselling
author Danielle Steel comes an uplifting novel
about an author who—to her surprise—
inherits a grand estate near London.

Chapter 1

Sabrina Brooks lay in bed with her eyes closed for a few minutes after she woke up, savoring the delicious limbo of being half asleep. She always woke up before the alarm went off at seven, and reached a hand out of the covers to turn it off before it rang. She rolled back slightly before getting up and she could feel the heavy form behind her, and hear gentle snoring as she opened her eyes and saw the brilliantly sunny May morning. There was a mop of white hair in the bed next to her, and as she turned over fully, she could see the round black eyes open and look at her, and the wet black nose of her man-sized Old English Sheepdog, Winnie. It made her smile every morning when she saw him sleeping next to her, and tucked in beside her the tiny white, long-haired Chihuahua, Piglet, who opened her eyes, yawned and stretched. They were her constant companions in the converted barn in the Berkshire Mountains in Massachusetts where she had lived for nine years.

Buying the barn and transforming it into her home had been her greatest reward and satisfaction nine years earlier, at thirty-nine. It was the result of the astonishing success of her second book. She had written her first book at thirty-seven, after a nomadic life and checkered career. She had resisted writing before that, because it seemed so mundane to follow in her father's footsteps.

Her father, Alastair Brooks, was English, and had written serious, respected biographies of famous British and American writers. She thought they were incredibly tedious and dreary, although painstakingly accurate. Alastair Brooks had a master's in history and a doctorate in literature. He'd been educated at Oxford, the University of Edinburgh, and the Sorbonne, where he had taught for a few years before coming to the States to accept a position as an English literature professor at Boston University. He had taught there for eighteen years, and died young, at fifty-one. Alastair had spent the last three years of his life in seclusion in a cabin in Vermont, where he moved after Sabrina had left for college at UCLA. He had dedicated himself entirely to his biographies then, with nothing else to distract him.

At her father's suggestion, Sabrina only visited him once a year at Christmas, which he seemed to experience as more of an intrusion than a pleasure, but tolerated for the two weeks she stayed. Once she left for college, her father informed her that she was an adult and shouldn't need much parental contact. She spent school vacations in L.A., and took a job in the summer for extra money. And as lonely as she was at times at school, she was never as lonely as she was at home with her father. She always suspected that he had contact with no other humans between her visits, except for bare necessities like the grocery store or the bookstore. He had no need for companionship and avoided it assiduously. Human contact always seemed painful for him, even with his daughter. She had never been able to bridge the gap between them, except when they spoke about one of his books, when he came alive momentarily, and then shut down again when the conversation ended. He seemed to exist only in relation to the historical literary figures he wrote about. The real people in his life were agony for him. He had been sent away to boarding school at Eton as early as they were willing to take him, as his older brother Rupert had been as well. Alastair had grown up without affection, and seldom saw his parents. Shortly after he'd arrived at Eton, when he was twelve, he had been brought home briefly for his mother's funeral and sent back to school immediately. His brother, five years older, graduated shortly after their mother's death and Alastair was alone at Eton after that. Having grown up without affection, he had no ability to receive it or express it later on in his life.

His childhood, his family, and his reason for leaving England were taboo subjects. Sabrina knew nothing about his family or early life, and he refused to discuss it with her. All she knew was that he had left England at twenty-six and completed his doctorate in Edinburgh, before moving to France and the Sorbonne. He had lived in Paris for three years, and met her mother there. She could only guess that his reason for leaving England was due to some sort of disagreement over his inheritance as a second son. His older brother had inherited everything, and Sabrina knew that once Alistair left England, he never returned, and had never seen or spoken to his brother again. She knew only that her father's brother was named Rupert, and that he had inherited whatever money and property there was. Her father never went into detail about it, and never spoke of his own childhood.

She knew only a little more about his marriage to her mother, although that was a taboo subject too. He had met Simone Vernier in Paris when he was twenty-nine and she was twenty-one. She had been a model, and Sabrina remembered vaguely that she had been beautiful. They married a few months after they met, around the time he was offered the teaching position at Boston University. After they married, they left for the States. Sabrina had been born in Boston a year later when Alastair was thirty, and Simone was twenty-two.

The marriage had lasted for seven years, and when Sabrina was six, Simone left. Alastair had offered Sabrina no explanation as to why her mother went away, and made it clear that he wouldn't discuss it with her. She was never sure if it was her fault her mother went, since they never heard from her. When she was thirteen, Alistair explained to Sabrina that her mother had gone off with another man, and he had no idea where she was after that, or even if she was still alive, but he assumed she was, since she was very young.

If he had other women in his life, Sabrina wasn't aware of it. When he wasn't teaching, he was writing, and communication between them was limited. He maintained the taboo on subjects about his past until his dying day. He never explained why he had left England, or what had happened with the brother he hadn't seen since and had never communicated with again, and he steadfastly refused to talk about Sabrina's mother. Communication with other humans was painful for him. As she matured, Sabrina thought of him as emotionally paralyzed, and didn't expect anything more from him. To the succession of psychiatrists she'd had since college, and once she was successful, she referred to her childhood as The Ice Age. There was no way to scale the walls around her father, or chip through the ice he was frozen into, like some prehistoric man from ancient times they had found frozen in a cave. The distance her father imposed on her, and his icy personality, made Sabrina silent and shy as a child, always feeling unwelcome and out of place. It had taken her years to feel comfortable in her own skin after feeling so unwanted as a child.

Alastair had wanted Sabrina to attend college in the Boston area, at one of the excellent universities around them, but she had been hungry for warmer weather and people. She had only applied to schools in California and been accepted at all of them. Alistair had had a rigorous study plan for her when she was growing up. He brought stacks of books home for her every week, and she dutifully read them all. Although he was unable to express affection toward her, he had fed, housed, and educated her adequately. He had cooked for her every night, and she ate in the kitchen alone. They lived in an apartment in Cambridge, and he had assigned her additional study projects. She had excellent grades, gave her father no trouble, and kept to herself, and as soon as she was accepted at UCLA, she left as quickly as she could, and their contact was reduced to her Christmas holiday. He had moved to Vermont by then, and in her junior year, when she came home for Christmas, he told her simply and directly that he had pancreatic cancer, and he was dying. He was surprised when she took the semester off and stayed with him. She was shocked by his illness, and she realized later that she was hoping to build some kind of emotional bridge to him before it was too late, but he continued to maintain his distance until the end. He spent his two final months frantically trying to finish his last book, which he did, and died two weeks later, without ever drawing closer to Sabrina. She waited for some final words of affection from him, but there were none. In his last days, he never spoke and slept most of the time, eventually heavily dosed on morphine for the pain. There were no words for her when he died, as she sat quietly by his bed. She was twenty-one years old and alone. It was the loneliest feeling in the world. He had remained an inaccessible stranger all her life.

He had left her a little money, enough to provide a cushion to live on, and to complete her education. He was dutiful about his responsibilities but never warm. She sold the cabin in Vermont, gave away his old, threadbare furniture and most of his books. She went through several boxes of papers in the garage, and found only a few photographs of him as a boy, with an older boy she assumed was his brother, but there was nothing written on the photographs. Whatever secrets he'd had he took with him to the grave. She found a box of her mother's modeling photographs, and she was as beautiful as Sabrina remembered her. Simone had raven-dark hair, was tall and slim with delicate features and big green eyes. Sabrina was blond and blue-eyed like her father, with a small frame and delicate features, and looked younger than she was. Coupled with her shyness, she appeared almost childlike, even as an adult.

What Sabrina remembered most about her mother was her bright red lipstick. She couldn't remember any particular affection from her mother, who clearly hadn't been deeply attached to her, since she had left and never contacted Sabrina or Alastair again. She vanished into thin air after she disappeared. Alistair had received divorce papers in the mail afterwards, but nothing else from Simone. There had never been a letter or a postcard or a birthday card to her daughter, and Sabrina believed her father when he said he had no idea where she was. Sabrina had some illusions about her mother in her early teens and wanted to meet her one day, hoping she'd be warmer than her father, but had given the idea up as she got older. A woman who had evidenced so little interest in her daughter couldn't have been much of a mother, and clearly wasn't interested in meeting her as an adult.

Sabrina had learned to live without parental

affection, or any at all, but unlike her father, she hungered for it. She envied classmates she saw with loving parents, and always felt like the odd man out. As she got older, she reached out to friends, who became the family to her that she had never had. She was a serious student in college, and her friends were almost like the siblings she didn't have. As a child she had led a very solitary life. Later, her shrinks agreed that she'd been love-starved. Her father had no ability to connect with other humans, which had been as much a tragedy for him as for her. Even when he was on his deathbed, she expected some sign of emotion, some indication that he loved her, and there was none. He lay in silence with his eyes closed until his final breath, while she prayed he wouldn't die so soon and leave her alone. He had remained an enigma and her mother a dim memory, a shadow figure in her life, who had abandoned her at six. It was heavy baggage to carry into her future when she went back to UCLA after he died, to make up the time she missed. She managed to do it over the summer and graduated on time with her class. She had no home to go back to, no relatives anywhere, except those in England she'd never met and knew nothing about.

After she graduated, she took a job at the Disney Studios as a production assistant, and eventually became a screenwriter, which was exciting for her. It was her first writing job, and she enjoyed it.

She moved to Venice Beach, which was young and lively. She learned to surf, and was good at it, despite her small size. She was a strong swimmer, and met a young surfer from New Zealand on the beach. Jason Taylor was fun and good-looking. It was her first serious relationship. He had a job at a surf shop. Within six months he was at risk of being deported, and he asked her to marry him, for as long as necessary to get a green card. She was in love with him and didn't want him to leave, so it seemed a reasonable suggestion, and she married him. She had no parent to object. He had dropped out of school at seventeen and other than surfing, they had no common interests. But it was exciting knowing that he cared for her, after years of her father's indifference.

The marriage lasted as long as it took to get his green card, almost two years, and by then, their feelings for each other had waned and there was little point to the relationship. He wanted to move to Hawaii to surf, which was of no interest to her. They filed for divorce, and Sabrina took a job in San Francisco, at Lucas Studios, which was a step up from her job at Disney. It was a great opportunity and challenged her writing skills, and she learned a lot. She started a new chapter of her life there. She had a few postcards from Jason after the divorce, and then lost track of him. He was living in Maui and loved it when last heard from. People had a way of slipping out of her life, without a trace, like her mother. She was twenty-four when she moved to San Francisco. It was a fun city with lots of activity and young people. She loved her job working on scripts, dated a few men without any great interest, and at twenty-eight, she met a doctor, Tom Wilkins, who was ten years older than she was. He was handsome, brilliant, charming, and interested in all the same things she was. Fascinating and intelligent, he loved to read, loved films, had surfed in college, and went out on the waves with her a few times. He was almost too good to be true, and an ER doctor, with a specialty in trauma.

Their life together was full and exciting. Because of his erratic schedule, Tom had few friends, but their relationship was intense, and he and Sabrina were constantly together when they weren't working.

They moved in together after a year, and he was desperate to marry her, which she did at twenty-nine, at City Hall. Tom had no family and neither did she, and he never spoke about his past. All she knew was that he'd grown up in Chicago, was an only child like her, and his parents were dead. They had much in common. From the moment she married him, he turned from Dr. Jekyll to Mr. Hyde, and controlled her every move, accused her of things she didn't do. Their marriage resembled the movie *Gaslight*. It was a nightmarish web. It took her five years to get free of Tom's control, which she finally did with the help of a group for abused women, and ultimately a safe house where she hid from him. It took her another year to recover and feel free and whole again. She had to leave San Francisco to escape him. Tom hunted her down wherever she was, and at thirty-five, divorced again, and feeling liberated, she moved to New York, to start her life over.

She had saved money from her job at Lucas, and with the money she had left from her father, she had enough to make the transition and move cross-country. Just as she had fled her father and the loneliness of her life with him, she headed east again, to New York, to flee the terrifying psycho-logical abuse of her ex-husband. She felt as though she was always running away from something, but this time she had no choice. She had realized how dangerous and twisted Tom was, and she knew that if she stayed with him, it would destroy her. He might even kill her. He had manipulated her until she lost all faith in herself, and as part of her recov-ery from her marriage, once she got to New York she started writing. This time she was no longer writing what she had to for her job. She discovered her own voice and wrote a terrifying psychological thriller, which was really about Tom.

She found a tiny apartment she loved in Soho, and a job as an assistant editor at *The New Yorker,* which was prestigious and interesting, and at night she wrote her thriller. She wrote it in three months, and spent another month refining it. It was a mesmerizing and frighteningly accurate portrait of a sociopath. She let her imagination run wild and the result was brilliant.

She contacted an agent, Agnes Ackley, through one of her colleagues at *The New Yorker*. Agnes was tough and smart, recognized Sabrina's talent immediately, and accepted her as a client. The two women got on well. Agnes was in her mid-fifties. She sold the book in four months. It was a very respectable success, although not a bestseller, and for the first time, at thirty-seven, Sabrina felt solid on her feet and headed in the right direction. She didn't feel lost anymore. She had survived the worst and come through it whole. And with her writing, she was never lonely.

With two marriages behind her, one of them to a sociopath, she had no interest in dating when she first moved to New York. Friends at the magazine eventually convinced her to try the dating sites on the internet, which felt dangerous to her. She was terrified of meeting a man who would turn out to be like the doctor she had divorced.

As soon as the book was published, the doctor tried to contact her again, but Sabrina's publisher shielded her, and Tom couldn't find out where she lived, and eventually stopped calling and texting her. She had kept the same phone number and finally blocked him.

Whenever she did read Tom's texts, he sounded

as dangerous and seductive as ever, and just as sick. During their marriage he had tried to taunt her into suicide, and had nearly driven her to it. She couldn't imagine another human as dangerous as he was. It had taken her five years to get brave enough to leave him, and find the escape route, and she didn't want to lose her way in those woods again, or any like them, with anyone like him.

Another junior editor at the magazine told her that the best way to get over a man was to meet another one, which sounded to Sabrina like curing the effects of one poison with another. Romance and dating seemed fraught with danger, but at thirty-eight, it seemed odd and a little sad to stay alone forever. She finally made a cautious attempt at internet dating but saw danger signs in every email she read. She met a few candidates for coffee in public places, and they seemed to her either odd, tedious, or not too bright, with lackluster lives, and some were even boring. Only one or two seemed crazy to her, but most of all they were of no interest. Some of them had lied and were taller, shorter, or older than they had claimed. She suspected that one or two were married. Lying seemed to be a constant with several of them. She couldn't imagine meeting anyone she could care about, and she had met no appealing men at work. She wasn't desperate to meet a man, but it seemed like what she was "supposed" to do. After her isolated childhood, and her bad marriages, she was comfortable alone.

After discussing it with her latest shrink, and two friends at work, Sabrina decided to make more of an effort and went to see a matchmaker who came highly recommended. Dating appeared to be far more complicated than she expected it to be. Gone were the days when you met someone at school or work or through a friend, found them attractive, went to dinner and fell in love. It was more like landing on the moon now, or attempting to refuel a rocket ship mid-flight in outer space. Highly technical and computerized, with algorithms, statistics, geography, and categories of desirability that had to match up. Chemistry was no longer relevant, and no one seemed to know people to introduce Sabrina to, and when they did, she wished they hadn't.

Sabrina paid the matchmaker an exorbitant amount for ten dates. She was a woman who had gone to Yale Law School and given up law for matchmaking because it was so lucrative. The men Sabrina met for a drink or coffee were stunningly inappropriate, with decent jobs which most of them were bored with. The age range she had opted for was forty to fifty, all of them were divorced, while many of them had children they complained about and ex-wives they hated, all of whom they claimed were crazy. Some of the dates were only trying to increase their existing stable of bed partners, while claiming to want a "relationship," which in fact was the furthest thing from their minds. She paid ten thousand dollars for the privilege of meeting them, a thousand dollars a date, which made it an expensive cup of coffee. She thought it was a worthwhile investment to pay homage to a biological clock she didn't actually hear ticking, since she had never wanted children, and didn't want to inflict a childhood as unhappy as her own on an unsuspecting child. She wasn't convinced that she'd be any better than her own parents at parenting. She had no experience with children and had never longed for one. Sabrina suspected a dog might suit her better and seem less frightening. You couldn't give a child away if it didn't work out, or stop seeing them, or divorce them. And her track record with her two marriages didn't encourage her, in terms of her own judgment.

After the tenth date arranged by the matchmaker, Sabrina made a decision to stop trying to meet the perfect mate. She thought that there was a good chance that a third attempt at marriage might be no more charmed than the first two, one of which had been foolish and harmless and a waste of time, a youthful mistake, and the second of which had nearly killed her. It seemed so much easier to be alone, and she had none of the frantic desperation other women had to meet a man. Her job and her writing seemed like enough, although she was embarrassed to admit it. It made her sound odd.

By the time Sabrina was nearly thirty-nine, she was sure she didn't want children. There was no appealing man of her dreams on the horizon, and she didn't want to go through the hormonal agony of freezing her eggs to save for a baby later, nor go to a sperm bank, which she thought served a useful purpose for women who were desperate for a baby before their time ran out. She couldn't imagine having a baby with a man she knew, let alone a stranger selected by a computer. She found the whole concept frightening, and remaining childless didn't frighten her at all. In fact, it sounded peaceful and comfortable to her, which set her apart from other women she knew, who were beginning to panic as they approached forty. She wasn't. She realized that she was a woman who didn't want or need children, and embraced it. She was busy writing her second book. It became an overnight bestseller. It was even more terrifying than the first one, and her readers loved it. She was making a career out of writing about twisted, disturbing people who did horrifying things, and she loved doing it. Her second book changed her life in ways she could never have imagined.

With the success of her second book, she was able to give up her job at *The New Yorker*, which wasn't a long-term goal, and write full-time. She had enjoyed her job, and the people she worked with, but she wanted to write her books without interruption or distraction, or having to go to an office to work for someone else. She bought a barn in the Berkshires and turned it into her dream home with a local architect, Steve Jones, and he and his wife Olivia became her closest friends. Sabrina was able to move to her new home in the Berkshires before she turned forty, and she was never lonely once she did. The ideas flowed, and she had a home, a booming career, a life she loved, and money in the bank, and she had done it all on her own. No one was running her life or telling her what to do. No one was trying to hurt her. She had felt insignificant and unloved for all of her childhood. No one was rejecting, belittling, or tormenting her. She felt competent and capable. She had failed at the dating game and marriage, but she was finally comfortable with herself, and had found the right path for herself with her books. Her life was full of the characters she invented, and the tortured lives she designed for them. Her own life had never been more peaceful, more fulfilled, or happier.

She met and enjoyed many of the locals, especially Steve and Olivia Jones, and she was a good sport about the odd single men they fixed her up with. They were almost as bad as the ones she had met through the matchmaker, or those from the internet. She had first (and last) dates with depressed widowers who missed their wives, men who hated their jobs, ex-wives, or children, or who wanted to have a slew of babies, which she didn't. Others couldn't keep a job, or didn't want to grow up, or wanted to control her and tell her everything she was doing wrong. She met commitment phobics, and reassured them that she had no desire to be married either. There were a few nice men in the mix, but she had her life just the way she wanted it, and she didn't want to upset the balance it had taken her years to achieve. She had come a long, hard road to get here, ever since her mother had abandoned her at six. She had tried to fill the void her father left by ignoring her and being unable to love her. And she had questioned her own judgment after escaping her second husband.

Sabrina tried to explain to her friend Olivia that she wasn't a good candidate for dating or a relationship and was afraid to make another mistake. She didn't want to get hurt again, or disappoint someone, or hurt anyone. She was so happy with her life as it was, she had no desire to take a risk. She loved her life as it was now, and the wrong man might ruin everything. Dating just seemed too complicated and risky, and apparently wasn't her strong suit. It was hard to explain that she really was happy. She worried at times that she was following in her father's footsteps, with her writing and winding up alone. But her father had been a deeply unhappy person, and she wasn't. She loved her life, her work, her friends, her home. It seemed greedy to her to want more. She didn't have a partner, but she had herself and the scars of the past had healed at last. What more could she want? And there was something blissfully comfortable about not being in love with anyone. She spent her fortieth birthday with a room full of good friends, less than a year after she'd moved to the Berkshires. On her forty-fifth, she went skiing with friends in Vermont. At forty-eight, she had seven bestselling thrillers to her credit, and had made a name for herself.

She groaned every time Olivia came up with a new man in the area to introduce her to. She gave in occasionally, just to prove to Olivia and her husband Steve that she wasn't a complete hermit, and now and then they came up with someone decent she went out with more than once, and even slept with. But her heart wasn't engaged. She hadn't been in love since Tom, the monster she had married nearly twenty years before who had almost killed her, and there wasn't a single thing in her life she would have changed if she'd had a magic wand. She was a survivor and had turned her life into one that suited her and made up for the past and her unhappy childhood.

Sabrina set down Winnie and Piglet's breakfast on the floor, and walked into her garden in the bright May sunshine. She had gotten Winnie the sheepdog eight years before, and Piglet the Chihuahua two years later. They were her constant companions. She was hoping to finish her new book in the next few days and couldn't wait for Agnes, her agent, to read it. Sabrina thought this one was even better than the others, and even scarier. In the end, her bad second marriage had spawned an entire career of terrifying books that people gobbled up like candy, and she loved writing. She just didn't want to live a story like it again, she only wanted to write those stories about sociopaths and serial killers and love gone wrong, with a fantastic twist at the end. Two of her books had been made into movies, and she was hoping for a series one of these days.

She checked her emails when she walked back into the kitchen, and saw that she had one from her publisher, asking her to call. She smiled at the dogs, patted both of them, and went to take a shower. She couldn't wait to get back to the book. Nothing else mattered when she was writing. She would call her publisher later. She knew it wouldn't be important. Probably a request for a book signing, or some detail about the paperback cover. Whatever it was could wait until she finished the book. She was humming as she stepped into the shower and Piglet chased Winnie down the stairs into the garden. As far as Sabrina was concerned, life didn't get better than this. And she was grateful every single day for how her life had turned out. She had worked hard to get here, and she was a happy woman.